_____ _____ _____ ____ohshop
in Porto. The shop
that inspired 'Flurish +

**RUDE ROUSING REVENGE** Blotts' in

Harry Potter.

# RUDE ROUSING REVENGE

## ROBERT HOBBS

The Book Guild Ltd

First published in Great Britain in 2018 by
The Book Guild Ltd
9 Priory Business Park
Wistow Road, Kibworth
Leicestershire, LE8 0RX
Freephone: 0800 999 2982
www.bookguild.co.uk
Email: info@bookguild.co.uk
Twitter: @bookguild

This work is entirely fictitious and bears no resemblance to any persons living or dead.


Typeset in Garamond

Printed and bound in Great Britain by CPI Group (UK) Ltd, Croydon, CR0 4YY


ISBN 978 1912083 121


British Library Cataloguing in Publication Data.
A catalogue record for this book is available from the British Library.

*I dedicate this book to my mum, Margaret and to my dad, Nobby.*
*A fine reward for bringing me up properly and for teaching me loyalty.*
*With much love to my amazing wife, Lindsey.*

# 1

A few people, some of the time, prefer something a little bit rude. Nearly everyone, most of the time, prefer something a little bit rousing. Everyone, without exception, whether they choose to admit it or not, enjoy some involvement with the art of revenge. Especially when the subject matter is personal. Very personal.

Prepare your approach to your thinking now, as it is possible your life is never going to be the same again, or potentially at the very worst, a little bit different. Have you ever been tempted to take revenge? I mean serious revenge, not feeble, effortless, wheel-banging road rage.

Revenge. I think you might like it when you taste it, allow yourself to get absorbed by it and feel the energy rising with your blood flowing a little brisker! Worried you might get tempted? Really, you just might…

The village of Hawkswold, sits in the glorious county of Kent. It is off the beaten track, and consists of a sprinkling of houses, a series of farmhouses, and a jewel of a traditional church as the centrepiece. That day was a grim milestone in Hawkswold history as it was six months to the day that Karen Verlander's sister, Helen Stansfeld and her husband Michael, were ruthlessly shot dead at close range, in their beautiful thatched cottage in the remote Kentish village.

Karen, knowing the significance of that day's date, the sixteenth of June 2009, visited the Stansfelds' cottage to reflect on events, and to try and make sense of the murders. The cottage had remained empty since the crime was committed, and the stuffy atmosphere inside definitely needed refreshing with a timely stirring.

Karen opened all the windows as she gingerly walked around the cottage, keen to let some of the gorgeous fresh June country air into the family dwelling. She was still heavily grief stricken. The two sisters were very close. She could not believe her beloved big sister, just two years older then her, had gone. The house felt so cold, so quiet and lifeless, it was so difficult to comprehend what had happened. The view from the windows upstairs, overlooking the slightly overgrown shrubbery and flowers in the garden, personified heaven on earth. It was perfect. How could such a ghastly crime be committed within such a glorious setting?

The question was of course why? What was the motive for murder? This question had filtered into Karen's thoughts almost every day since the senseless act had taken place. This cottage had sinister secrets and it was not unlocking its history easily.

Given the couple had been murdered whilst they were both in bed, the police had removed the blood-sodden duvet and bed sheets with the mattress for further forensic examination. Cream rendered bedroom walls, splattered with blood following the shooting, had been given a simple wash off, none too cleverly. This had quite an impact on Karen, as Helen had always kept an immaculate home, and her bedroom was normally a stunning focal point to her cottage. The contrast in presentation from how the police had left it, following their hasty mop-up operation, compared to how Helen would have presented the master bedroom, was stark with crudeness to the point of being

2

emotionally shocking. The room did not fit or feel in unison with the rest of the cottage. Life went on, however it was not the same.

Karen was executor to her late sister's estate and she was sifting through paperwork downstairs when there was a knock at the front door. Karen opened the creaky door to find Detective Chief Inspector Chris Cattermole standing on the doorstep.

"Hello, Chris. How are you? Please come in," said Karen, in a very positive, expectant voice. The visit was a surprise and Karen hoped the Detective Chief Inspector brought encouraging news of a gainful development.

"Thank you, I am fine," said the inspector, in a rather unconvincing, uncharacteristically downbeat delivery, as he entered the Stansfelds' cottage. His half-forced smile and lack of eye contact, contrived with his sheepish mannerisms to convey a message stronger than any of his official statements could. This was not the same warm DCI Karen had got to know freely over the last six months, this was a very different man.

Karen was on edge with the change in his persona she was witnessing. It was clear the DCI was on a mission, and whatever that quest was, it was not likely to be good news for her.

DCI Cattermole, in Karen's eyes, was a sensible trustworthy man. He was straight down the line, and very sincere. He had shared confidences with Karen regarding processes and developments during the police murder investigation. They had built up a very good relationship, even verging on friendship, certainly more engaging and progressive than a normal professional, customer service footing.

Chris always told Karen what he wanted to tell her, rather than what he thought she wanted to hear. He was a rare policeman in that respect, and appeared genuinely caring. Most policemen clocked off at seven in the evening and went home to their wives and family, Chris took some of his work and emotional baggage with him after work. She sensed he never totally switched off from being a detective, which was commendable, for such a demanding role.

They respected each other, and had a mutual liking for one another. They appreciated and valued how each other handled themselves and coped with whatever the world threw at them. Neither of them had experienced an easy time of life recently.

"Can I get you a coffee, Chris?"

"Yes, that would be lovely, thanks."

Whilst Karen walked into the kitchen to pour the Detective Chief Inspector's coffee, Chris admired the photographs on the living room wall of one of Helen and Michael's holidays.

"I see Michael and Helen went to Rio de Janeiro. When was that, Karen?"

"A few years ago now. It was Michael's fortieth present to himself. He claimed he always wanted to go to Rio, ever since Roger Moore fell out of that ambulance."

"Oh," replied Chris, not really getting the quip.

"They both loved it out there. They were full of stories detailing romantic meals on Copacabana Beach, first-class beachfront hotels, climbing Sugarloaf Mountain, dancing in cable cars, they surrendered their souls to Christ the Redeemer. Brazil has got it all."

"The only downsides on their holiday I recall were an incident on a tourist schooner out in the bay which collided with a fishing boat and a near-death experience during the flight back home. Four hours of turbulence apparently! They often spoke about that holiday for months afterwards."

The DCI took control and adjusted his delivery to a more purposeful tone. "This is not a scheduled visit, Karen, it is not part of our normal follow-up or crime solving progression report, I am afraid."

"Oh really?" said Karen cautiously, passing the chief inspector his coffee.

"Come through to the living room, Chris. Take a seat," she

4

said, bracing herself as she was not sure why but she was sure that whatever Chris was about to tell her, it was probably not going to be welcome good news.

"Thank you, I would rather stand," said Chris, his demeanour was decidedly uncomfortable, his descriptive hand movements and fidgeting becoming more pronounced.

"Karen, I wanted to see you today for a number of reasons. Firstly, I am aware of the date. Six months has passed so quickly since Helen and Michael passed away and knowing how close you all were. I wanted you to be aware our thoughts from myself and my immediate team are with you."

"Thank you, Chris. That is kind of you."

"In terms of an investigation report, in truth we are no nearer discovering the murderer now than we were when we started the case six months ago. In twenty years of policing, I have never known a murder, or any serious crime for that matter, where we have had so little evidence to work with or been able to make so little progress. I am here to tell you, Karen, that we have exhausted all lines of enquiries and unless a witness or more evidence presents itself, we really cannot move forward with the case."

"I see," said Karen, wiping a single tear, trying hard, unsuccessfully, to mask her disappointment from the harshness of her predicament.

The DCI continued. "The other part I need to tell you is strictly confidential. We have had our force resources budgets reduced and some of my team are being redeployed to other challenges within the county. We have new initiatives with anti-terrorism actions I need to support, and as a consequence, I cannot keep your sister's murder investigation at the top of my agenda. I am very sorry, Karen. I could not bear you thinking and hoping it is only a matter of days before the police get a breakthrough, I cannot see it happening. I would, however, remind you the case is definitely not closed. You have always been very straight and helpful to me, Karen, and I wanted to be the same to you. I am sorry."

"I see. It was expected really; I always knew in the absence of more evidence, it was only a matter of time before you had to wind the activity down. I just did not know when the cut-off was likely to be."

Karen reached out to Chris and let out a distressing shriek. "God, this is a bloody mess. Who would do this? Who would hurt my family? We have never hurt anyone in our lives. Why is it left to me? Why do I have to pick up all the pieces. It is simply not fair. Why?"

There then followed what seemed like several minutes of uncomfortable silence, and warm embraces. Rolling eye movements from Karen failing to connect with reality highlighted the distress she felt in her heart. The realisation of the detective's few words and resultant impact confirmed to both parties that everything which needed to be said had been said.

After an awkward pause, the detective chief inspector declared, "I am sorry, Karen. I need to leave. I must see my deputy. Would you like me to call someone to be with you?"

Karen replied, "No, thank you, Chris," wiping her tears. "Time does not heal as quickly as I thought it would. I am amazed at how hard the recovery from all this is. I try and convince myself I am getting better, moving forward, the reality however is quite different. Hope we speak again soon."

As the inspector turned away to face the front door, Karen grabbed at his hand expectantly, and commented in tearful desperation, "Find the killer, Chris, find him."

The inspector offered a knowing nod, turned, and made his exit through the large wooden front door. As the eye contact between them was lost, a sinking feeling began to drag Karen down. The gravity of the reality confirmed her feelings were not getting better, answers were not forthcoming, and life for her was not progressing as it should. Closure from her loss was as far away now as it was six months earlier. Karen needed inspiration, not to mention a distraction. She decided to visit her nearby sister's grave for comfort, as she had done on numerous occasions before.

Karen's sister Helen was buried with her husband in the grounds of the village churchyard. It was less than a two-minute walk from the thatched cottage. Karen enjoyed the brief moment of anticipation prior to seeing the grave for the first time of every visit. She had visited her sister's grave almost daily since the murders.

Karen was clutching some freshly picked roses from the Stansfelds' garden. She always found a visit experience to be uplifting, she felt close to her sister again, it was a rare private moment for them both. Memories would flood back, thoughts of the good times, the fun and pleasure they both had growing up together. Stupid fun things they did, which were insignificant really, suddenly became very important and valuable. There was strength in her thoughts, and love in the recollections.

Karen cherished the experience she gained from these private visits, it was necessarily therapeutic to her grieving process. Karen displayed the roses in the flower holder by the gravestone. She kissed a rose goodbye, a tear flowed, and she stood up to take one final look at the grave before she turned to start her walk back home from the churchyard.

"Hello, Karen," said Father Ham from behind her. "I hope I did not disturb you. I saw you kneeling at your sister's grave, and just wanted to say hello and enquire as to how you were."

"Thank you, Ham," said Karen all glossy eyed. "I think my tears say it all really. I had a visit from the police. DCI Cattermole saw me this morning. He told me the police have scaled down the murder investigation. I have also told the marketing agency I work for that I want to take a sabbatical. We have agreed for the moment, to part company. Quite frankly, my mind is not on my job – I think this option is for the best."

Father Ham replied, "That sounds like a bad idea, you need

normality and definition in your life. What are you going to do if you do not work and keep yourself occupied? Wrapping yourself in tearful memories and pondering the past without a distracting purpose will not be helpful."

Karen responded, "No, you are right. I am aware of this. I have done enough sulking, draping myself in self-pity and tears. It really is time to move on. I want to do something productive."

Karen paused for a moment then the following tripped off her tongue. "I want to find Helen's killer, Ham. I do not know yet how I am going to do this, I do not know where to start, to be honest. All I am certain of is that I want to find the killer, I want justice."

Father Ham was slightly bemused by Karen's comments, certain her statement was a short-term knee jerk reaction, rather than a deep-rooted desire to turn into a super sleuth. Sensitive to not wanting to distress Karen any further by probing her or challenging her comments, he thoughtfully paused, allowing his eyes to wander around his grounds, then changed the subject to his last week in office.

After seven years of being the vicar for his parish, he wanted to ensure her attendance at his last gathering of his congregation, planned for the following Sunday. "Will I see you in church, on my final day, next week?" enquired Father Ham.

"Oh yes," Karen replied. "I would not miss it for the world. Do you know who your replacement will be yet?"

With a non-committal smile, Father Ham offered, "I am sure the next vicar of Hawkswold will be announced shortly."

Father Ham, which was short for Hamish, was a popular vicar and extremely likeable. His friends in the borders gave him the nickname of Hammerite, reflecting his robust opinionated outlook and ability to get involved with anything the parish would throw at him. Hamish or Hammerite, Ham suited him just fine.

# 2

The sun rose high in the sky and shone majestically down on the village church. That beautiful June morning was the calling card announcing that this was the day that the parish was to say goodbye to one of its most favoured priests.

The vicar of Hawkswold, the Rev Ham Thompson was a larger than life character, and in many ways a most unusual vicar. Physically he was a big man, his extra large frame would make any body mass indicator spin off its results gauge in disgust. He was a very caring, honest, and as you would expect, a fastidious people person. He was totally committed to the community and his enthusiasm to make things happen within the village was legendary. He was a most unusual salesman, but sell the good faith he did, he sold it well.

Beneath the ministerial church branding was a likable man who was both humorous and engaging with the potential for being, outside of the confines of the church arena, a little risqué! His confident manner and ability to test political correctness was a breath of fresh air. With a dash of flamboyancy, Father Ham was a far cry from the stereotypical staid, disciplined, and dare I suggest, boring clergy, you may sometimes witness holding court in churches of *your* local parish.

A vital ingredient to the resident vicar's popularity was that Father Ham originated from the Highlands of Scotland. His resonating regional tone not only added interest to his delivery but added urgency to resolving the important issues in his congregation's lives and parish. Some women of the parish may have made comments his accent was even sexy, it was unusually soft and purposeful, not at all aggressive or intimidating. He playfully maximised and exaggerated the historical conflict between England and Scotland, often suggesting his time spent in the small Kentish village of Hawkswold, was merely respite from battle or border fury. He also enjoyed a glass, and was a welcome visitor to a number of public houses in the surrounding area. He found this a perfect way to keep in touch with his parish, enjoy the company of others and to spread the good word of the lord at every opportunity. A good local brew provided more leverage to spread the good word, than many a month of Sunday sermons ever could.

The vicar had declared in the May edition of the parish newsletter, following events of the last few months, that he had decided to take early retirement, and relocate to his first love, the wonderful Highlands of Scotland. He thanked everyone for their support and kind wishes in a letter he had written within the newsletter, encouraging everyone to attend his final address.

Within no time at all, the vicar's last day fell upon the local community. The church was brimming with parishioners and the mood was upbeat with anticipation, masking the sadness that the village was soon to lose an exceptional pro-active companion. The turnout was strong as over the years Rev Ham, as he was affectionately known by most of his parish, had dipped into the lives of so many friends within the community. Providing service as a result of births, deaths, marriages, and untold support when a shoulder may have been required due to difficult family circumstances. Above all, Ham was generous with his time, when his community needed it, and this meant a great deal to all the people who were gathered around the church on this memorable day.

Rev Ham stood up at the lectern and gazed down to his congregation, smiling with pride. He fought back a tear, forced his lower lip to stop quivering, focused on controlling his breathing, and savoured the silence. Ham was a confident public speaker and had delivered important messages in church before without drama.

That day, however, was different. Soaked in sentiment and deep-rooted pride, Ham was battling with his emotions. That day meant a lot to him, and it showed. His composure and professionalism was a credit to him.

Ham began his address to a packed church, many people attending from further afield than the local parish, such was the popularity of the man.

"This is my last day," the vicar said, holding his nerve and clearing his throat with purpose. Holding both arms outstretched reaching for the heavens, then clutching either side of the lectern, he braced himself to continue.

"I want you all to know, this is a beautiful day, and you are beautiful people. I wish you could stand where I am now, and witness yourselves in the flickering sunlight, gloriously filtering through the stained glass windows, shining on the bright stars of the parish below. This wonderful church really knows how to provide a magical theatre. I want you all to know I will miss you all and will cherish this moment forever.

"When I first applied for this job with God, it is the words from an enthusiastic Bishop which have stayed with me through my career.

"As I was handed the keys to my first parish from the Bishop, he said. 'I warn you now, it's not until you start dealing with the general public that you realise how many nutters there are on this planet!'" The congregation laughed with generous passion, in typical upbeat village unison, smiling at each other in the pews approvingly.

The vicar continued. "It was not inspirational guidance or indeed the most profound energising statement to launch oneself into a career, but I learnt not to take life too seriously. Do what you can well, and help others. That was another statement made by the same Bishop, but I forgot those comments!" More rumbles were heard from the pews, again in glorious chattering of approval.

"Our thoughts today should not be with me, and my desire to retire and leave the parish, and to return home to the Highlands. Our thoughts and prayers today should be with Karen Verlander. As we all know, six months ago in the village we all love, she lost her sister and her brother-in-law in an act of unrivalled cruelty. None of us can imagine the horror, despair, and amount of loss Karen has felt since the double murder in the village." Ham looked squarely into Karen's eyes as she sat in her seat facing him, making a connection with her and the rest of the congregation.

"The graphic events of that night have been well written and publicised so I will not dwell on them here. What I will say is that Karen has tremendous fortitude. I think the way she has conducted herself and dealt with this truly horrific incident should give strength to us all."

The vicar paused again, looked approvingly at Karen one more time and watched the tears stream down her face. A fellow member of the parish put their arm around Karen to comfort her.

The vicar, fighting his internal emotion, then continued with increased volume. "My job has always been to remain positive, and to encourage the good souls, and find the good in the other people. Yes, my job has been a very hard one at times! For twelve years, I have been supportive of all my congregations and of my wider parish. For the last seven years based in Hawkswold, I have delivered my unique style of parish leadership, which I hope has been well received. I have lent my ears, and offered what I hope have been genuine words of wisdom. Where appropriate, I have also provided a good old-fashioned cuddle, and an armful of support.

"With sadness, I confirm to you all, this is to be my closing address. The events of the last six months in this village have left me emotionally winded. Ask any priest about murder and he will talk to you about prayers and forgiveness. Ask me about murder, and I am sorry, but forgiveness is not something I think of with ease. Justice, however, is something I think of, and it is regrettable our under-resourced police force, led by the hugely capable DCI Cattermole, have not been able to identify the perpetrator of this callous crime. Our thoughts and prayers are with Karen. I pray the police successfully bring this criminal investigation to a close very soon and normality of sorts, outside of the glare of the media, returns to this pleasant little cluster of villages within our parish.

"This small village has great strength of character, and of spirit, good honest spirit. I have enjoyed serving you all immensely, we have had a lot of fun, and I take some truly fantastic memories with me.

"Finally, I would also like to extend gratitude to my staff and would ask you all to join me and raise a glass outside in the churchyard shortly to these three marvellous pillars of our society. The lovely Doris, seventy-five years young and the best one-armed pianist this side of a Soho jive bar. Jeff, the groundsman, who confidentially admitted recently, he knows less about plants and gardening than I know about our solar system. In fact I do not know anything about our solar system, aside from the heavenly bodies, of course. Then I come to our beloved treasury secretary, Mollie. It is fair to say with Mollie's guidance, we will never have enough money for our needy church roof fund during our lifetimes, however you can be sure Mollie has put some of these funds collected over the years on some of the fastest greyhounds and well-chosen racehorses with unrivalled boldness and enthusiasm. I salute you all, I thank you. Amen."

For one final time, Father Ham raised his head high, closed

his bible and notebook, and walking down the aisle of his church, shook hands and enjoyed the spontaneous applause as he led his followers to the large oak entrance door. The congregation filtered outside the church onto the front path and surrounding churchyard lawns. Father Ham shook hands with his entire parish and for one last time, joyous light-hearted banter filled the grounds. It was like a glorious wedding celebration, without the fuss, ceremony, or complication of a marriage.

After ninety minutes of circulating, laughter, words of gratitude and plenty of goodbye kisses, Father Ham met up with Karen once again.

Moving away from the rest of the crowd, Father Ham shuffled Karen into a more secluded part of the grounds and challenged her regarding her declaration to try and solve her sister's murder herself. "Is it still your intention to investigate the murders, Karen?"

"Yes, I have never felt stronger or more focused about anything," she replied. "You do not think I will be successful do you?" she retorted with purpose.

Father Ham thought carefully before continuing. "You're a sharp lady, Karen, and I am sure you will rise to the challenge. I have reservations that if the professionals, namely the police, cannot find the murderer, with all their knowledge, access to data, forensic ability, etc. I wonder what makes you think you can solve the crime?"

Karen replied, "I have a passion for results. This crime involved my sister. It is not just another crime file on my desk or statistic on an investigator's whiteboard. I do not want to discredit the actions the police have taken. I am sure they have done their best. My life has been dramatically affected; it has been changed by these events. I need to make a contribution to this investigation. I need to find the killer. I want closure. The police must have missed something."

Father Ham offered an olive branch. "Assuming you are going

to go ahead with this, you will have an extremely daunting task ahead of you. There is someone I know, who I think could assist you."

"Who?" enquired Karen with interest.

"His name is William Radnor. He is an accountant," offered the father, looking around and smiling at his guests as they walked past.

"I do not need an accountant," replied Karen, "The world is full of them! I need answers, not a bloody accountant."

"Just because he is an accountant, Karen, it does not make him a bad person!" said Father Ham with a wry smile, moving them both away from other people milling around them.

The father carried on. "Look, I helped William many years ago, when he had problems," the reverend said, stumbling on his words feverously. "I think he would help you too. He originates from Eltham, South London. He relocated to the Highlands, with my guidance, to get away from a bad influence. The fresh air and generous breeze did wonders for his outlook, not to mention a lucrative partnership deal with a leading Scottish accountancy firm, once he gained his qualifications."

"Okay," said Karen. "Tell me more about William."

Ham continued, "His life was in free-fall chaos, that is probably an overstatement. He got distracted from the morally correct highway we all know and love, and got involved with the wrong sort of people and he was forced to surrender his young innocence, and got involved in an illegal pastime. That is all."

Karen thought Ham was the master of telling her everything, without revealing anything!

Ham continued, "William knew his life was not heading in the right direction, and was leading increasingly on a catastrophic course which, ultimately, was likely to see him getting locked up in jail."

"He sounds charming, Ham. He sounds like a rogue. I do not need help from a no hoper. I need… " turning with tears in her eyes as her emotions got the better of her. "I do not know what I need, that is the problem."

Ham sighed. "I am sorry, I know how to sell someone to you, don't I."

Then Ham paused, thought about his suggestion, and then delivered a final throw of the dice. "William is a fine fellow. I always see the best in people, and more importantly, in those who make mistakes in life, I try not to prejudge. In my line of work, you give people the benefit of the doubt, and entrust them with your faith. As you know, Karen, I do not suffer fools gladly, and I find you can tell if people are bad people, or if they genuinely slipped up, and want to correct the error of their ways. What I look for in people is positive potential. If they have the qualities and courage to distance themselves from their misdemeanours, combined with the ability to learn from their mistakes and make a serious effort to recover their predicament and move on, I am willing to assist them.

"William is such a man. He regrets some of the things he did and why he did them. He is basically a good person, who got distracted. I offered him a way out. He got an accreditation for accountancy from an acquaintance of mine, and joined a local practice twelve years ago when he relocated to Scotland. He has never looked back since.

"The point I am trying to make to you, Karen, is you are a good person. You would never do any wrong. You want to start investigating a serious crime you are emotionally involved with. I believe you have the strength of character and mindset to manage yourself successfully and an ability to conduct some liberal digging. However, bear in mind, the people or person you are trying to find will not want to be found. They will be devious, calculating, and not to mention, potentially incredibly dangerous. The voyage you are about to embark on could be a very risky one.

"I believe it would be helpful for you to work with someone who has overstepped the line of the law in the past. You see,

William's experience with crime, and previous knowledge of people who led their lives by a different set of rules, would be invaluable to you."

"Your partnership could be a marriage made in heaven. Bless you, Father," said Rev Ham, joyfully looking skyward with a cheeky smile and a glint in his eye, as only priests can when they tread on the coat tails of spontaneous humour.

Karen, who started to show signs of being interested in meeting William, asked, "Tell me what William did wrong, what crime did he commit?"

"I am sorry, I cannot tell you that," stated Rev Ham, pausing his delivery. He started again. "If I told you, I would have to kill you." They both finished the statement in unison, looking at each other, laughing and smiling. "If you want to know William's past, why don't you ask him directly?"

Without any further suggestion, Father Ham turned his back on Karen and started to walk away. After six paces and without turning back to face her, Ham hollered "Besides, Michael is bored stiff of being an accountant and wants a new challenge. Do you want me to ring him and fix up a meeting?"

Karen, relishing the pressure of a wandering priest putting distance between them, paused, then declared with volume, "Yes, why not. I would love to meet him."

The good work of the parish priest had once again been done, and the intricate wheels of blind faith were put in motion to instigate a meeting. Deep joy!

# 3

A week later, Rev Ham, who by then had concluded his duties as the parish priest in Hawkswold, was back in Scotland. At long last, the popular Scot was the right side of Hadrian's Wall. Accompanying Ham was Karen. They found themselves outside the house of the reformed character, now-turned accountant, William Radnor. Ham had fulfilled his promise to introduce them, and hoped their meeting might create a few positive sparks.

Radnor's hillside chocolate-box cottage was a traditional block stone affair, with pretty white wood window frames adding definition to character. Situated by a meandering road-cum-track, elevated on the side of a hill and supported on both sides by a rich deep forest, Radnor's home overlooked one of the many lochs in the beautiful West Highland region. The cottage with its landscape as a backdrop was truly stunning. Karen fell in love with the place immediately.

Red deer and other forms of random wildlife would often be seen walking by the cottage and grounds. This was a truly idyllic setting. As Karen and Ham approached the front door, location envy was already on Karen's agenda.

Karen was not sure what to expect in the mystery man William Radnor. Ham had driven Karen to the Highlands from

Kent. Whilst they shared some of the driving, Karen used the opportunity of travelling in Ham's car to do plenty of thinking. Ham had not been very responsive to Karen's digging and repetitive questioning regarding Mr Radnor, which intensified her quest for knowledge. If she was shortly to work closely with an accountant, especially one with history, she wanted to know all she could about him, and it was likely to be a long night.

It was eight-thirty on a delightful warm June evening, a sharp knock at Radnor's front door announced Ham and Karen's arrival. William Radnor opened his front door, and welcomed them both warmly into his home. Karen could not help but feel disappointed with the initial first impressions presented to her. Here stood no knight in shining armour, no bronzed exotic waiting to carry her off on horseback and fight her battles majestically for her. William Radnor did not even look like an accountant! He was very much Mr Average, so, so, disappointingly, Mr Average, scruff! He had not even had a shave and his hair was unkempt.

She reminded herself that, in reality, an accountant was normally one step removed from a geography teacher on the grand scale of excitement. She really had to get to grips with herself, and focus on whether William Radnor could cut it as her partner in solving the murders. It was rather obvious he was not likely to induce a cheeky tingle or an unscheduled adrenalin rush. Shame!

After twenty minutes of friendly banter between Ham and William discussing mutual friends at the local pub, catching up on Scottish football, rugby and recent fishing trip exploits, Ham requested an opportunity to use the bathroom, and freshen up. This gave Karen an ideal opportunity to get to know William on a one-to-one basis, and to offer herself a more balanced appraisal of the new man in her life.

Karen's assessment of the inside of William's house was revealing. Whilst the two men had talked, Karen walked around the lower floors of the house, soaking up information. Here lived a man, who clearly lived alone, There were no family pictures on display, no tourist trinkets of a well-travelled individual to be seen, the furniture finished in poorly matching colour schemes was functional, not homely. The fridge was full of beer, the kitchen had more beer, wine, and the finest malt whisky in plentiful supply both on the table tops and stored on the kitchen floor. There were two immaculate guitars on their display stands pride of place in the living room, and strong stacked cardboard boxes, which by the amount of dust on top of them indicated they had probably been there years, residing at the far end of the very long drawing-room-cum lounge. There was no fruit anywhere. You didn't need to be Sherlock Holmes to work out the demographics of Radnor's homely arrangement. It amazed Karen how he managed to get himself such a lovely house, in such an amazing location, and screw up the interior design so badly. Men! Single men!

William pushed a generous glass of fruity white Chardonnay in Karen's direction, offering "Cheers" as a starting point to the evening's proceedings. This was her favourite tipple, and the refreshing offering was well received.

"Thanks, William. Ham tells me you're an accountant." She tried not to laugh or snigger, itching to know what act he had committed prior to this to antagonise the police.

"That's right. You can call me Will, my friends do." William was very direct, and answered in a sincere friendly tone.

"What made you relocate to Scotland, Will?"

"Ham suggested I should visit once. I came here and simply fell in love with the place. I love the location, you can get lost in the beauty of the place."

"What did you do before you were an accountant?" asked an inquisitive Karen, eager to find out what Ham had refused to divulge.

"I did many things." William paused. "However, that was well in the past. I have been an accountant in the Highlands for over twelve years now."

William's delivery this time was quicker and sharper. He stood up and looked out the living room bay window. He was avoiding eye contact with Karen at all costs, and was clearly uncomfortable with a lady asking pertinent, searching questions.

Sensing where the next question was going, William took the opportunity to lead the conversation. William ramped up his vocal delivery and had a useful edge to his tone. "Ham has made me aware of the events in your village, and I was sorry to hear of the distressing murders of your sister and brother-in-law. The murders do not make sense, Karen. I mean they truly do not make sense, something does not add up, something's missing."

It was clear in William's eyes there was no such thing as a random killing with such precision. There is always a motive, and this shocking double murder was clearly no accident and no random act. Or was it?

Capitalising on the fact both of them were alone, William turned and looked Karen pointedly in the eyes. "Did you kill your sister, Karen? Did you pull the trigger?"

Karen's eyes lit up in stunned surprise. She exhaled sharply and loudly in disbelief at what her ears were telling her. Her pitch and vocal volume amplified in anger. "My god, how can you ask such a thing? Have you any idea what I have been through in these last six months? Do you think I have driven with Ham all this way to be insulted? Who the hell do you think you are? What place do you have to ask me such a question?" Karen was in no mood to wait for answers. She grabbed her jacket and headed for the door, her face a flood of distress and tears.

William repeated with urgency, "Did you kill your sister, Karen? Did you?"

Karen responded, "No, I did not, you bloody fool."

Before Karen got to the front door, Ham appeared, and blocked her path and offered his arm in support. Ham held Karen in his arms and said, "Please do not leave, Karen. I want you to listen to William."

21

William, standing unruffled as if they had first met, and still as calm as if nothing more than a friendly fireside chat had occurred, enquired, "Karen, You asked me who was I to ask that question of you, did you kill your sister? You want me to help you find the killer, don't you? It is not going to be easy, Karen!"

William continued. "I needed to know how you would react to challenges and difficult questions. I have asked you a direct question, however I am none the wiser. I do not know you Karen. Do I think you killed your sister? No, I do not believe you did. But as I said, I do not know you. You could be a good liar. You could be telling the truth. Who knows? When you question a suspect, they will not tell you they committed the murder. They will lie. How will you deal with that, Karen?

"We would have to do a lot of digging behind the scenes. The problem with digging is it can prove to be dangerous.

Are you up for that kind of risk? Are you up for that kind of partnership, Karen? Can we work together? Have you got the stomach, determination and bloody-mindedness to do that?"

In hopeless disappointment, Karen walked back into the living room and flopped down in the well-worn comfy armchair. She could not believe she had travelled so far, to be insulted and let down. The reality of what she had hoped to achieve had hit home. In her mind, she was questioning herself: did she have what it took to be a detective? Could she handle the pressures this work would entail. Could she confront the personal side, could she handle the day she stood next to the person who committed the murder? How would she react?

Ham was a good man, and Karen trusted him. She thought the qualities she would find in Radnor would be uplifting, offering strength in direction and character, with useful support. In the man she had just met, she found nothing but disappointment, seriously tinged with frustration and annoyance. Karen was not impressed. Silence followed, and for a few moments, which seemed like an age, only eye contact between the three bounced round the room, nobody being sure what was going to happen next.

With calmness, Karen declared, "Look, I have travelled a long way today and I am very tired. Where can I sleep tonight? I need some sleep."

William asked Ham to escort Karen to the guest bedroom, the first on the left upstairs. Ham duly obliged.

Whilst Ham was upstairs, Will poured Ham a large Scotch and was eager to discuss Karen when he returned. He was sure they both needed a strong drink.

After approximately fifteen minutes, Ham returned downstairs. "That went well, William!" said Ham. William turned away momentarily, as unprovoked poker-faced as ever.

Both men sat either side of the fireplace, facing each other, eyebrows twitching aloft embracing their crystal tumblers of Scotch. The sumptuous red leather chairs creaked, anticipating the next round of prognosis.

William pierced the silence with, "Karen is not strong enough, Ham. She really has not thought this through. Besides she cries too much. I think she believes solving a murder is easy, a few well-chosen questions will do the job. That is her view? She is out of her depth and I do not want anything more to do with her. You should not have brought her here."

William directed his eyebrows into the ceiling in a visual expressive gesture indicating, I told you so.

Ham defended Karen's position. "Karen is upset, that is all. She was not expecting you to ask the questions you did, she was not prepared for it. I think you were a little hard on her. She has lost her sister. This is a big issue; she needs a little more time."

William continued. "I do not mind a challenge, I am willing to help. Trying to work with a stranger who is emotionally involved, with no experience in searching and completing the spadework, could be a recipe for disaster and a valuable waste of time. Karen is still grieving, she needs more time to adjust to her circumstances.

She means well, however this partnership will end in tears, literally. What is the point of it?"

Ham finished his glass of Scotch and put the tumbler back on the table. He looked at William as he collected his travel case to climb the stairs to enter the other guest bedroom.

"Karen is a talented lady, who you could work well with. She wants results and I believe she might just pull this off. The pair of you could be brilliant together, you might be terrible, however I sense you could be brilliant! I am disappointed you cannot see this and you are not prepared to work with her. You better check the train timetables tomorrow, Karen will need to go back home. Goodnight, William."

Ham wore an unhappy face as he spoke these words to William, a rare expression he very seldom used. He hoped his no-nonsense delivery and downbeat undertones of concern would spur William into re-assessing this situation in the morning.

As Ham left the room, William was left to ponder. Ham and William had always seen eye to eye, and William could not think of another occasion when both men had disagreed so passionately.

The next morning, it was going to be an interesting conversation around the breakfast table!

# 4

A fine selection of tasty jams, toast, cereal and fresh fruit greeted the new arrivals downstairs, as William's spectacular orangery played host to their much-anticipated breakfast. A generous square table with sitting room for four overlooked the inviting garden in all its splendour. The light and airy striking extension, with raw timber frames and a glass roof, provided an excellent uplifting atmosphere. This really was the best room in the house. William had done his visitors proud and joyfully poured the fresh coffee, and let the aromatic vibes fill the air to do its trick.

"Would anyone like something cooked for breakfast? I have some cracking traditional Scottish sausages which love to be sizzled!" offered William.

"Why not," responded Ham enthusiastically. "Sizzle away."

"Karen, would you like something hot?"

"No, I am fine, thanks, William. I will just have cereal."

Karen was very thoughtful that morning, very careful of her actions, sensitive to all parties monitoring her reactions and her comments made. To some people, the thought of coming downstairs to breakfast, following the previous evening's exchanges, could have been labelled intolerable. To Karen, however, it was merely a small test, an assessment she was not only willing to participate in, this was a trial she was determined to win.

She decided to wear her hair up, in a more glamorous, professional pose. She thought long and hard about William Radnor and his approach to things. She was aware, following the lengthy conversations in the car the day before with Ham, that William Radnor was a complex animal. He had lost both his parents as a youngster, and never really got together with any of his wider family. He was very self-centred, courageous in some areas, but he never let anyone get too close to him emotionally. He clearly enjoyed a distant remote lifestyle and liked his life on his own. It appeared the comments she received and his current status reflected these thoughts completely.

Unsurprisingly, he was not in a current relationship with anyone else, and was living alone, as he had been consistently for pretty much most of his life. There had been some female partners but none of the relationships seemed to last. He was one of those guys who was destined to be single, and he savoured every minute. He loved being in control of his life with no compromises, that was what being alone was all about. Doing what you liked, when you liked, with no strings or commitments to tangle with your self-centred desires.

William finished cooking Ham's sausages and joined them both at the breakfast table.

Karen was busily slotting her early morning deliberations into place, she had learnt a lot about her immediate demands and needs for her future in the last twenty-four hours. Initially, fuelled by the grieving for her sister, she thought naively she could launch her own private investigation into Helen's murder on her own with little thought given for the complexities of the task or the potential for risk which was very real. Following a flippant remark from Ham, at Helen's graveside, just over a week earlier, Karen started to think in terms of a joint effort, potentially with the unknown suitor, William Radnor.

26

Karen was puzzled as to why Ham had suggested the pair of them work together in the first place. Perhaps Ham was aware of his hidden talents and abilities, which Karen had yet to uncover. At best, William was capable of mild annoyance. At worst, he was a full-blown pain in the arse with an uncanny ability to get ones back up with ease! That said, he did have a slightly bizarre appeal. He was a little cheeky, almost charming at times, but the accountant label did not stick. Karen would need to dig a little deeper with William Radnor, should the pair of them be able to work together. Surely a man who lived in such a lovely house, with fantastic surroundings, had to have something positive going for him! At least that morning he had sharpened himself up; he was clean-shaven with neat hair and a roll neck shirt. Very James Bond stuntman style, she secretly thought.

Karen realised she was now on the back foot. She was at a strategic disadvantage. She thought she would come to Scotland, meet Radnor, have a discussion, and agree terms to work together or not. Simple. The reality was a disturbing volley of questions, with Radnor well and truly putting the squeeze on. Karen simply lost it and caved in. She was sure to be more disciplined in the future as she would not allow a repeat performance to work against her. She knew she had to be more robust and she would not disappoint.

The morning after was now the return match, and Karen was eager to get both of their attentions. Karen smiled at both of the men and started the serious element of their morning dialogue.

"I did a lot of thinking last night!" said Karen in an upbeat confident voice. "Yesterday's exchange was a bit of a wakeup call for me. It made me realise, if I am to seriously move forward and put myself in a position where I can investigate the murders, I have got to get myself emotionally detached from the reality of it all. In short, I need to get stronger. Moving forward from today, I will be a more devoted person, a challenger with extra grit. I have also realised there is no more time for tears, now it is time for decisive action."

Ham and William looked at each other in approval; they liked what they were hearing. Karen's assured rhetoric was impressively delivered. Whilst William accepted Karen's comments with open arms, he was doubtful a leopard could change its spots. She could talk the talk, but could she walk the walk?

Karen continued, "For avoidance of doubt, I did not kill my sister. I am keen, however, to use this visit to the Highlands as a springboard to get my emotions and thoughts in order, also to launch my very personal investigation. With that in mind, William, I would like you to demonstrate to me why I should consider working with you?"

Ham and William were slightly mystified by Karen's comments, the tables had been turned, with some style. Credit to Karen, Ham thought.

Karen loved the dominant attention, and maximised her air of control using her piercing eye contact on William to full devastating effect. This was not only an act of distant manipulation, it was also very sexy. Karen loved it and worked it to the max. "I am sure you will understand, William. As a result of your poorly structured questioning yesterday, my belief is such that the world would be a better place with one less accountant in it."

Ham choked, hardly believing what his ears were telling him had just happened.

Karen turned and focused on Ham, noting he was pre-occupied, slowly fighting and chewing his last sausage, almost choking again on both his food and Karen's thought-provoking statement. She offered "More tea, Vicar?" in recognition of Ham still wearing his clerical collar, allowing Ham the opportunity for his mouth to catch up with his thoughts, after his distraction with his tasty food.

William responded, "I make no apologies if you felt my level of questioning was upsetting yesterday, however I wanted to expose your depth of character. For what it is worth, I would very much like to work with you, and help you solve the murders. I think we would work well together. Your hunger for results, combined with my history and ability to assist you, would make us a formidable team. I would be a useful colleague with which to bounce ideas and work solutions together. I would be much more use to you alive, rather than dead! It was not my intention to upset you yesterday. I wanted you to think about your answers and what you were capable of achieving, that is all."

Karen enquired, "What about your history, William? Will that get in the way of your progress. Convince me your past conquests will not get in the way of our working partnership."

William thought carefully, then replied slowly making careful eye contact with Ham. "You do not need to worry about that, Karen."

Karen, relishing her power from being centre of attention at the breakfast table, wanted to stir her newfound courageous stick, well and truly into Radnor's hornet's nest.

"Come on, William. What did you do in your past which was so bad, and yet so helpful to me now?" Karen sat back pleasingly self-assured, waiting for the silence to be broken.

William looked apprehensively at Ham, knowing he knew what was coming next. He swallowed hard then said, "I used to kill people, Karen. That is my history. I used to be a hitman." William had well and truly lit the fuse to Karen's firework. The question was now, would she be about to launch a rocket, or fizzle out in disbelief as reality dawned?

Floods of questions ran into Karen's head. She could hardly believe what she had heard. She did not know what to ask first.

Karen looked at Ham, then at William. She knew he was not lying. She was in a room with a killer. Ham had brought her to a killer. Why? Was this a masterstroke or a mistake?

William knew Ham trusted Karen implicitly. He would not

have brought her to his house if he did not have faith in her. William also knew Ham would find himself involved with the police should Karen get vocal, as harbouring a criminal and withholding information was still an offence in this country.

Both men monitored how Karen absorbed the revelation, flicking eye contact between themselves. She remained sharp, but silent. Her cogs were turning.

Ham knew William's statement was another test. Whilst his declaration was a statement of fact, his timing was perfect.

William looked at Karen. "Ham told me about the murders in your village. I was interested in all aspects of the case and how it unfolded. To be honest, I found it quite shocking. When Ham told me about the police downscaling the investigative operation, he told me what you had said to him and I wanted to help. I wanted to get involved. For once, I wanted to use my experience and history, to good effect. My understanding of what makes a killer tick may be useful in your private investigation. I am very experienced and resourceful. I assure you now I am no threat to you. My killing days are well and truly over. As a further endorsement to my good intentions, I will happily answer any questions you may have about my past. My only proviso is this: you can ask me what you wish, and I will be truthful in my response, however once you have finished extracting the juicy bits, I do not want any more discussion on the subject. It is a part of my life I would rather forget. The matter will then be considered closed. Agreed?"

Karen nodded. "Agreed. You know how to hit a girl for six, don't you. Just when I get myself together, and think I am on top of things, you drop a bombshell, which takes me to another level. Thank you, guys!"

Ham, who had been very quiet that morning, busy listening and chewing, was starting to feel a little smug, now his pairing was starting to work. At least they were not throwing ornaments, furniture, or smart remarks at each other, he playfully thought.

Ham declared, "I have been doing some thinking too! I find

this whole thing very exciting, and at the risk of sounding like an invitation to a select swingers club, could I join you both too, for a threesome? This probably sounds all wrong, however I am genuinely very keen to get involved. I do not know what I could do for you both. Let me just say, now I have retired from the clergy, I am ready to go to work! I would be willing to help if I can."

Ham raised his teacup in approval, in typical persuasive style. "Are we partners, or are we partners?"

After a brief contemplation, William raised his coffee mug, side up to Ham. "We are partners."

Ham and William looked to Karen for mutual support. "Well, will you join our select club, Karen?"

After a teasingly short pause, Karen agreed. "We are partners." She raised her morning coffee cup in approval too. Karen's crime-solving partnership with Ham and William was born.

Karen was very eager to find out the full detail of William's history following his disclosure. The added dimension of a killer, hunting a killer, put a very positive creative twist on the investigation moving forward. Karen had ideas for progression, however they were relegated into second place, behind her newfound pre-occupation, which was to extract all the scandalous details from William's past as a hitman. Karen found herself in a fascinating position to be able to talk to a killer. A fully house-trained tame one at that!

What William Radnor did in his past was wrong, very wrong. However, what was it that made someone overstep the mark to that degree? Then switch it off, seemingly never to trigger the need to kill again. Karen was keen to find out. Would William Radnor reveal his past in all its gory entirety? Time would tell. Karen could not wait, finding it hard to conceal her excitement to ask a raft of direct questions regarding William's past.

# 5

Ham decided a day out was in order. All three of them agreed, and after one hour travelling from William's house, they climbed aboard the local gondola cable car, and took a ride to the summit of a prominent local mountain range. A lady has never truly experienced real glamour until she has been trudged up a mountain, wedged in a cable car with two burly men, accompanied by a strong south westerly. Welcome to the real Scotland. Karen loved it.

Knowing Karen had never been to Scotland previously, Ham was very keen to show her the jewels in the Highlands' crown. The coffee shop at the summit of the cable car was one of Ham's favourites. The location was remote, fresh, and the views were stunning, the strong coffee and delicate iced buns an added bonus.

Ham, Karen and William, sat at a table, in the summer sunshine, overlooking one of Scotland's awe-inspiring mountain ranges. Their coffee cups were fully charged and Karen's anticipation was at breaking point. The spotlight soon turned to William.

Karen could hardly contain herself any longer. "How did it all start, William? When did you first kill someone?"

Ham was eager to set the tone correctly and before William could draw breath, Ham's introduction was flowing with facts.

"William's upbringing was difficult. His mother died when he was five, his father was a drunk and spent most of his time between prison stretches and rehabilitation centres. As a youngster, William was bounced from one group of carers to another. He felt unloved, lonely, and isolated. He felt he was very different to everyone else. He was an only child with no family, his life experience was crushing him. The authorities did their best; he was labelled a 'problem child' and very few people took the trouble to get to know him."

William used Ham's slight pause as an opportunity to get his side of events aired. "Thank you, Ham, for those few kind words, and for a fine glowing introduction."

William began to tell his story, with his own words. He was fourteen years old when he first picked up a gun. It was peer pressure really. A group of older boys had a gun, and wanted a drunk man who was a notorious bully, killed. This guy, the bully, had picked on some of the younger girls from school. It was alleged this guy had abused children. He was not well liked. He was a nasty piece of work who shouted a lot. He had clearly been taking drugs and alcohol all day, and was vulnerable when he stumbled across William's group of school friends by the riverbank. It was after eleven in the evening and overhead street lamps flickered their reflection in the numerous puddles on the ground. This vagrant had stolen some drugs and booze, from the older boys, and they wanted to set the record straight by doing him in. At first they tried to get a younger ten-year-old boy to shoot the bully in the stomach whilst he was overcome and confused rolling and squirming on the ground. Fearful of what would happen if he did, and what the group of lads could do if he didn't, the young boy broke down in tears and was clearly very frightened and distressed. William, however, was keen to impress and strangely he was devoid of emotion. The older boys gave William the gun and told him to kill the nasty man. They wanted to see what he was made of, never believing William would do anything to harm the roaming nuisance who had fallen before them.

As a child, William had always felt so isolated, he had had a hole in his life where most others had a family. He never felt any love, no warmth, no moral compass to guide him. Suddenly, late at night, by the riverbank with these other kids, he had this chance to belong to something. He wanted desperately to belong to a welcoming crowd or a group or gang. Actually, on reflection, he did not know whether he wanted to be part of a gang or not. He just wanted to be part of something. There must have been a group of a dozen schoolkids round this bully lying on the floor. The bigger boys told William to kill him. He thought 'big deal'. William proceeded to put the gun to this man's head, and pulled the trigger without hesitation. Bang, it was over in seconds.

Then followed silence. Deadly silence.

Everyone just stood there looking at everyone. Someone asked was he dead? Then it turned into a frenzy. One of the kids grabbed the gun, and they all ran off in different directions. William was left staring at the body of the dead man on the floor. He calmly turned around and walked away. He got a lot of respect from the others after that, he never got picked on by anyone. That episode was never discussed again.

William had captivated his audience. He continued. "I can always remember feeling the weight of the gun in my hand for the first time, the sense of power, the precision of the thing and the smell after firing. Inducing fear in my victim, watching them squirm prior to the death sentence being activated, had its sordid appeal."

When William turned eighteen years old, he was approached by a guy in a pub, who had been one of those kids who had witnessed him kill the bully all those years earlier. The proposer was distressed and was very keen to offer William up to ten thousand pounds to kill a man who had muscled in on his drug-dealing patch. William agreed, thinking it was a one-off contract for easy money. He found the task simple, although he knew it was wrong. After his first contract killing, the phone just kept ringing and the work just piled in after that. It is amazing how quickly word gets around that you can do something rare, very well.

William's mindset was different back then. He was devoid of emotion, killing was quite clinical. He only killed so-called bad people or criminals. Whilst he was a hitman for hire, he never accepted contracts from jealous wives who had caught their husbands with their pants down, or over exuberant legitimate businessmen, trying to gain a commercial advantage by contracting William to wipe out a key competitor. Countless times, William would meet a stranger in a pub, they would offer all manner of different prizes, sometimes as high as twenty thousand pounds per hit, anything from cash in an envelope, or the latest Jaguar, an offshore account, luxury watches – the list and creativity of the offers were endless.

William found revealing his history quite therapeutic, it was almost as if his soul was receiving a well-needed cleansing. On rare occasions, he was able to reveal his historical notoriety. He felt invigorated with fresh energy. Committing a crime gave him an adrenalin rush, which sharpened his senses and fuelled his desire for survival. Telling his stories, again and again, recharged his distant batteries. His history was his drug, and he enjoyed the blast of the brief fixation.

William continued looking at Ham and Karen square on, his posture very well pronounced with a professional edge, similar in delivery to a trusted financial advisor revealing the next big opportunity to his clients.

"You might be surprised to learn I had high standards, I would only deal with really filthy, unsavoury individuals, drug dealers, extortionists, people traffickers, money launderers, and generally nasty people. There were enough bad people trying to get even with one another or gangland contracts to murder one another, or trying to teach one another a lesson, to give me a very good living for the best part of ten years."

William was keen to promote the view he was very good at what he did. He normally got his target on the first hit, and he was one hundred percent successful. He always killed with a gun. He was scrupulously careful. He took full control, and took the job on his own terms and timeframe. He had awesome influence. He had power, and he enjoyed harnessing the power accepting the contracts offered to him. Some of his peers made the mistake of not using a gun, perhaps trying to sabotage the target's car, or by arranging a fire or using generous quantities of C-4 explosives in spectacular fashion. These amateurs got involved in extremely messy affairs, which heightened the risk of innocent individuals getting harmed. Not to mention leaving catastrophic trace evidence behind, which William was very careful not to replicate.

"Why did you stop killing?" Karen asked.

William responded, "One day something snapped inside, and I said no more. A bit like when I gave up biting my nails; a little voice inside my head said no, so I stopped. Just like that. In truth I was aware that despite the best-laid plans and all that, the unexpected could and often did happen. Killing is a risky business and there are no guarantees. I no longer wanted to risk exposure to getting caught. Simple as that. So I stopped."

Karen reached out and held William's hand to the light, stating approvingly, "So you did stop biting your nails, and you have perfect half moons too."

William responded and smiled. "Yes, a man would never have noticed that, only a woman."

Karen enquired, "So was giving up contract killing, and the enjoyment, earning the money you did, as easy to give up as you thought?"

"No, and not for the reasons you might think!" William replied in a serious edgy tone.

"The problem is this, when you are involved with nasty,

unscrupulous people, you cannot stop being bad just because it suits you. I thought, rather naively, I could just switch it off. I was not sure what I was going to do; I just knew I did not want to kill anymore. I accepted in my heart that what I had been doing was wrong, and thought, that is it, no more contracts. It was time to move on."

William revealed he was living in London at the time, and had an expensive apartment overlooking the Thames. He was a confident bastard, swanning about in sharp suits and sharp cars. Not your typical undercover, trench coat-wearing let's-blend-in-with-the-scenery hitman. He was a nightmare. He enjoyed having a good time, got distracted with strings of girls, chancing his arm in casinos, and he started to overlook the basics of gun-for-hire survival.

"Such as?" Karen enquired.

"Well, always using a fresh batch of ammunition and from a different supplier per kill, using a different gun per contract, ensuring the serial number on the gun was always removed etc., it helps keep the ballistics people away from your tail when they think they are on to something. I had a friend who had his own lock-up garage, he used to break the guns down, 'chopping', he called it. He would then conceal the gun parts in household rubbish and hand deliver it to the landfill crusher. Towards the end, I might use a gun for two or three contracts. Once I tossed a weapon into the Thames after I used it, which was stupid. These things have a habit of coming back to haunt you. Luckily it has not been found or if it has, I have not been linked to it!"

Karen asked, "I do not understand why you could not just stop contract killing. What prevented you from ceasing to lead the life of an assassin when you wanted to?"

"When you have been accepting contracts for killing, for ten years or more, people get used to it, they expect to be able to call on you, and for you to accept the job. If you are dealing with prominent figures in the underworld, and they approach you, and one day you turn around and say no, they do not like it. You need to think how these people operate. There are not really asking you, can you kill someone and we will give you some money. They are telling you to kill someone, then they seal the deal with money, they buy your silence with assumptive mutual agreement.

"The other issue is reverse admittance. If you decline their offer, then you expose yourself to being a target. You see, they have confided in you, that they want someone killed. It's transparency of contract. If you choose not to accept it, you have that contract knowledge. That level of knowledge is extremely dangerous. The fewer the number of people who know, the better. Top-ranking villains do not like to be messed around. When a decision is made to *remove* someone, swift action speaks louder than words."

William, sensing retiring from hitman duties was not going to be easy, approached an old friend. That old friend was Reverend Ham, and William approached him for spiritual guidance. William confided in Ham, and he advised him to move away. Start a new life, a legal new life, before his past, his enemies, or his victims' associates, got even and caught up with him.

William was barely thirty years old when he decided to throw the towel in. Ham took William under his wing, and was instrumental in taking him away from the temptation of London, by exposing him to another way of life. A better way to lead his life, if an accountant's professional can be classified as better!

William found it a real tug leaving London, he loved the place. He knew it well, and he knew how to make things happen, and where to go to get things in life he needed. He found moving to Scotland a real upheaval. He knew it was necessary and invaluable for his long-term survival. The pace, however, was painfully slow in comparison to the bustle, diversity and complexities of modern London.

William confided with Karen playfully. "It is one of life's paradoxes; do you carry on with an exciting life in London, being totally in control, living on the edge illegally taking risks, knowing you might just be one step away from the police arresting you and locking you up. Every day I stayed in London could have been a day closer to winding up bloodstained and beaten in an alley. What is the alternative? Do you confine yourself to a life of boredom in Scotland? It is a difficult call to make!"

Ham came to the rescue of the Scottish Tourist Board, defending his corner, with an ever-broader Scottish accent, announcing, "With Scotland, the drama is in the scenery, and in the golden liquid we Scots hold so dear to our hearts. Then there is the warmth and generosity of the local people, the community spirit, and ample fresh produce."

Karen was like a dog with a bone, her questions increasingly broadcast in a more intense tone, came thick and fast, asking William, "Do you miss killing people, William?"

William responded, "No, I do not miss taking people's lives. That was wrong. I loved the thrill of accepting a contract, and for getting well paid for doing something I was gifted with. You see not everyone can deal with the emotional and moral side of things, not everyone can fire a gun well. Not everyone can shoot and be accurate. When you sprinkle the pressure of getting caught with the additional focus of a short timeframe to target, balanced with the deep water, you would get into if you failed in your task. You needed to be quick, successful, and obviously not get caught. Simple! It is pointless having lots of money, then spending a lifetime in prison. I got a tremendous buzz and satisfaction from killing at the time. It is a shame it is not a legal sport."

"Did the police ever get close to catching you?" asked an ever-inquisitive Karen.

"The police interviewed me on a couple of occasions, which I thought was purely routine rather than targeted interrogation. My findings seemed to reflect the fact, as a criminal had been killed, did it really matter? You see, if a drunk driver kills a mother and her baby, this person needs to be found and charges brought. If an arms dealer or people trafficker winds up in a ditch, is it a big deal? Morally, yes, it is, but the reality is, it is one less problem for the masses to deal with. Who cares about a drug dealer rotting in a gutter?"

Ham raised his arm to attract the attention of the resident waitress, to recharge their coffee cups.

Ham then stated, "You see, I knew there were hidden qualities in that mixed up kid William, who was desperate for change all those years ago. It is now time to put those ill-gotten gains behind you and use your knowledge and experience to good effect and get Karen a worthwhile result. We have a killer to find."

The three of them pondered the future, enjoyed the Scottish mountain backdrop and the strong tasty fresh coffee. Following some lively chit-chat, more intricate tails and playful banter, Karen had one final question to ask. "What about women, William? What happened to the ladies in your life?"

William, for once, looked slightly uncomfortable with Karen's questions, his eye contact became erratic and his arms moved oddly, highlighting his awkward predicament. "That is private. There is no lady in my life at the moment."

*Oh*, Karen thought, *here is a man willing to tell his deepest most tantalising secrets regarding highly illegal activity, namely committing murders, and yet he is not prepared to discuss something less complicated or casual than his relationships with other women. How odd!*

Karen decided to keep her questions firmly on her back burner, she was sure there had to be some stories to tell here.

William, keen to put some distance between Karen's romantically linked grilling, enquired, "It would be good to have an overview of your sister's crime scene and I would like to see the room where the murders happened."

"That's fine," said Karen as they made tracks back to William's house for a full update on Michael and Helen's murder.

# 6

The village of Hawkswold had never seen a sunrise like it. It was seven twenty-two in the morning when police were first notified that there had been a murder. The Stansfelds' housekeeper, Mrs Brown, had raised the alarm after finding the two lifeless bloodstained bodies of her employers, Michael and Helen Stansfeld, in their master bedroom.

Police immediately closed the village to through traffic. Police Range Rovers, normally the preserve of the Motorway Division, were used in spectacular fashion; sliding at speed to a halt sideways across the access roads to the village. The high-profile roadblocks cut off all immediate traffic flow with urgency, and leaving no doubt to onlookers that a serious crime had been committed in the vicinity.

Before chattering neighbours had chance to air their inquisitive opinions, a line of police cars and two ambulance vehicles blocked the single-track road, which formed the main arterial route through the village. Slamming doors from the emergency services and skidding tyres from abrupt stops from investigative personnel was a most uncharacteristic start to the typical calm country village dawn of a bright fresh day.

The Stansfelds' home, a picturesque thatched cottage, was

sealed off with familiar blue and white police tape. Uniformed police immediately made house-to-house enquiries, gathering data. Forensic teams collected evidence inside the cottage and combed the garden and pathways for material clues. The Kent police helicopter circled above, adding to the intensity of the crime and stirring attention.

As the drama unfolded, excitement and concern was in rich abundance as the glare of media publicity hit home to the sleepy Kentish village and its inhabitants. Remote broadcasting vans, equipped with the latest satellite technology, were queuing up and ready to broadcast sketchy details of the crime, nationally and globally.

Gun crime is rare in this country; it's practically unheard of in the Kent countryside. Make no mistake Hawkswold was well and truly on the global map, featuring on all the major television and radio news programmes. Media chatter was everywhere.

As details of the victims had been leaked to the media, and reference made to a significant lovers' quarrel noted by a neighbour, news reports gathered momentum that Michael Stansfeld had killed his wife Helen, and then turned the gun on himself. Another theory gaining traction was that the Stansfelds had been burgled. They were known to be fond of expensive antiques, and it was totally plausible a thief, caught in the act, had used a gun on the unfortunate Stansfelds, as they were woken by the crime in progress, with disastrous tragic consequences.

The vicious crime had been committed in the early hours, the time of death was estimated at approximately one o'clock in the morning, the appalling events unfolding in the couple's master bedroom. Forensics confirmed three bullets had been fired into each victim, resulting in almost instant death to both parties. The aggressive nature of the close range firing of the high velocity bullets resulted in significant blood loss from substantial skin tissue damage and irreparable damage to key internal organs.

It was likely both the victims were making love to each other at the time of death; forensic details confirmed there were signs of sexual activity between them. Karen remembered thinking cheekily to herself, what a way to go, and good on you, sis! My sister would have liked that, brazen to the last. This detail was not relayed to the general public of course.

The victims, Helen and her husband Michael, lived in a thoroughly charming Kent village. This was not an inner-city turbulent area, with a history of violent problems. Far from it; you simply could not wish for a more idyllic, quieter place to live.

So why kill Helen? Why Helen and her devoted husband? Why this village? A question the deceased's sister Karen, the police and the media were anxious to find out.

The facts were stark, and clues minimal. There was no apparent break in, no locks were forced. No apparent attempts of theft of personal effects. No items in the house appeared to be moved, certainly no evidence of a struggle. There were no fingerprints. The murder weapon was never found, the bullets retrieved from the bodies and walls were standard 9mm bullets. The likely murder weapon was a 9mm semi-automatic handgun with silencer. None of the local residents saw anything suspicious, or witnessed any noise, and nobody witnessed anything unusual prior to the double murders. Rumours of a quarrel between the victims the evening before seemed to evaporate once the police started asking direct questions within the community.

The killings had the hallmarks of a highly organised contract killing, but why? Was it a case of mistaken identity? Was it a totally random, unprovoked attack?

The police of course looked closely at Helen's and Michael's family arrangements and business dealings, but nothing appeared unusual. Their private life was private, and relatively problem free. They were well liked and certainly did not have any enemies; this whole thing did not make any sense. What were the motive for the murders? No obvious reason could be found. Could this awful turn of events really have been a dreadful mistake? How else could anybody explain it.

Karen and her sister Helen were extremely close. If something was wrong, or if Helen feared something or someone, she surely would have told Karen. There was never a hint of any problems in their relationship, or with any outsiders. The fact the police were no closer to solving the murders, with the lack of hard evidence, was a real strain. Without reasoning or evidence, and no obvious killer, there was no closure and there were no answers.

# 7

Ham and Karen travelled south with William to take him to the scene of the crime, the destination the Stansfelds' cottage in Hawkswold. It was an opportunity for all of them to start to work together, and for their investigation into the double murders to flourish or flounder. This was William's first visit to the village, and he was notably quiet as he soaked up all the information around him.

The first stop was Karen's house. Ham brought his car to a halt on Karen's drive following the long journey from the Highlands and all three of them got out and stretched their legs with pleasure. Karen lived alone at the other end of the village, in a very nice, modern four-bedroom detached house. Karen was two years younger than her late sister Helen, and she preferred the younger more modern home, with easier maintenance and less fuss and glamour in the garden. They both loved the freshness of the country, and enjoyed the quietness and exposure to nature the village life afforded them.

Karen led the way for the two men to follow. It was a brief two-minute walk through the village to reach the cottage. Karen was very keen to let William do some prodding, prior to her making an evening meal, back at her house for her two new, illustrious partners.

William's first observations, stating the obvious, was that Hawkswold was a very small village. As Karen had detailed previously, the village was remote, and was served by a single-track country lane only. A sprinkling of period listed homes and farmhouses formed the backbone to the village. Some newer houses had been built in the last thirty years or so, developing the character of the village along the central, arterial thoroughfare with a solitary phone box at one end of the village, the church in the middle, and a farm and numerous agricultural outbuildings at the other end. Typical of modern cutbacks, the village school had long ceased teaching pupils as it simply was not big enough to compete with modern efficiency targets, and the local post office in recent years had morphed back into service as a residential dwelling.

Situated opposite the prominent village church, was the Stansfelds' delightful thatched cottage, presented perfectly and complimented with well-established truly beautiful gardens. In truth, the Stansfelds' foliage was a touch unkempt, however the overall impact of the gardens were still delightful all the same. If ever you wanted to fall in love with the archetypal English thatched cottage with playful character eyebrows surrounding the top floor wooden windows, then this was it. Its only historical tarnish being the unsolved mystery of the recent murders.

Karen opened the front gate to the garden, and proceeded onwards to open the large wooden front door to the cottage. The front door never opened smoothly, or closed snugly without a generous shove. Helen had often referred to this as homely character.

Once inside, you were hit with the wonderful smell of an open log fire, even though the cottage's fireplace had not seen service for several months. The exposed wooden beams dominated the internal structure, providing very pleasing aesthetics, as well as obliging structural reassurance. The massively thick outer walls, typical of the period, reduced the internal dimensions of the property tremendously. The downstairs area was effectively split evenly in two halves, consisting of a living area with large inglenook fireplace, and a dining room filling the other side of the cottage.

Karen, keen to demonstrate some knowledgeable flair, stated to her assembled guests, "This village harks back to medieval times, and this cottage where we are standing, which is over four hundred years old, at some point in its past, used to be the village bakery."

Ham could not resist. "Bloody good job it never caught fire. Thatched cottage used as a bakery, whatever next!"

William and Karen, ignored Ham's subtle attempt at humour, and continued without allowing their serious demeanour to be dented. Once they had completed a ground floor tour, Karen led Ham and William up the creaky wooden narrow staircase to the master bedroom, where the crime had been committed. The constricted access route to the first floor was notable for being precarious, full of character and a noisy way to manoeuvre around a property. Sensations sure to be totally alien to a homeowner used to a modern-built or recently designed property.

"What did the ballistics report from the police say about the killers weapon?" enquired William, sticking his head into the master bedroom.

Karen read out part of the report she had in her briefcase – DCI Cattermole had given this to her in confidence. "The origin of the firearm is unknown, a 9mm calibre weapon had been used to commit both murders. Standard specification ammunition was used, it was noted typical examples of the bullets recovered from the scene are freely available commercially. No unique signatures found."

William again was very considerate, and measured in his response. He knew full well 9mm handguns were plentiful, and even if he knew what type of handgun was used, he could not draw any helpful conclusions. He knew gunmen used different weapons for different reasons. Availability of a model is a factor, how the firearm feels in the gunman's hand, how comfortable and positive is the grip, is the trigger mechanism well weighted for the user? Every gunman had a favourite, and unfortunately the ballistics revelations meant nothing. Handguns come in many shapes and sizes, and this group of would-be detectives would never know whether they were looking for a common handgun, or the 9mm pistol which could claim to be the choice of champions.

William turned to Karen and said, "All I can tell you, Karen, is this is no contract killing. Whoever committed these murders, in this bedroom, was passionate about killing the victims. That is all."

William knew the risk was far too great for a contract killer; to enter this cottage, climb the crooked wooden stairs, then find the right bedroom. To do this without knowing if anybody else was in the cottage, other than the victims. The risk with this kind of shooting going wrong was immense. Lack of plentiful, sizeable exits, and working in a confined area was a recipe for disaster. He knew the killer almost certainly knew the cottage well, which meant, the killer probably knew the victims too.

William asked Karen matter of factly, "Who do you think killed your sister, Karen? Who do you know who is capable of this? I am certain the killer knew every inch of this cottage, which means they could possibly know you."

Karen was stunned by his authoritative statement, adding in a non-agreeable manner. "This killing could be totally random, by an unknown psycho," she reasoned, not being totally prepared to accept that she may also have known the perpetrator.

Ham then commented, "If we are all prepared to accept this murder was random, carried out by a local *nutter*, then we might as well call it a day, and go to the pub now. No amount of head scratching and thought provoking analysis will help us solve this crime today. However, it is my belief we are dealing with a very dangerous calculating killer, and that killer had a motive. We need to find out the killer's motive."

William offered his viewpoint. "There are two things which

could get you killed today: a relationship which has gone wrong, or the fact you owe somebody lots of money. These murders could be as simple or as complicated as that."

William turned to Karen. "Did the Stansfelds owe money to anyone, Karen? Or were either of them having an affair or involved with anyone else?"

Karen defended Helen's position. "Absolutely not. Their marriage was strong. Helen would not have had an affair; she was not the type. I am certain Michael would have remained faithful to her too. The business Michael was running was doing well. I do not know too much about his business other than he bought the odd classic car and he ran a horse transport business. I do not believe they had any money worries. Whatever Helen wanted, she got, within reason."

Ham sighed. "Karen, are you aware of any heated arguments or problem phone calls Michael took?"

Karen responded, "There were occasional colourful exchanges with suppliers, but nothing aggressive, unusual or intimidating. Barely a day went by without me speaking to Helen, she was my sister after all and we were very close. If there was a problem with something or someone, she would have mentioned it to me."

Karen sighed in despair and flopped into one of the fireside armchairs, turning towards William and Ham. "I have been a bloody fool. To think we can stand a chance of finding Helen's killer. Where do we go from here? You said it yourself, Ham, if the police cannot find the killer, what hope have we got?"

Ham walked over to Karen, and approached her chair from behind. He leant over and outstretched his arms and rested his hands on her shoulders in support. "Remember what you said to me, Karen, when I made that comment. You told me your passion and your desire fuelled your pursuit for justice. That is an edge you have, over and above the police. You have an energy for this, Karen, and William and I will help you."

A tear ran down Karen's cheek as she wrestled with her emotions. She raised a hand to meet Ham's hand on her shoulder, and smiled in approval of his comments.

William was convinced the police must have missed something, something trivial, which could have major benefits to solving the crime. At least he hoped as much. Uneasy with Karen's emotional twist, sensing the proceedings needed direction, he offered his thoughts. "Karen, I think it would be useful for you to write down all the contact names from both Helen's and Michael's mobile phones, also state next to their contact names, what their relationship with each of them was. Think about calling patterns, there could be some clues here in the mobile phone bills. Also find out who spoke to them both on the evening prior to their shooting."

William continued, "The police would have done this already, I know, however you have the benefit of knowing who some of the contacts are, and something might stand out as being unusual. See if something surprises you." Karen nodded in approval, wiped her eyes dry, and set about finding the phones, chargers and bills.

William, by now on something of a roll, looked at Ham. "Why don't you go to the pub, Ham!"

Ham responded, "You serious?"

"Yes, go to the pub and interrogate the locals. Find out what their gut feelings are, and find out if anyone has gone missing or acted strangely since the murder. Also whilst you are out and about, get some milk, we need some coffee in here."

As Ham left the cottage, William reminded him not to tell the villagers why he was asking questions. Ham accepted his mission with relish, and could hardly believe his luck. An invitation to go to the pub, be inquisitive, lay on the charm with a hidden agenda and drink beer. Life really did not get any better for this ex-man of the cloth.

William then asked Karen, "Where can I find Michael's

50

business accounts? I would like to review your sister's personal accounts too."

Karen was a little hesitant at first, the bank details and entries were personal, personal to her family, however she knew if there was a clue in the detail, then the contents would be worth sharing. Again the thought entered her head, the police have reviewed these already, so would they have not flagged something up. Anyway, she did as she was asked.

Karen passed over the mass of paper remarking, "The top statements are the business accounts, and the bottom section statements are my sister's private account."

William sat down on the large sofa, and started sifting through the large binder of paperwork and bank statements as he set about searching for potential clues.

Three and half hours passed in no time at all. Ham arrived back from his adventurous public house mission, brandishing three very enticing bottles of quality Italian white wine.

William enquired, "Ham, good you are back. Did you find anything interesting out?"

Ham replied slightly bashfully, "Yes, the pub does not sell any milk!"

William and Karen knew Ham was likely to have had a few too many pints of beer and forgot the reason for venturing out in the first place. His return with three bottles of wine was, however, a welcome gesture, even if it was quite a predictable outcome.

Ham's return alerted Karen to the fact it was time for her to prepare some food. They all agreed to regroup back at her house, enjoy an evening meal, and discuss their afternoon's findings. Would their collective digging amount to much?

Sustenance would have to take the form of something quick that evening, Karen thought, wedging a large ungrateful-looking frozen pizza into her faithful, well-used oven.

With a generous token salad bowl to accompany the Italian

themed feast, within half an hour, dinner of sorts was served, much to the delight of her new men in her life.

Following the meal, the three of them sat down on the sofa and armchairs in Karen's agreeable, self-styled front room, each of them eager to enlighten the others to their findings.

Karen started with her analysis. Helen's mobile phone had predictably been little used. She had her close circle of friends, many of whom Karen knew. Helen did not speak to anyone regarding Michael's business dealings, Karen felt sure of that. With Helen, girly chit-chat and rich gossip, appeared to be the order of the day looking at her mobile call log.

Thinking about it, Karen could never recall a situation where Helen took a call at home in her presence regarding their commercial activity, all business calls were routed to Michael's mobile. Was this a deliberate act of a control freak or a brutal undertaking of concealment?

Karen's analysis of the phone bills revealed, unsurprisingly, Michael made a lot more telephone calls than Helen. One name kept cropping up with frequency on Michael's mobile phone; a man Karen had never met, a guy called Alfonso. She did not know how he operated, however he provided Michael with lots of work. He cropped up in lots of conversations when Karen had been round Helen's house, enjoying liberal chit-chat and numerous coffees with copious lady gossip.

Karen revealed, "The evening before their murder, Michael rang me, and nobody else. We discussed a birthday gift for a family friend. There were no other outgoing calls made after that."

So Karen had made progress of sorts, and Alfonso was definitely on the group's radar for a future meeting. Ham recharged everyone's glasses with a fresh refill of the fruity Italian wine he had so carefully sourced.

William injected his approach into the evening's proceedings by prodding Karen with lots of questions, in what was reminiscent of a quick-fire round. "Did Helen ever have large bundles of cash or currency? Did Helen and Michael ever do anything unusual? Did they hold other bank accounts, business or otherwise? Were they involved with any dramas in their lives, any confrontation with any individuals? Did they have financial pressures? Did they ever handle large sums of cash? How well was their business doing?"

William's tactic was to try and get Karen thinking again, spontaneously. Was there something critical she knew, which she had failed to recognise as being important?

Unfortunately, the tactic did not appear to work, as Karen's non-committal response said it all for her.

William fired a few other queries at Karen. "Who came to the funeral? Did anyone arrive you did not know? Was anyone there out of place?"

Karen remained calm and focussed, delivering a very solid blow to William's avenue of questioning. "Nothing struck me as being odd, nothing appeared out of place, everyone at the funeral seemed full of love and genuinely saddened by the events which had unfolded. I can never recall Helen talking about large sums of cash. I cannot help you, William, sorry."

It was evident William had a real energy for getting answers. However, it would appear his chosen route taken for progress was sadly misplaced. Karen remained unflustered, thinking it must be the cheese in the pizza that had affected him.

William fired one final question at Karen. "Who found the bodies?"

Karen replied, "Mrs Brown, the elderly housekeeper, found them both when she started work just before half past seven in the morning. She worked three hours per day, two days per week, and had done so for the last five years. She was a lovely old lady from an adjoining village, she was very loyal and enjoyed keeping busy. She was devastated with her find, and no, she is not a valid suspect."

William absorbed Karen's answer and went on to detail his findings, noting the police had copied lots of the bank statements, and left comments and their reference numbers on some of them, however, interestingly, not all of them.

William went on to explain that Helen and Michael had had a joint bank account, a household account, which appeared to be used like a traditional account. This account checked out fine, appearing normal in all respects. There were monthly electronic transfers of four thousand pounds, credited from Michael's business account, on the button, every month. These were the same account statements the police had scrutinised, leaving tell-tale investigation evidence reference numbers all over it.

Michael's business account made a lot less sense. William's observation was that Michael's business account were not the accounts of a traditional business.

It was clear from what had been presented to William that Michael was no accountant. In fact, given the slap dash nature of the few presented supporting commercial invoices and lack of substantive entries, it indicated a qualified accountant had probably never been close to these business accounts previously. It was apparent none of Michael's business financial paper flow had been audited professionally. They had not been audited for a reason. It was unlikely the tax authorities were even remotely aware of Michael's business activities. It was William's suspicion there was a reason for that. It was not just a tax dodge, there was a greater depth to this, a worrying degree of holes and lacking in valuable turnover.

William offered the following summary to Karen and Ham. "Tax office, HM Revenue and Customs, lack of income tax declarations, lack of VAT payment, and a can of worms! Then throw into the account, large deposits of forty-five thousand pounds, three times per year, and another deposit of seventy-five thousand pounds sterling. Vast credits into a business account, with no connection with an invoice or any detailed services, in between long periods of dormant activity. Michael was on the fiddle."

William's assessment gained gravity from his findings that

Michael had made circa one hundred and ninety thousand pounds income, in one twelve-month period, importing one classic car and operating one journey in a horsebox from France. The accounts looked so good, they had to be wrong.

Karen tried to plead support. "Could it just be a simple case of ignorance?"

William replied in a true qualified accountant authoritative tone. "There is no excuse for ignorance in business. I have no doubt Michael knew exactly what he was doing. He was not doing well enough to do the job well!"

It was clear from William's findings that Michael's commercial enterprise did very little business, however earned very well. Michael was clearly up to no good.

William unquestionably excited, rubbed his hands together in a token gesture of personal glee, "In fact I am very satisfied with what I have found here. This is good work, good progress. I feel very positive and I have not even shot anyone yet!"

Ham and Karen looked at each other, wide eyed, aghast and slightly worried. William of course was only playing.

Ham quietly reminded Karen, "William is not only an accountant, he is a person, a real person with feelings and a sense of humour. When he is good, he is very good, when he is bad, he is terrible."

William, sensing he had caught Michael out with mismatched accounts enquired, "What sort of man was Michael? Was he articulate? was he trustworthy?"

Karen responded, "Michael was an honest, kind person. He was very likable and a loving husband. My sister had been married to him for twelve years. Michael clearly was definitely not an accountant. He was a very private man, he kept most things close to his chest. Just because a man keeps untidy accounts, it does not mean he is a villain?"

William prodded Karen again. "Were your sister and brother-in-law insured?"

Karen replied, "I am not aware of their insurance status. They may not have been insured. Then again they may have been?" Karen thought for a private moment, perhaps they were insured – who would benefit from that?

Ham interjected, "Was Helen actively involved in the business, Karen, or was it totally Michael's domain? Was she knowledgeable, or was she out the loop with his business dealings?"

Karen enlightened both inquisitors. "Helen was the most silent of partners. She provided some financial assistance, however Michael was the driving force and dealt with the operational side. He did all the negotiating and worked the deals out. Helen hated numbers and disliked the likely confrontation that cropped up every now and again in business."

William declared in a statement to Karen and Ham, "If Michael was squeaky clean, we would all be looking at one another, reaching out for the next clue, probably in despair. My findings with these accounts are significant. These anomalies indicate it is well worth us scratching beneath the surface to reach new available clues within his business activity."

Ham, aware of the difficult personal connection between Karen and this case, enquired with sensitivity, "What have Michael's family said regarding the murders?"

Karen informed Ham that, whilst Michael was a fine gentle man, he did not blend well with his family and none of them were particularly close. Michael's family were shocked with his murder as you would expect, however there was no obvious friction or cause for concern with his immediate family.

William still had comments to get off his chest. He made his view clear that when people wind up dead, these sorts of extreme actions often came down to money. "Were they financially strong? Did they borrow money from an unregulated or unofficial source? Were they forced to borrow funds so quickly that their credit status could not support them? Did they fail to make the repayments?"

Karen shook her head. "I do not believe debt was a problem.

If my sister and Michael had financial difficulties, I am sure Helen would have said something to me."

William, always keen to get a reaction, offered, "People are not always as perfect as their home life may be portrayed. Trust me, things are not always as rosy as their family unit persona may dictate or project. Walls keep secrets."

William was concerned that Karen was very protective of her sister, even if this was understandable and to be fully expected. It might mean Karen could potentially fail to identify facts or approach circumstantial evidence with the unbiased eye, critical for solutions to their dilemmas and challenges.

Ham quizzed William. "The police knew the issues with the accounts, they have seen them. They may have acted on these enquiries already?

William's response was quite direct. "The police may have took one look at this amount of untidy paperwork, and skipped across the surface. Worse still they may not have realised the distinction between the two accounts and the queries the entries highlighted. The police reference numbers and comments only refer to the household accounts, not the erratic business accounts, there are no formal endorsements on those. I think they missed it."

Ham's thoughts were equally disturbing. "The police have suffered budget cuts, staff shortages and lack the number of experienced staff their departments need to function effectively. Is it conceivable a junior member of staff, tasked with looking at every shred of paper evidence for this case, missed this glowing opportunist clue regarding the mismatch in accountable income, against the service Michael provided. Why were questions not asked?"

Ham and Karen were full of respect for DCI Cattermole and his enquiry, they were sure he was a very capable detective. Questions however were now raised regarding the quality input of the fact-finding resources used within this murder investigation, leading to this posing thought to be launched. If the police missed this detail, what else could they have neglected to have seen? In a murder investigation, oversights are unacceptable at this level, and any negligence regarding a lack of progress from available substantial evidence had to fall squarely at the feet of the officer in charge, namely DCI Cattermole.

Ham, William and Karen reminded each other their quest was one of resolving the mystery of the murder and providing closure for Karen. Their goal was not to pick holes in the police force or to try and make excuses for them, or try to understand the pressure they were exposed to every day. Although William quietly liked the idea of taking on the police, head to head, playing mind games and hopefully beating them.

Ham looked at Karen, and she was tired. Between the three of them they had, enjoyed some fun, and made some real progress clue hunting and putting the overstretched police to rights.

That night in Karen, Ham saw a lady gripped with pain needing a hug. "Are you okay, Karen?"

"Every day I think about the murders. It distracts me, it disturbs me. I have got to do something about it. That is my angle. I need my life back. I am not interested in scoring points over the police, even if they have made mistakes. Helen and I were extremely close sisters, we had the odd cross word, but our closeness developed over the years. We were friends, confidants, and enjoyed our time together immensely. I sorely miss her and I want the bastard who committed this crime. That is all."

Ham and William, sensing enough was enough, put on their coats and said their goodbyes. Karen was genuinely very happy with the headway made, even if she was slightly aggravated by William's seemingly senseless questioning and enthusiasm for accounts data. His heart was in the right place, she thought, even if his brains were irritatingly elsewhere.

# 8

Three days had passed since Karen, Ham and William had met and trawled through all the paperwork at the cottage. Karen was driving back home alone after an evening out with her lady friends. Her cross-country trek would take her twenty minutes to reach her drive and would normally be a non-eventful journey, a precursor to a late- night bath and opportunity to catch up some much-needed sleep.

That night the rain had started with a vengeance and the wet roads had the potential to be very slippery. Karen was in no rush to kill herself and was taking her time, driving steadily.

After a while, Karen was aware that a car was following close behind her. It had been pursuing her for quite some distance. As the headlights played in her mirrors, her focus on the car behind increased and a tingle of tension began to creep in

Why did the car not overtake? she thought. She slowed her car from a solid fifty miles per hour to around forty miles per hour. The car behind her still failed to overtake. It just stayed on her tail, too close for comfort.

Karen then decided to increase her speed, this time raising her speed to sixty and then onto seventy miles per hour. Whilst she was more than capable of driving at that speed, she was on a country A road and the sweeping bends presented little problem for her in her little Roadster sports car.

The noise from the rain hitting the fabric roof increased in its intensity as the weather worsened. The sparkling lights from oncoming traffic appeared and disappeared with increasing momentum. The driver behind responded by maintaining the closeness to Karen's tail lights. The chase was on!

Who the hell would be driving so close to her? Karen's mind tripped into overdrive, digesting the options as her focus and firm grip on the steering wheel went up a gear. Was it another motorist displaying road rage tendencies, following a minor traffic-related issue, Karen was not conscious of? Was it youngsters or joy riders trying to scare a lone lady driver, or was it something more sinister? An option too worrying to contemplate.

Karen decided a dab of normality was in order and decided to slow her car back to her more comfortable fifty miles per hour. Given she had unwelcome visitors escorting her, she chose not to drive straight home, but sensibly decided to carry on to friends she knew who lived ten minutes away.

As Karen's car straightened a bend, bang, a loud crack and surge of energy pushed her car from behind. Karen screamed, and hung on for the ride of her life as the car following behind had rammed her. The driver pursuing her had decided to demonstrate their intent by forcing Karen into corrective action. She immediately felt the steering of her car go light and the seat of her pants slide alarmingly as her car skidded from one side of the road to the other. In advance of the pendulum effect turning into a devastating tank slapper, Karen demonstrated highly impressive car control and amazing presence of mind she quickly turned the steering into the skid, and dropped a gear ratio, pushing the engine revs, accelerating to maintain control.

Before Karen could fully grab her thoughts, bang and crack again. The driver behind gave another ram to her rear. This time the physical impact was less severe, however Karen's heartbeat raised in unison with her rev counter as she desperately tried to get away. She decided to damn the consequences and floored the throttle.

As the journey continued, the risks became more frequent and numerous. Her heightened heart rate and adrenalin rush taking her to a new level of terrified, pushing her above the realms of normal thoughts and reasoning. She began taking uncharacteristic risks, carrying dangerous doses of speed into challenging corners.

Screaming engines, increasing road noise and spirited exhaust tones filled the evening air. As Karen's speed increased, so seemingly did the intensity of the pursuing car's headlamps. Karen became increasingly distracted with the following car's looming silhouette and irrepressible glare in her rear-view mirror. She tried to anticipate the next attack, her lack of focus with oncoming traffic and roadside obstacles were taking its toll on her car.

Oncoming traffic sounded their horns in protest as Karen's car became more unstable at speed, dangerously crossing the central white line, glancing a passing motorist, sparks flying. Roadside hedges and embankments were hugged to the point of despair, certain to inflict terminal damage to her car with prolonged enthusiastic contact.

Karen negotiated a series of bends, comfortably in excess of the speed limit. As a straight piece of road emerged, she braced herself as the pursuing car closed in for a further ramming. This time the impact was more severe, louder and frightening. Karen's car's chassis was past anxious and slippery rubber tyres could not fight the laws of physics any longer. The resultant spin sent Karen's car pirouetting across a road junction and seventy-five feet into an adjoining unfenced, muddy field.

The perpetrators of the chase had stopped in the road with urgency, the driver lowered his electric window to improve their view of the spectacle. The driver looked momentarily at the car in the field and Karen exchanged glances with them.

It was dark, it was raining, she froze in horror with her

predicament. Karen's car was silent, the engine had ceased turning. The lights were still on, and broken coolant lines provided a cloud of steam for her headlamp beams to cut through, all adding theatre to her accident.

In silence, Karen remained seated. Karen had witnessed her first serious road traffic accident, and tried to allow her thoughts to catch up with the reality of the situation. The resultant spin could have been catastrophic, had an oncoming motorist been using the junction, the junction Karen had just passed over at speed, rotating and facing the wrong direction.

Without warning, the other car driver raised his electric window and drove off at speed. Karen was a wreck, she was left in tears and grappling for her mobile phone. She then rang the police for help and recovery, totally terrified, however thoroughly relieved her immediate drama was over.

She was left pondering a lot of what ifs whilst she waited for the police to arrive. What would have happened if she had hit an oncoming car head on? What would have happened if she had hit the embankment head on and gone airborne? What would have happened if her car had been flipped over, during her spin?

To cap it all, Karen found herself in the middle of a muddy field, wearing her best shoes, and nowhere to go. She calmly got out of her car, threw her designer shoes onto the roof of her car, allowed her bare feet to sink into the wet mud, looked up to the stars, and said, "Shit, what a night. I am a mess, my car looks like a write-off and I am on my own in the rain. Fantastic!"

The police, an ambulance and a recovery truck all appeared within fifteen minutes of her telephone call to the scene of Karen's accident. Having dismissed medical attention, Karen left the required statement to the attendant policeman and was given a lift home.

Karen reflected to herself on the evening's events. She had not expected to be rammed off the road following a lovely evening out with friends. She had not expected to find herself the centre of attention with the local emergency services, whilst getting extricated from a mud flooded field. Nobody deserved that kind of treatment, surely?

Karen said her goodbyes to the policeman as she was dropped off at her home. As she walked up her drive, she removed her house key with anticipation, and was eager to open her front door and put the awful events of the last ninety minutes behind her.

As Karen entered her house, she noticed an envelope on the floor, which had clearly been delivered by hand through her letterbox.

She removed her coat and sat down. The envelope was blank. Inside was a computer-written note, it read:

*I want my money, and I want it now. If you do not pay me, then next time you may not be so lucky?*

*I want my money!*

*C*

Karen went straight to her front door, opened it and screamed into the darkness. "Who are you? What do you want. Why are you hounding me?"

Karen did not expect anyone to listen, or to return her shrieking cries, this was an extreme demonstration of frustration venting more than anything else. Besides, it was now well past eleven in the evening and only the odd badger and resident fox family were guaranteed to hear her.

Her fears that the ramming incident was purely joyriders, had been quashed. Someone clearly had an agenda, and the thumbscrews were turning.

After a pause, and a return of silence, Karen gently closed her front door, she put her television on quietly and opened a bottle of white wine. Her thoughts which penetrated her mind were a combination of surreal disbelief, blinding bafflement, topped off with raging anger.

Karen held herself together well, she did not lose control of her actions or cave in under pressure. Her emotions and her composure held up impressively. A blip in her blood pressure and a punishing migraine from hell were the only factors offering side effects. Knowing she needed to get her head around these recent traumatic events, she chose, rightly or wrongly, to keep the experiences of the last two hours to herself. She did not want to burden Ham or William with this episode. Not yet! She certainly did not want any distraction to cloud their judgement regarding finding Helen's killer.

Was Karen demonstrating a master class in observation and self-containment? Or was she acting stupidly? Only time would tell.

Pondering her evening, Karen consumed the Chardonnay with vigour, and with her trusty glass of white wine by her side, the calming qualities of the grape did the trick. Karen sighed and soon enough started to fall asleep on her sofa. She needed the rest and longed for a fresh start for another day. A positive, new day. That new day could not come soon enough.

# 9

Karen knew from studying Michael Stansfeld's mobile phone call log history that Michael had spoken to Alfonso frequently. The dialogue between them increased sharply every time Michael came back from a business trip abroad. This further added fuel to her belief that Michael was working closely with Alonso regarding his commercial activities. The question was, were these consignment shipments, whatever they were, legal? Whilst Michael's outward persona was totally respectful, law-abiding and polished, his business related financial transactions, which were well hidden, were at best truly messy and told a different story. Michael certainly had fiscal fudgery down to a fine art. Much to William's annoyance initially and pleasure shortly afterwards, Michael's lack of a crisp recordable paper flow had provided more questions than answers.

Was Alfonso the key to unlocking more details regarding Michael's large payment deposits? Karen, William and Ham were keener than never to find out.

Karen had made contact with Alfonso during the previous day, and advised him of Michael Stansfeld's death. Alfonso did not sound shocked or surprised at this news, however he agreed to a meeting at his home in Epsom, Surrey.

Karen was very enthusiastic at the thought of meeting Alfonso, and it was decided William would make a good chaperone to accompany her. Sensing they did not want to appear mob handed, it was decided Ham would stay back in the village. Ham not wishing to be left clicking his fingers, decided he would spend some time checking over Michael's horsebox. Would that reveal any clues? Karen and William were happy to leave Ham to it. William hated the smell of horses and Karen's description of the thing was that it was an aging death trap on wheels and best avoided.

As William pulled into Karen's drive to collect her, the absence of Karen's sexy sports car disturbed him. They had agreed to meet at ten in the morning and it was now nearly ten minutes to ten, perhaps Karen had gone out, this irritated William as he knew this could potentially make them late for their meeting with Alfonso.

William knocked on Karen's door, not fully expecting an answer, grappling for his mobile phone in anticipation of giving Karen a hurry up call.

To his surprise, Karen answered her front door, she was ready to go, dressed to impress, buzzing and excited and ready to set off. They had a good two-hour drive in front of them.

"Where's your car, Karen?" William enquired.

"Oh, I had a small accident last night. I got a puncture and the car went into a field. It was not at all dramatic, the car got towed to the garage."

"Are you okay?" asked William, in a concerned voice, trying to make eye contact.

"It was nothing," replied Karen, walking out of her house with strides of purpose, hopeful that her confident actions and lack of interest in answering would deflect further questioning. Whilst Karen was happy not to tell William and Ham what had happened to her on the previous evening, she certainly did not want to lie to them and hoped further invention would not be necessary.

William assumed Karen was slightly embarrassed about her

accident so decided not to push the point any further. She was clearly unhurt, so that was all that mattered.

In an attempt to get Karen on side with him, he offered, "You certainly look stunning today, Karen," as she got into his car.

Karen flashed her eyes as she looked at William, she smiled and nodded with approval. Karen was thrilled with that comment, and commended herself quietly inside for swerving William's attention.

William, pleased with his effect of his comment, decided he would leave it until later to find out what really happened regarding Karen's accident. He felt there was more to the accident than Karen was letting on. It was probably her driving that caused it, not a puncture! That teasing thought amused him as he smiled to himself.

Karen enthusiastically punched the address of Alfonso's home into William's in-car satellite navigation system. Destination Alfonso was one hour fifty-three minutes away.

William offered reassurance that as his sat nav was engineered by Italians – William drove a Maserati – it could not be relied upon to get them to their destination by the most direct or quickest route! William's Maserati offered exceptional chassis dynamics and effortless power delivery, which made up for any shortfall in his car's technical mapping ability.

Karen missed the point of the joke and sat back, seemingly relaxed, and prepared her mind for their impending meeting.

"So what's the plan, Karen? What is the question track you want go down with Alfonso? What do you want my role to be?" enquired William.

Karen suggested, "I think we should play it natural, and respond to Alfonso's responses. If he fails to open up, I think we should try and rattle him."

William continued driving, not quite sure what that comment meant and wondered whether Karen really knew what she was getting them all into.

They were not going shopping and Alfonso was sure not to be a pussycat. William concentrated on his driving, watched the scenery whoosh past, braced himself, and waited for the sparks to fly. He counted down every mile on his sat nav with a degree of trepidation. If Karen felt the same, she never showed it. This either highlighted Karen's impressive range of qualities with tenacious reserve or could reveal her naivety.

William guided his beloved Maserati into Alfonso's avenue, it was quite clear Alfonso lived in the posh part of town. Here they drove slowly down a very exclusive long, tree-lined avenue, with every house protected by an electric-gated entrance. Both their heads were twitching; each progressive house down the avenue seemed to get bigger and more impressive the further they travelled along it. These houses were massive, and given the postcode area this was definitely millionaires' row.

At the end of the avenue, William turned right into Alfonso's entrance, stopping at the large wooden entrance gates. Before William could press the trigger on his electric window to allow access to push the entrance buzzer, the gates majestically opened, beckoning them into Alfonso's drive. With the gates open, the full impact of Alfonso's home became apparent. It was bloody enormous!

William drove the fifty metres from the gated entrance, past the steps to the elevated front door, to park carefully to the far left-hand side of the drive. The gravel crunched with enthusiasm as the wide tyres made their progress. With a quality drive that large, you certainly did not need a doorbell to announce your arrival.

Karen excitedly looked and smiled, shaking her head at William in disbelief. "Wow," was all she had to say in wide-eyed amazement.

Whilst William and Karen knew very little about Alfonso, they never really knew what to expect or the kind of house he lived in. They never imagined it would be as imposing or as grand as the grounds they now found themselves in.

Alfonso's home was vast and stately with monumental touches such as double height Neo-Georgian columns supporting his massive porch. What a welcome statement! Karen remembered she had stayed in smaller hotels. This house was truly colossal.

Once William parked the car, he passed something small, weighty and solid to Karen. She looked down at her gift, pupils fixed in alarm; William had passed Karen a loaded handgun.

William reassured Karen, "Take it, keep it in your handbag. It is your insurance in case things turn ugly."

Karen did not say a word in reply, her eyes said it all for her. Inside she felt uncomfortable, however she realised a gun might provide a solution to circumstances she had not imagined possible. She did as she was asked.

William and Karen got out of the car and they were aware a man was coming over to see them, complete with a playful black Labrador in tow, bounding all over the drive.

"Hello," said the man, with proud passion and a distinctive Italian tone. "I am Alfonso, greetings. Welcome to my home."

With boundless enthusiasm, Karen was keen to make an impact. She reached out her hand and smiled to formally introduce herself, and shook Alfonso's hand. Failing to hide her flurry, grinning, she turned. "This is my friend and partner, William."

Karen then declared, "Your house is gorgeous, Alfonso, *you* are gorgeous," with a laugh. She gave Alfonso a cheeky peck on the cheek and walked with him arm in arm across the gravel drive, climbing the steps to the grand entrance of his house.

William was a little surprised by Karen's flamboyant over-familiar greeting; she greeted Alfonso like she would have greeted an old friend with a big cheque for her in their pocket. William was ever cautious; he patted Alfonso's warm welcoming dog and kept a low profile, walking behind, ever observant. William reasoned the Labrador was most likely an English dog, and was likely to be a lot less slippery and more genuine in friendship than the Italian fellow in their group.

Alfonso was a short Italian in stature. He was tanned, of slender and slight physique. Not macho, not imposing, more cheeky, toned and mischievous in appeal. The Alfonso package was topped off with a stylish crop, at the sharper end of the grading scale. Very smart and articulate in profile, and comfortably in his late forties, Alfonso was reassuringly experienced at what he did, had reason to smile a lot and by all accounts was living life well from the proceeds. William immediately hated him for his success and was pleased Alfonso was considerably shorter than him.

Karen seemed to immediately like Alfonso, whether this was genuine, an act or a result of celebrity fever now she had seen the size of his house, was a difficult one for William to fathom. Women seemed to like Italian men. Was this because they have a permanent tan, they were super stylish or had that rare ability to be able to talk and offer a warm inviting smile at the same time. Whatever, Karen and Alfonso seemed to be getting on just fine. William noted the Labrador had the ability to display energy and looked happy even if it did have big black sad eyes. Now William had met Alfonso, he tried the same visual trick.

Alfonso held out is arm, as if directing traffic, and led the way to his two massive oversized period white wooden entrance doors. These double doors would look out of place on most houses, but suited the front of Alfonso's residence to a tee. Forget for one moment this is a monster of a house, then look at the superfine character detailing on each door, you know you are about to enter a world, that is a little bit special. Alfonso was certainly a man who was used to dining at the top table.

Inside was a major let-down for Karen; she was expecting vivid colours and super stylish furniture from out of this world. The two front rooms which fed off the amazing vast entrance hall had their doors wide open. The house was clearly going through a renovation and decorating phase. There was no furniture evident. Painters' sheets which covered the floors were everywhere. The smell of paint was pungent and the stark absence of carpet made the place seem even bigger than it probably was, amplifying an audible echo. The inside rooms may have been bare and devoid of luxury trinkets, however due to the size of them they had the wow factor in spades.

Alfonso explained, his delivery with his typical Italian smile, "When you live in a neighbourhood like this, it is important your house outside is well presented and looks the business. If you have not got carpet on the floors, that is not a problem, if you have a skip on the drive or weeds out of control in your garden, your neighbours' curtains really get twitchy. Inside I still have a lot of work to do, the problem you have is every job you undertake costs a small fortune. I think I am close to running out of money!"

Alfonso walked the two guests through his house at a pace, keen they would not linger in any part of the house for too long. Leading the way onwards to his home office, Alfonso pointed out to his guests that he was very proud to own a very rare oversized Persian rug. "This cost me thirty-eight thousand pounds. Bloody shame to walk on it really, but it really is super quality. Please look at the detailing and colours. This is truly remarkable global craftsmanship. When this room is finished, this will be my dining room."

William muttered under his breath in a disapproving questionable tone, "Thirty-eight grand, on a rug!" Karen elbowed him in the ribs as they walked.

Alfonso picked up on William's remark, continuing to grin in true Italian fashion. "I have another three Persian rugs much the same upstairs, which I will display when each room is finished down here. Now please, come into my office."

William and Karen both had their eyeballs out on stalks, trying to take in all the surroundings in Alfonso's office and the content of his desk. There were neat shelves of general books, pictures of boats and Italian scenery, and endless quantities of A4 binders all around him. Nothing seemingly unusual, just a busy, typical man's home office, which like all men's home offices could probably benefit from a bit of a tidy up. One stand-out detail was a gilt-like golden border around the top of the room. An unusual feature in a home office environment. Alfonso's place of work could quite easily have been a doctor's surgery or solicitor's place of work, there was nothing else distinctive to highlight. Beside Alfonso's desk on their own dedicated table were two screens for his computer – one for his emails and PC access, the other relayed security camera images from a variety of buildings, no doubt from his wider empire.

The three of them sat down, Alfonso, the master of all he surveyed, sat behind a magnificently tasteful Italian style wooden desk. This was a quality imposing desk with beautiful inlaid marquetry, finished to a very high-gloss standard, a proper work of art which was clearly very expensive and was sure to be extremely heavy.

Karen and William took the vacant guest chairs facing Alfonso from the other side of his workplace. As they sat down, William and Karen tried to scan the contents of Alfonso's table top, a selection of paperwork remained stacked neatly in various piles. Most correspondence appeared to be from banks or solicitors. They both knew, as this was a scheduled appointment, anything Alfonso did not want the two of them to see would have been well hidden, so any attempt to grab a cheeky glance of something important exposed on Alfonso's desk top was likely to be futile.

"I am sorry to hear of Michael's death," said Alfonso, in a not very convincing voice. "What happened?"

Karen went on to explain that Michael had been shot. A victim of a cold-blooded murder whilst in his own bedroom at home with his wife, Helen, both killed by a mystery gunman. Karen reminded Alfonso that Helen was her sister, and the loss had a massive impact on their close-knit family.

In recognition of these comments, aiming to demonstrate an understanding, Alfonso, nodded his head and looked Karen squarely into her eyes. Alfonso then enquired in a more concerned, measured tone, "Did the police find the murderer?"

72

William replied, not giving Karen an opportunity to answer. "No, the police enquiries are still ongoing. However we understand they are making progress with the case."

Karen then continued. "When I phoned you the other day, Alfonso, you did not sound surprised with Michael's murder. I assumed the police had been in touch with you, following his death months ago."

Alfonso responded in an agitated, typically Latin manner. "Why would the police contact me? Do you think I killed your sister and her husband?

Karen went on to explain that she found it surprising the police had not been in touch with Alfonso, not because he was a suspect, but because he was a close working associate of Michael's. Close working associates often held useful information!

William looked at Karen, and kept his thoughts to himself; he knew either the police had not dug deep enough, or they genuinely had not known about Alfonso, which was a deeply concerning state of affairs. Given the severity of the crime and the importance the victims' families entrusted with the police investigations being uncompromisingly thorough. The other variable alternative was Alfonso could be lying, either about a police visit, or knowing about the murder from other channels, before Karen had called him! The thought had not escaped William's mind that Alfonso could have been the killer too.

Before images of worms and a can could form in William's increasingly frustrated and tangled thought processes, Karen took centre stage and grabbed Alfonso's attention.

Karen stated that her visit, with William, was not about digging for details regarding the murders of Michael or Helen. That task was for the police to handle. The reason for meeting was to see if they could assist Alfonso.

Karen offered clarity. "Alfonso, William and I would like to work with you."

Alfonso scratched his outer ear, and rubbed his chin with his hand, the way all men do when they want to buy extra seconds of time before delivering a carefully constructed answer.

Karen continued, before Alfonso had an opportunity to speak. "William and I provided Michael with funding, to assist him when he was working for you. Michael trusted us, we were effectively silent partners. Michael told us things about what he was doing for you in confidence. He knew he could trust us. We are here because we want to fill the void, left by Michael. We would like to carry for you."

William's eyes lit up, he could hardly believe what he was hearing. What the hell was Karen saying? Inside William was fuming, and he was struggling to contain his anger. His face was focussed, however it was not a happy one.

William knew if Karen was addressing the killer, or the instigator of Michael's murder, doubts would now be bouncing around his mind as to what they did or did not know. Karen was playing a very dangerous game here and they were exposing themselves unnecessarily to potential trigger-happy mayhem. William and Karen could become the next moving targets, spontaneously.

Alfonso stood up, and started pacing slowly around his office. He was not about to embark on a business relationship with two individuals he regarded as being inexperienced amateurs. Michael did have his faults, however he was exceptionally good at what he did for Alfonso and his wider connections. Shuffling his thoughts before making his delivery, Alfonso stated, "There are a few things you need to know, Karen."

Alfonso went on to explain that Michael worked with him for a number of years, possibly five or six years. Alfonso was the logistics man, the planner and the broker. Alfonso was also the brains of the outfit, putting end users, buyers and sellers together for a variety of different products. Alfonso had that rare ability to influence and control commercial relationships, he could keep distant, however he kept close enough to be integral and involved.

His partnership with Michael started off well enough. Alfonso would buy goods from all over the world, often having them shipped in with Michael's assistance.

The product would be sold and Michael would get his cut. In recent years, Alfonso confided, Michael started doing his own thing, he arranged his own consignments, often conflicting with established dealers, muscling in on their territory. This was not welcome.

Another negative tendency developed with Michael. When he was shipping product some of the consignment would go missing, or get watered down. This trend was not healthy either. There were instances where Michael would request an increase in the amount he was being paid for a job. He got greedy, and tried on more than one occasion to hold product to ransom. Whilst Michael never did anything wrong by Alfonso, he ruffled plenty of feathers within the black market. The sort of people working with these commodities do not care for a ruffling from a fellow peddler. These types take action, fast ruthless action.

Alfonso sat down again. "So you see, Karen, when you tell me Michael has been murdered, I am saddened and my heart sinks a little for you. However, flipping the other side of the coin, I am not totally surprised. Hopefully my position now makes more sense to you."

Alfonso paused, reached over his desk to cup Karen's hands with his own, then continued. "On a personal level, Karen, I am sorry to hear of your sister's death. It is such a shame she got caught up in this. My dealings, and those of other associates I know, have only been with Michael and Michael only. I never met your sister. I am very sorry to hear your news."

Indicating the short encounter was now over, Alfonso stood up. He made his apologies in a hurried voice, and made claims he had other urgent things to attend to.

Karen gave Alfonso her business card with her phone number displayed. "If you change your mind, Alfonso, or you can recommend anyone we can work with, please let me know. We are reliable and keen to work."

In closing the meeting, Alfonso walked Karen and William back through his house, over the rare and expensive rug to the imposing main entrance hall. Opening his decadent double front doors, Alfonso smiled and shook Karen and William's hands in a purposeful farewell handshake.

Alfonso looked up to the heavens and shared his thoughts with them both. Yes, Alfonso was smiling when he directed his final address to them. "Clumsy questioning to one side, you are both bright people. You can do better than this. Be careful who you form partnerships with. Good luck to you."

Karen gave Alfonso a final, lingering peck on his cheek, a kind of thank you, and they both said their goodbyes. William was so relieved to be outside again without being shot at, he could have kissed Alfonso's dog goodbye, he was wrapped in personal euphoria.

Pleasingly, as Karen and William walked across Alfonso's drive for the final time, there were no flying bullets in evidence and the trusty Labrador was nowhere to be seen. Perhaps Alfonso was not such a bad guy after all.

Sitting in William's car, ready to depart from Alfonso's impressive drive, Karen waited for the silence to break. She sat motionless, looking completely forward, avoiding looking at William. She now waited for the silence to shatter with William's tirade and delivery of superior judgement. She anticipated a rant, giving her the benefit of his experience. Instead she got nothing. Just William's burning eyes and devastatingly powerful silence.

Karen could not hold herself any longer, seconds felt like minutes, it could have been several minutes. The fact William had not started the car alerted Karen to the fact William was anticipating something. What?

Karen broke the silence. "Okay," she said. "I know I was reckless, I know I should not have said the things I did. I do not want to get involved with a smuggling racket any more than you do. But do you know, for one brief moment in there, I tasted a new life I thought I wanted, I tasted excitement and adventure!"

William fired back in an untypically calm, unimpressed monotone response. "You got carried away with the moment, Karen. That is what happened. What you tasted was a cheap Italian with expensive taste. You are a nightmare, a nightmare with a penchant for tiny Italian curiosities!"

Karen continued. "Well, I think Alfonso is a nice guy."

William smiled and shook his head playfully in disbelief, pointing to the entrance they had just walked through. "Nice guys do not live in a house like that!"

Karen, sensing more than a tinge of jealousy from the other side of the car, laughed out loud.

William started his Maserati and they drove off, back down millionaires' row. The burble of William's car's V8 engine and the sound of gravel tossing up from the wheels, pinging on the sexy bodywork, made their own farewell statement to the Alfonso estate. Karen looked at the large houses flashing by outside her passenger side window and she started contemplating. *I wonder...*

# 10

Later that evening, Karen and William sat down for a bite to eat in their hotel restaurant. The pre-prepared plan after meeting Alfonso was to stay in a hotel for one night, touch base with Ham, and start digging with whatever leads they got from Alfonso.

William had tried to phone Ham on his mobile several times with no connection. Ham's phone was notoriously unreliable, so the fact they could not speak was not a major concern.

Karen and William tucked into their starters for their evening meal. Karen was a little glazed in her facial expression, she was annoyed with herself that she had got carried away earlier when asking Alfonso questions. What was she thinking of, asking Alfonso if she could be one of his carriers. Did she really want to break the law, embarking on a criminal career, peddling something unspeakable? She got carried away with the moment all right.

William was not sure whether they got away with that encounter or not, he was certain however, Alfonso only told them what he wanted them to know. He was definitely sharper than your average rogue scoundrel.

Karen had learnt a lot from that day's events. She had learnt it was very hard asking the right questions to complete strangers, and even harder trying to extract the juicy answers, especially when dealing with slippery Italian villains. It was also very hard not to get distracted from the primary objective.

Karen and William had moved on and started their main course with enthusiasm. They were only staying in a budget hotel, however the food was surprisingly tasty. They both acknowledged Michael Stansfeld had stepped on too many of his associates' toes, too many than could be considered healthy. Karen took some comfort learning her sister Helen appeared to have no direct involvement with Michael's business dealings or knowledge of the food chain of gangsters Michael felt compelled to get involved with.

It was conceivable that Michael had become troublesome to Alfonso, which at the lighter end of the scale could have resulted in mild annoyance. If Michael's insider dealing and home-grown profiteering had wider ranging consequences, then Alfonso may well have found Michael to have been a more serious problem. A serious problem which required dealing with! Alfonso could have provided the coercion needed to pull the trigger on Michael, either directly or indirectly!

So if Alfonso's version of events was to be believed, Michael Stansfeld was a chancer, a dealer, and a trafficker of sorts. A bad man without scruples. How on earth could Karen's sister have ended up being married to a man like that? Did she even know she had married a man like that? The assumption Karen was keen to make was that she did not.

Then she thought, *How many other women really know the true depth of their husbands' businesses. The true goings on? Could an illegal activity like this really be concealable? Are men really that good at covering their tracks from their loved ones?*

Karen's thoughts strayed back to Alfonso. Karen was aware he had supreme confidence. Any man involved with an illegal business, who was prepared to let total strangers into his home, did so because he was confident, and in total control. She also accepted that under that cheeky Italian's charm was likely a robust layer of hard edged nastiness, that tier of wonderment was best left uncovered.

William, ever keen to share his wisdom, asked Karen, "Do you know what I think about today's meeting?"

William carried on before Karen could air any comment. "I think today, where we have been is akin to a visit to a tarantula spider's nest. If Alfonso was head tarantula, he could have pounced on us and incapacitated us at any time, he could have displayed his sharpened claws and injected some venom, and killed us quite easily. For some reason however, he chose not to. Today he was not in his attacking mode and he has let us walk free. Why would he choose to do that?"

William smiled at the waitress as the dessert arrived at their table.

"My god," said Karen smiling. "You really do have some deep and concerningly elaborate thoughts, don't you."

Without any warning, two men walked through the hotel's restaurant quite briskly. As they approached Karen's and William's table, they made eye contact with Karen who was facing them, they made a beeline for her then sat down and joined them, warning them not to do anything and act natural.

Karen and William were sitting opposite each other on a four-seat table. The taller of the two men sat next to Karen, the stocky man with short cropped hair sat next to William. Both the men were dressed in smart casual dark clothing with jackets which could have concealed all manner of nasty surprises.

Before they could both grab their thoughts and protest the intrusion, the stocky man sitting next to William told them both in an assertive purposeful tone, "Keep quiet and eat your food." He then pressed a sharp object into William's groin area. William threw his spoon on the table in disgust, making a loud noise, sufficient to momentarily arouse the attention of other guests and an attentive waitress from across the restaurant.

William looked down to see the barrel of a well-used handgun impaled between his legs, with force, pointing at a valuable part of his anatomy.

In a moment of automatic reflex, William moved his hands from the table, intending to drop them to more natural and protective state beside his legs. He was told by the gun-wielding thug sitting next to him, "Keep your hands on the table or you will lose your cock." William did not need to be told this twice, his heart rate raced as he maintained his hands uncomfortably on the table. William watched the man's every movement and aimed to do everything he could to appease the gunman.

The stocky gunman was uncompromisingly muscle laden, tarnished with attitude gristle. The taller of the two men however was the more polished, purposeful of the duo.

The brains of the outfit, Mr Tall, introduced himself. "My name is Collard. Please forgive this intrusion, I have no wish to disturb your delicious food any longer than necessary."

Collard then went on to explain that he had taken a delivery of opium from Michael Stansfeld, a fifth consignment from the same originating supplier. However, this last batch being the more valuable consignment was the more important. Complaints down the franchise pecking order had escalated to some unsavoury exchanges between smaller dealers and their sub-suppliers regarding the quality of the merchandise. This unwelcome last problematic consignment was traced back to the last batch supplied by Michael Stansfeld.

Collard continued. "Now I am not looking for compensation, I do not even expect a free holiday. All I want is my money back. I want my seventy-five thousand pounds back. I assure you, I am deadly serious and best not messed around with. I want you to reverse the transaction, reverse the transaction or else."

William protested, wriggling under the strain of being confined in an area he would rather not have any restrictions. "We have not got your money, you are crazy, leave us alone."

The gunman pushed his gun, with uncomfortable increased

potency, into William's groin. Collard winced in disapproval as William doubled over, clearly in acute pain, telling his gun-toting friend, "Be careful, we do not want any accidents. Not on this carpet."

Karen looked at Collard. "Michael Stansfeld is dead, we have not got his money, we are not Michael's suppliers. We have no connection."

Collard responded. "You are Stansfeld's sister-in-law, you have full power of attorney over the Michael Stansfeld estate. Sell the house if you need to, just get me my money or suffer the consequences – it is your decision."

Collard was quite a cool character, William observed. Totally under control and completely unruffled by his ad-hoc gate-crashing dinner party interaction routine. He certainly had presence and was a few rungs up the ladder from a conventional hooligan. He was definitely a classy villain, and from the cut of his suit, his sharp shoes and well-presented dialogue, a reasonably successful one too. He obviously had good coaching, good schooling, or wealthy parents. Commendable comments given his delivery was somewhat abrasive and not to everyone's taste.

William sensed this was not the first time Collard had laid the law down in such circumstances. William looked at Karen. She was visibly distressed by the unwelcome interruption to their evening. They both realised at this point, that this was likely the first spin off from the meeting earlier with Alfonso. They had clearly been followed back to their hotel. Round one to Alfonso.

Collard continued, making purposeful eye contact firstly with Karen, then with William. "Now I do not know what you two are intending to achieve by visiting this patch, or by asking penetrating questions. You need to realise your presence here is not welcome, and some of us do not like giving answers."

Before leaving, Collard left the following remark. "You have seven days to get my money. Please do not let me down. My men will be calling on you. We know where to find you."

Collard stood up, and as he slowly walked past their table, he grabbed Karen's arm, squeezing it just enough to inject torment and encourage a juicy bruise. "I have got better things to do with my time than embark on ball-breaking lessons in life such as these. Make sure I do not have to repeat myself."

Collard was definitely a man with a sinister edge, an edge they were both not keen to see again for a while. William reeled with a sigh of relief as the gunman stood up, removed the gun from William's groin, and took the pressure off William's balls. For the moment, his cock was safe, badly shaken, but safe.

William grabbed his thoughts, checked his projection and thought, freedom of movement never felt so good, nor did that feeling of remaining intact feel so pleasurable.

Karen stated the obvious with renewed agitation. "Well, that is great. What the hell are we supposed to do now?"

William, looking behind to ensure their two rogue patrons had definitely left the restaurant, conceded public ambushes of this calibre were rare. Whilst they were in a budget hotel that evening, William could not help but feel the guest list was not as exclusive as it should have been. He then picked up his dessert spoon and continued to eat a mouthful of his chocolate sponge cake, his favourite. He never said a word, he just carried on eating his dessert. He had obviously been kept away from his culinary delight for far too long.

William was digesting his frustration at not being armed that evening, so much so that he did not rush a reply to Karen's question. He prided himself on being a sharp guy and yet he never foresaw the meeting taking place in their hotel restaurant, with two opportunist visitors. A consequence of his lack of foresight being his lack of a handgun by his side. William, in a previous life, always went about his business armed. If he was armed he was ready for any eventuality. In much the same way most people would not dream of going anywhere without their mobile telephone, it was second nature, and William was the same with his trusty handgun. Maybe it was the company he kept, or a discipline he grew a fondness to. Whatever, it worked for him, and that night he felt he had let himself down by lowering his guard. He knew when he was in a tight spot if you could not offer a cheeky smile, and try and talk your way out of a situation, your handgun might just assist. If all else fails it was the most valuable addition in your final chain of defence.

Having digested his tasty finale to their meal, William summarised their predicament in candid perspective, answering Karen's question. "If you do not pay Collard, and his threats are genuine, he could kill us. If however you pay him, he might ask for more money later or he could kill us anyway. It is a tricky dilemma, isn't it."

William highlighted to Karen the realisation that even if Collard's life was to come to an abrupt end, other associates of his could come chasing afterwards. He was sure to have a network of underlings ready to pounce and continue the thrill of the chase, if things did not work out well or if Collard suddenly expired. If Collard's statements were true, other dealers down the food chain could conceivably want their money back too, with gory interest!

William, whilst not wanting to say I told you so to Karen, knew full well all three of them needed their wits about them. This was no longer an amateur investigation, it was a mission of survival. William was interested to see how Karen handled this additional pressure, now developments were hotting up. Poor Ham did not have a clue what he was missing, or what he was now implicated in.

Karen was understandably shaken by these events, she was also extremely annoyed. Aggravation poured on bloody frustration for her. The distraction of maniacs walking around with guns, demanding money, threatening her life and dislodging her appetite for her primary focus, to find her sister's murderer, were reason enough for her to contemplate, enough was enough. Was it time for Karen to accept she had got involved with something well out of her depth? Hell no. Karen was not about to let grown men, with bullyboy tactics, walking around waving guns around, dictating to her what she could or could not do.

She knew she had to come up with a sensational plan to sort this lot out. She was well up for it, and best of all, she had a suitable strategy. The idea was not fool-proof, it had a few holes, however it was a plan, and Karen was determined to push on with it. For the moment, however, she wanted to keep her scheme close to her chest. She did not want to frighten William!

*It is funny*, Karen considered. She expected to be pondering clues, and following up leads to her sister's murder, not quite in the same mould as Miss Marple. However, she certainly did not expect to be trying to formulate smart arse tactics to keep a villainous community at bay. Such was life.

Full marks for William, she thought, for holding his own, whilst faced with the realisation that he might just get his cock blown off. Karen was pleased he had remained composed and never lost his appetite, or anything else!

# 11

The next morning, Karen, William and Ham all agreed to meet up again. This time, Ham had requested that they all meet in a field, behind the village church, back in the village of Hawkswold. Behind the church were farmers' fields and in one of the corner plots, was an old disused barn. Shoring up one side of the open fronted barn was Michael Stansfeld's horsebox. The horsebox had not been started or moved since Michael's murder six months earlier, it may even have remained dormant for many months prior to that and it was the trio's hot favourite vehicle of choice for Michael's smuggling activity. Michael had used the horsebox on numerous occasions – he ran it as part of his business, transporting horses around the country and across Europe. At least that was the official front for the vehicle's use. Two or three times a year, Michael would transport horses from France, import them for covering purposes and take the horses back afterwards.

Ham was very much like an excited schoolboy, in a fantasy toyshop, and he was very interested in telling Karen and William what he had found, and the fun he had had with the horsebox the day before. Ham, certain the previous day had gone well for Karen and William, dismissed any notion of an Alfonso hiccup. Ham's enthusiasm suited Karen and William as they were not totally sure how to tell Ham what had happened when they met Alfonso, and then Collard, and what kind of twisted plot the three of them had now got involved with.

Ham loved his engineering, and his new passion was Michael Stansfeld's light-blue horsebox. The horsebox was reasonably large, full of character, and had more than a few rattles in evidence. In Ham's view, it was, mechanically speaking, quite a sweet piece of engineering. Was this a true appraisal of a twenty-five-year-old vehicle or Ham getting carried away with the romance of an old truck? Time and patience would tell.

Ham loved to hold an audience, and with Karen and William standing in a field, next to the horsebox, eagerly awaiting his presentation, Ham went about his twenty-four-hour update with some flair and gusto. Ham really was the master of his craft, and he loved to be the centre of attention. Whether he was preaching to the converted, praising the Lord, or rattling on about an old horsebox, this vibrant ex-member of the clergy, really knew how to work his material.

Karen looked over to William with a facial expression that told him, My god this is going to be painful.

Ham started his address. "What we have here, is a twenty-five-year-old Bedford, five-stall horsebox. However, my findings would suggest that what we actually have here, is much more than merely an authentic livestock carrier.

"It may be a bugger to start and gear selection may be a tad recalcitrant when cold, but when you get that mighty diesel lump warmed up, it runs through its cogs with real pride, it is a genuine joy to pilot, and I am convinced it has got plenty of life left in it."

William was starting to roll his eyes in frustration, then he started pacing and announced, waving his arm about, "Ham, you do not need to sell the thing to us. Have you found any evidence Michael used the vehicle for smuggling?"

Ham ignored William's interruption and continued, using

his eye contact with William to good affect. "The obvious assumption is that Michael used this vehicle to conceal drugs when he came back into the UK. Now I have looked at the floors, tried to remove the side panels, looked at the partitions carefully, and rummaged around under the insulation material in the cab, and I cannot find any evidence that this is the way he used to work. If he did use the vehicle for smuggling, then there must have been another way."

Karen peered into the back of the load area where the horses would be held. "Ham, it smells disgusting."

Ham agreed, sharing his view that he felt the horsebox made a lot of sense to be used for smuggling. The vehicle's bespoke construction lent itself well for harbouring areas of concealment, although these areas were clearly very well masked, as none of them could be found. The smell from the hay, straw, and the horses was sure to act as useful aroma camouflage when concealing the unique scent from the contraband cargo, assuming some form of drugs were the commodity Michael was unlawfully importing.

The smell of the horses would also act as a useful distraction to sniffer dogs. The other rather clever angle, was that as with perishable goods, livestock was treated with priority as far as clearance through Customs and Excise was concerned, which would put additional pressure on the port officials to get the vehicle on its way as swiftly as possible. So there were indeed a lot of benefits for would-be smugglers to use such a method of entry into the country.

Karen in a rare act of tactile interaction, ran her fingers down part of the side of the horsebox's bodywork in a suggestive manner. Looking at William and Ham, she agreed, teasingly. "For a smuggler, this vehicle sure ticks a lot of boxes."

Ham then went into the horsebox's cab, and removed some paperwork. He showed Karen and William details of the equestrian centre in France, which Michael used as his collection point for the horses. The stabling was located approximately seven kilometres south of Reims, and it was a high-class centre, specialising in working with the best thoroughbred horses available.

Ham highlighted two interesting points. Firstly, he had found ferry tickets in the glovebox, dated the seventh of January. Michael had a trip prepared two days after his death, so the vehicle was likely prepared for the journey and transit plans were well advanced. Secondly, there was an abundance of invoices from a local French garage. Ham noticed the dates, and every time Michael took his horsebox to France, it always went to the same rural French garage for a service. Conveniently, the garage was only two kilometres down the road from the equestrian centre.

Ham declared, raising his eyebrows in query, "Who in their right mind, takes their vehicle to another country for a service, especially an aging horsebox like this one?"

It was quite clear the horsebox was likely getting more than just a fresh service from Michael's popular French spanner-wielding artisans.

William asked Karen, "What did the police think of the horsebox? Presumably they thoroughly checked the vehicle over following Michael's murder."

Karen responded, "The police carried out some forensic tests initially, however, given the vehicle was little used and there was no attempt to steal it, they ruled it out of their investigation quite early on. The police never saw the horsebox as being of interest and never saw any mileage in pursuing it. More probably the stench from the thing put them off."

Ham was quite chuffed he had found something useful from his day's activities, being left alone with the horsebox had proved invaluable. Finding something which warranted further investigation, another lead for them all and worthwhile interest from Karen and William. Ham was pleased he had now proved his worth as a member of the newly formed investigative trio.

Karen asked, "You're quite confident driving this horsebox then, Ham? How do you fancy a run to France?"

Karen was very pleased with Ham's work. It was quite clear a visit to the garage in France was worth a throw of the dice.

Ham was over the moon. He loved the old bus, and he relished the thought of a proper run out with it. Okay, it was never going to be a sterling drive, never an opportunity for Ham to sample pedigree engineering. There was no rifle bolt precision gear change here, more like a mop in a bucket agricultural transmission, however it was an opportunity for Ham to drive something imposing and large. As all big boys know, it is a wonder to behold, getting your hands on something bulky and wieldy to navigate.

Ham was also very keen to visit Champagne country. "What better excuse to fill up an empty horsebox with cases of champagne, fine wines, cooked hams and the odd baguette," he revealed.

Karen was less enthused about this, and quashed any attempt to turn an important stepping stone in their murder investigation, into a lads' outing or a booze cruise.

"You can stop licking your lips, Ham. It is not going to happen." Karen was firm and enjoyed keeping the men in line, and perversely, she also took some pleasure from withholding something they both enjoyed. Would Karen eventually soften? We will see. It was not really in Karen's nature to be a bitch. However, she quite liked the sensation. She was learning.

William had other concerns and addressed these with Karen. "What can we possibly gain, driving a tired old lumpy horsebox to France?" William could see the benefit of checking the French garage out, but surely it would make more sense to travel to France in the comfort of his car. The horsebox was slow, fuel-thirsty, and wafted around corners like an untethered ship set loose in high winds. William was pleased he was not driving it, however it certainly was not going to be any fun for him following behind it.

Karen was quite insistent. "If we arrive at the garage with

this highly recognisable horsebox, that will hopefully open a few doors for us. I think we will learn more and someone there will be very keen to speak to us. It is the ultimate calling card, and we can almost guarantee a reaction."

William retorted, "It might be the ultimate opportunity for us to get shot at! Michael was not Mr Popular remember. Someone might be very keen to kill us!"

Karen ignored that remark. Ham had no option than to remain quietly bemused, as he did not fully appreciate the gravity of that comment. At least not yet anyway.

It was agreed Ham would drive the horsebox, with Karen by his side. William would follow them in his Maserati. It would be a source of comfort for them, knowing they had William's fast car at their disposal as backup, should things go wrong and they needed it.

Ham could hardly contain his excitement and jangled the horsebox keys to promote maximum annoyance. He then tossed them into the air with a flamboyant playful lob and waited for gravity to return them to his eager clutches.

Ham then asked, "Anyway, guys, how did you get on with Alfonso yesterday?"

William and Karen looked at each other pensively. The uncommon silence, and piercing eye contact between them was enough to suggest to Ham that the visit was not as smooth as it could have been.

Karen explained to Ham that Alfonso was not fully co-operative. Superficially he seemed like a nice enough guy, however it was clear he only divulged selective information. It was also clear from the size of Alfonso's house, that whatever business interests he had, they were financially very substantive. Karen also brought Ham up to speed with Collard, who must have been the next step down in Alfonso's considerable product pyramid distribution network. Karen divulged Collard's concern that his consignment quality delivered by Michael was not up to scratch, and he was demanding his money back. All seventy-five thousand, full English, pounds back.

Karen reflected on Collard's meeting at the restaurant with William in their hotel, was no accident, and Alfonso must have tipped Collard off. It was likely Collard followed them from Alfonso's house, eager to inflict a squeeze.

Ham enquired, "Do you think Collard's claim regarding the substandard consignment is genuine or are these just scare mongering tactics to increase his wealth?"

Karen replied, "Who knows, all I can tell you is that Collard has the ability to display a very nasty streak. He has a hard edge which is a problem for us, what he would like at the moment is seventy-five grand from me."

William was in a prime position to offer valuable guidance to Karen and Ham, from his standpoint as a retired hitman. William explained to them both, "In my view, Collard and Alfonso are both bloodsuckers on society. They need to be eliminated."

Ham raised his eyebrows in disapproval. He could hardly wait for the next bit.

William continued. "My concern with you Karen, is that you are now dipping your toes into a very dangerous world, a world I left behind many years ago. The type of people I used to deal with, day in and day out, are just like modern-day Collards. They are ruthless bandits with no respect for the laws of the land or people's mortality or feelings. They are heavy-duty villains, they are worse than parasites."

William then went on to explain to them both, the following predicament which engulfed Karen. "Imagine this: Collard wants seventy-five grand, his challenges will not stop and his chasing will be relentless. Your life will become hell. You could pay a hitman today ten thousand pounds to kill Collard, and another ten thousand pounds to kill Alfonso. You will then be fifty-five thousand pounds better off, and you stay alive, potentially without any further aggravation. In your final account of life, you then juggle your moral conscience with the inevitable police investigation. Can you handle that, Karen?"

William then reasoned, "Let us assume the hitman makes a mistake, and also kills an innocent bystander, in the same way a killer almost certainly mistakenly killed your sister Helen. Where do you sit on the moral high ground then, Karen? Inflicting the same loss and pain on another poor, unsuspecting family?"

Karen fired back, "Your suggestion is nonsense William, we do not even know whether Collard or Alfonso killed Michael and Helen. They may have had a motive, but we do not know for sure. I am not about to hire a hitman to sort my problems out for me."

William moved over to Karen, put his arm on her shoulder to support her. "You're right, we do not know for sure, however they have the capability, they have the motive and they are bad people. Is that not enough stir in the mix?"

William knew Karen's quest for answers into her sister's death was deeply distressing, however her actions were totally reasonable. Her commitment to her cause was undiluted, and it seemed her appetite for answers was unabated, regardless of what obstacle was put in her way or what danger lurked around the next corner. Karen carried on regardless, that was her inherent strength.

William's concern that her current campaign was leading her deeper and deeper into complicated vendettas and villainess acquaintances, a by-product of her unique mammoth task. She was also getting drawn into illegal activity, the distraction and attraction of which she could well do without.

Ham and William had both observed Karen becoming less rational in some of her thinking. She really was chasing answers to her questions at all costs. William and Ham's alarm bells were ringing, however Karen could not hear them, or, more shockingly, she chose not to.

She turned away from Ham and William, and started to walk the short distance through the village to her home.

William, in a rare moment of self-conscious guilt, noting Karen had gone quiet, enquired, "You all right, Karen?"

She replied in a confident, bubbly manner. "Oh yes. We leave for Dover in one hour, and if Ham expects me to sit with him in this damn horsebox, I am getting a cloth, some disinfectant, and some air freshener from my house."

Ham lifted his head up high and responded, "I have had a bath this week, you cheeky mare!"

"But today is Thursday, Ham."

Karen flicked her hair and smiled. With an air of confidence, she continued walking with a purposeful spring in her step down the village lane, allowing her eyes to wander, and eventually settle, glimpsing inside her handbag she was holding. Her vision locked onto the small handgun William had given her. As she walked, she slipped her hand inside her bag, and she felt for the grip as she took the holding position, with one finger lightly taking the tension on the trigger. She marvelled quietly to herself, in awe of the power she had when holding the gun. She especially loved the weight of the thing and the coldness on her skin of the shiny barrel. She also loved the power of concealment.

No self-respecting villager would dare imagine Karen could be caressing a concealed handgun as she walked through the village. It certainly was not sexy, however it did feel a little kinky, she confided to herself, as she marched along to her house. Karen continued to smile as she walked; she loved being in control, she loved the sense of power she had. Even if she did not know what step was coming next, she was however enjoying the twisting journey. Well, at least most of the time.

Firearm power trips to one side, Karen was pleased her investigation with Ham and William was moving in a different direction to the one the police had embarked on. Whether her quest would take them to Helen's murderer would remain to be seen. It certainly felt like progress anyway. Karen's life was definitely entering a new phase; she was becoming stronger and more self-assured each and every day. Karen was proud she did not allow challenges from William to penetrate her ladylike resolve. She believed William, whilst very supportive in some respects and of course very knowledgeable, especially when dealing with toxic members of society, was often trying the push Karen's boundaries, trying to tip her over the edge.

Karen liked William, and she was growing fonder of his prickly charms daily, however it was still a distant fondness. Like a gamekeeper prodding a crocodile; fascinating and just a little bit scary, all the same it was rewarding being so close to the action.

In no time at all, Karen returned to the horsebox, clutching her cleaning materials to set about tidying up and freshening up the dreary cabin. Once again, Ham found it hard to contain his enthusiasm for the impending journey and could not resist running his hands down the flanks of the truck, lightly polishing some of the very rare glitzy chrome trim, covering the wheel arches. William found Ham's activity very odd, as after all, this was a very tired old truck, and it looked like it needed more than tender loving care and divine intervention to get it through the next MOT.

Karen had used the opportunity, when back at her house, to review Michael's mobile telephone bills and logged calls at the time of his last overseas movement with the horsebox. Interestingly, there were several calls made to Alfonso, and many calls directly to the small French garage. The link and timings were far too strong to be purely co-incidental; there had to be a commercial connection, this lead had to be progress, surely.

The slam of doors, a grunt from the gearbox selecting an appropriate cog and plenty of start-up smoke, told the world the Stansfelds' horsebox was once again ready to hit the road and cut a few moves on the continent.

After a thirty-minute drive, Ham at the wheel of the horsebox, all three of them arrived into Dover port. William brought up the rear in his trusty Maserati, groaning incessantly at how slow the horsebox was in comparison to his Italian sports car. With typical brisk passenger management efficiency, they had flashed their passports, gained their boarding passes, and were speedily lined up to board the Dover to Calais ferry.

Boarding procedures were disciplined and energetic, and soon enough the three of them were looking out from the ship's balcony, over the stern of the ferry, facing back to Dover. They watched as the white cliffs shrunk in the distance as their motor vessel carved its well-trodden path through the glorious English Channel.

Karen's plan was a simple one in her head. Take the ferry from Dover to Calais, drive to the small rural garage outside Reims, then wait and see what happens. Perfect.

William remained very calm, and very quiet. You could be sure he was factoring in all sorts of different reception scenarios in his head. Would the staff at the French garage interact with them? Would their reaction to their arrival be hostile? Would the French mechanics be typically relaxed and not take a blind bit of notice? This next chapter could be a learning curve for all concerned.

Ham sat down on one of the bench chairs, on the top deck outside, legs outstretched and arms crossed in typically relaxed fashion. Wearing a happy face, he was clearly enjoying the freedom of the moment.

Ham declared, "You know, as a youngster I loved the jaunts to France on a ferry. With lovely weather, such as the sunshine we are having today, the wind in your hair, the effortless gentle pitching motion, you really feel you are going somewhere. This trip almost has a jolly schoolboys outing flavour about it."

Karen retorted playfully. "What about fellow schoolgirls, Ham? Do you have any vivid recollections surrounding schoolgirls?"

Sounding mildly serious, "No, not really. Women are

wonderful creatures, however when a boy is exposed to fantastic engineering such as this roll-on roll-off ferry, little boys seize their imagination in an instant and little girls simply do not stand a chance. I think it is the size of the thing that overwhelms."

William, not for the first time, nodded in disbelief, indicating his schoolboy trips were a totally different ballgame.

Karen looked away and smiled.

Whether it was the vibrations from the massive boat engines thundering up his trouser legs or the wonderfully fresh sea air, causing nostalgic thoughts, Ham certainly had a different viewpoint on things.

Karen declared it was time to get a coffee, so the three of them made their way to the on-board restaurant for refreshments, before calls were made for them to re-join their vehicles and continue their onward journey on French soil.

As the mighty cross-channel ferry docked in Calais, the massive bow doors opened, letting fresh light burst into the darkened vehicle-holding deck area below. With welcome signals beckoning traffic to leave the ship, engines were started and with a stirring of the gearstick, the horsebox with Maserati in tow, was once again in motion, looking forward to a fluid section of open continental road with billiard smooth tarmac.

The target destination was a garage situated seven kilometres south of Reims. The journey was a five-hour trek, the roads thankfully were largely uncluttered and as one kilometre, meshed into another, the garage silhouette eventually loomed on the horizon.

There had been very little communication during the journey. William was pretty isolated in the trailing Maserati on his own, verbal exchanges between Ham and Karen, were a lot less enthusiastic than normal. Perhaps Karen's inner tension was starting to show, whether it was pre-meeting nerves, or the result of Ham's antics behind the wheel of the horsebox was a difficult one to call.

Ham slowed the vehicle to a walking pace, and Karen directed Ham to park the horsebox in a very prominent part of the small car parking area, to the right of the main garage.

The garage was a very traditional slab-sided affair, typical of a nineteen seventies design, which showed very little evidence of receiving any form of an update since its original build. To the left was a small showroom area which had enough space to display two or three cars. To the right was a couple of large wooden double doors, looking slightly worse for wear, offering a glimpse behind of a grimmer-looking workshop. Not very enticing and certainly not the place you would randomly drive five hours in France to reach to have your English horsebox serviced.

For all its faults, the garage was busy. There was a young couple in the showroom area, looking at one of the used cars displayed within, and four or five cars could be seen in the workshop, receiving the motley mechanics' attention. There also appeared to be quite a few staff walking around, almost looking occupied. Twin petrol pumps formed the centrepiece of the front forecourt, with a small display of twelve used cars lined up to the left of the premises. The garage was located right on the edge of a light industrial area, forming the perimeter of what appeared to be a larger, nondescript town. Whatever the appeal was of this place, it concealed its charms well.

Ham observed as William drove past, surveying the locale as he continued along the main road, passing the garage slowly and continuing well beyond the parked horsebox.

Ham looked at Karen. "Was William overshooting the garage part of the plan?"

Karen put Ham's inquisitive nature to rest, offering her own unique blend of assurance. "The plan is, Ham, there is NO plan."

Ham remained silent, and for once looked a little bit worried. This is where the French connection gets serious. Unpredictable, but most definitely serious.

Karen was taking one hell of a risk visiting this garage. She could almost imagine four or five spanner-wielding maniacs heading towards them at any minute, Karen hoped whatever form the reception committee took, there really should be someone who wanted to talk to them, and they needed to appear soon. All three of them knew the tone of the reception party, assuming someone was even going to approach them, depended greatly on the relationship Michael had with his French contact, prior to his death.

Ham and Karen got down from the horsebox's cab. They both looked around gingerly, expecting someone to meet and greet them. Nobody came, their awkward bait failing to catch a nibbler.

Karen, without warning, walked over to the showroom window. She paused slightly and then walked inside, heading for the reception area.

Ham, not quite sure what to do, decided to walk over and befriend a local dog, tied to a post by the garage workshop entrance. The playful dog was certainly not a pedigree, although it looked like it had descendants from the Border Collie family. Ham's new canine friend was certainly more pleased to see him than the rest of the garage workforce. A step into the shade, away from the limelight, was a welcome relief for the both of them.

William duly arrived on site and parked his car, next to the used cars displayed on the other side of the garage forecourt. His car was facing the way they had come from, and William, for the moment, remained in situ with the engine running. Watching heads began to turn and if there were any curtains in the neighbourhood, they were sure to be twitching. This part of France was typically rural in presentation, feeling underdeveloped and enchantingly crude.

There was not another car worth more than a couple of thousand euros within a ten-kilometre radius. William's thoughtful ability to be sitting in a car worth at least eighty thousand euros afforded him the privilege of blending in with his surroundings like a distress flair in full flight, lighting up the nights sky. His ever-so-foreign English number plates, a further beacon alerting locals to his arrival, provided more visual impact than a big red neon sign, flashing in the shape of an arrow placed on his roof. He would have been less conspicuous if his car was a blaze. If ever there was a dedicated accountant who wanted to be a getaway driver, who ever so slightly lacked the full understanding of subtle subterfuge, then William was this man.

Ham, ever observant, peeked between the open wooden doors fronting the workshop, and slipped a hand inside to open the doors further to widen his field of view. A mechanic closed the doors with a gesture of speed that indicated Ham was not welcome. If ever 'bugger' could be used to describe a situation, then this was it.

Whilst William was gaining attention outside and Ham was doing his utmost to make a nuisance of himself, Karen was standing at the front of the service counter within the small showroom, waiting to be served.

"Bonjour, Madam," said the young man, a smart attendant.

Karen responded. "Hello. I would like to see someone regarding having my horsebox serviced."

"One moment, Madam." The young attendant scurried off, almost in panic. Karen noted the young man spoke to numerous other members of staff, they all peered outside, looking at the horsebox parked in their customer parking area and then disappeared from view.

Karen deliberately spoke in English, with volume, even though she was fluent in French. She detected she was centre of attention, all eyes were on her, clearly English visitors to this garage were not the norm. She was also well aware that garages liked nothing less, than unannounced visitors, that were not pre-booked. Throw potential for a smuggling ring into the mix and you are bound to get a reaction. Karen was certainly out to ruffle a few feathers, William would be proud, or not!

Predictably, the service manager arrived and introduced himself. "My name is Jacques. Please follow me."

Karen was ushered into the service manager's office, well out of the way from other customers. She had been whisked off to a cheerless, grubby non-descript half-glazed room at the far end of the building. The dirty fingerprint-lined walls, featured inviting smears of unsightly grease with a table top adorned with out-of-date local newspapers folded, with dog-eared pages detailing the horse racing fixtures and runners.

Jacques was an amusing-looking French man. He was short, quite tubby, aged about fifty-five years old, and spoke English in a comical French accent. He looked ruffled with life, apparently succumbing to the pressure of his endeavours and was sure to have had a story to tell. His grey receding hair, which appeared waxed back, complimented a grey moustache, topped off his typically French persona to a tee.

Jacques enquired, smiling, "How may I help you?"

Karen made Jacques aware that she was Michael's sister-in-law and at Michael's request she had come to France, to meet him, and to have the horsebox serviced.

Jacques was puzzled with the total lack of communication from Michael, however he was keen to oblige. A customer after all, is a customer.

Jacques asked for Karen's passport – this was just a formality – and requested the keys for the horsebox, so his team could get the service under way. Karen sat with her handbag on her lap, she briefly inched her fingers inside, intentionally caressing the barrel of her gun momentarily, then passed the spare keys to the horsebox and her passport over to Jacques.

Jacques left Karen alone for several minutes in his office. Typically, Karen had a brief rummage around, sighting only car-related invoices and parts inventories. There was nothing juicy for her to get her hands on, only unspeakable engineering lubricant residue.

Karen was heartened that her direct approach had paid off. Jacques scurried off without question, and the lack of interrogation regarding what service her horsebox required indicated that her strategy was taking shape.

In the distance the unmistakable clatter of the Bedford horsebox diesel engine firing into life filled the air. A commotion could be heard in the garages workshop as other customers' cars were juggled to accommodate the horsebox for its service.

Jacques arrived back after a short period in his office, clutching Karen's passport. He had photocopied her booklet, and returned the original to her.

Jacques enquired, "How is Michael?"

Karen retorted, "Michael is dead."

Jacques rolled his eyes, and then locked his vision with eye-to-eye contact with Karen. Jacques was visibly surprised by her statement, and appeared genuinely shocked. "How? What happened?"

Karen made Jacques aware of the murder, and also the police involvement and the lack of forward progression with the case. She made Jacques aware she worked closely with Michael and she was happy to bring the horsebox over to France for him. Karen enquired, "Can you help, Jacques? Do you know of anyone who could have killed Michael?"

Jacques nodded in apparent disbelief, looking downwards, clearly being careful what to reveal and refused to show any significant emotion.

Karen asked, "How well did you know Michael?"

Jacques was very uncomfortable with Karen's line of questioning. "I have dealt with Michael solidly over a number of years. We worked well together, with no problems."

Jacques reminded Karen, "In this business, you must be very careful with the people you choose to do business with. Perhaps

Michael got careless with some of his contacts? Who knows? I will miss him, he had character. English type, awkward character"

Jacques gave Karen his business card and he asked her to contact him if they had any further business for each other. Jacques confirmed Michael had been a good customer over the years, and Jacques was happy to start a fresh business relationship with Karen, so long as she was reliable.

Jacques told Karen the horsebox was likely to be two hours until it was finished. He suggested she visit the restaurant, two hundred yards down the road on the right. It would give her the opportunity to sample some quality French cuisine whilst she was waiting for her truck. Jacques commented that food locally was very good and it was highly recommended by all visitors.

Karen agreed. She thanked Jacques for his help and walked outside to see what Ham and William were up to.

William was nowhere to be seen, and Ham was looking at the used cars, having parted company with his French-speaking dog.

Ham enquired, "How did you get on?"

Karen responded, "Jacques, the manager, is a nice enough guy superficially. However, he was not super keen to talk. Funny that! Where is William?"

William had disappeared round the back of the garage to see if he could find anything interesting. Ham made Karen aware that it was noted the mechanics were very protective of what work they were doing in the workshop. Maybe it was just the way they did things, however it was quite noticeable the horsebox was positioned in the workshop at the far side of the inner retaining wall, well out of the way from view. It might have been normal practice, as it might have been the workshops designated area for trucks, who knew? It was hoped the horsebox was positioned as it was to receive some special attention from the men with the spanners.

Ham meanwhile was going gaga over a lovely 1972 Fiat 124 Spider prominently parked in the customer car parking area.

"Now, Karen," enthused Ham, showing off his newfound treasure. "This is when the Italians made proper traditional sports cars. How sexy is this?"

"Yes, it's very nice, Ham. Let's go and get something to eat."

The two of them walked over the road and set about finding the restaurant Jacques had recommended. Karen sent William a text, detailing their whereabouts, urging him to hurry up. Ham and Karen set about interrogating the local menu, and enjoyed some quality food and a friendly chat together.

Ninety minutes passed and there was still no sign of William. What was he doing? Ham was in danger of getting the bill when William eventually turned up, looking more than a little shaken.

Karen greeted him with typical affection. "Your soup's cold, William!"

William responded. "I do not want any food, however I could kill a beer."

A round of drinks was ordered and as Ham did the pouring, William started talking.

"Karen, I think it is best for you to come back to England with me, in my car."

"Why do you say that? Have the grease monkeys loosened my brakes," said Ham, laughing in typical, jovial fashion.

The serious look on William's face and Karen's concern was enough for Ham to realise something odd was definitely on the cards.

William continued. "In some ways, I do not want to tell you this, however I fear I have no option."

The scene was set for drama, a pause followed, then William started to elaborate regarding his findings.

He went on to explain that Jacques' workshop did not have air conditioning and to increase air circulation in hot weather, such as that day, staff left two fire doors wide open at the rear. The staff were so preoccupied keeping their eye on the front doors and making sure no customers could see what they were doing, including Ham, that they failed to notice William, perched behind two industrial bins at the rear of the building. As the horsebox was worked on at the back of the garage, William had a perfect view and could see everything.

The horsebox was reversed onto a large four-poster ramp, and elevated into the air. From underneath, mechanics with air tools and plasma cutters cut through the underneath of the chassis sections. This gave them access to large metal cases, there were eight in total. All intricately removed, and stacked carefully to one side. Two ladies then arrived and opened the cases. Inside was a stash of euros, genuine hard currency and lots of it.

The money was stacked on the mechanics' benches, neatly put into bundles and bagged. Once the money had been counted and processed, it was placed in a tatty old oil container, ready for onward banking.

The garage van was then reversed into the workshop, the front workshop doors securely closed behind it. Inside the van were a lot of small packages of various commodities. They were like slabs or small bricks, neatly wrapped in something similar to cling film. These were then placed into the eight aluminium cases which had previously held the money, and re-inserted into the truck chassis. The cut sections were then welded back up, painted, rubbed over with dirt and old oil for good effect, and the horsebox was then wheeled out, ready for collection.

William looked at Ham. "It is clear your horsebox chassis rails and other hidden compartments are full of drugs of some description. We are not talking Paracetamol here, Ham."

Ham remained silent, and swallowed hard.

"Oh, my god!" shrieked Karen. "This means we unwittingly smuggled a vast sum of euros out of England. I wonder how much our hoard was worth."

It had never occurred to the trio that Michael would have concealed currency in the horsebox prior to his death. In many ways of course, the technique made perfect sense. A flawless exchange for the trade in drugs or whatever the packets concealed.

Perhaps naively, an image of a sharp-suited mystery man, wearing aviator-style sunglasses, laying a briefcase on a table top, flipping the case open, revealing a stash of used notes would be a more romantic image of a dealer purchasing the drugs. Ham had no difficulty visualising the middleman handing over the briefcase, for his ill-gotten gains, whilst a dry ice machine created drama by allowing a mysterious fog to swirl around the villain's silhouette in full widescreen cinematic style.

The reality however was a lot more complex, and much better executed. Frightening well executed. Whilst this team may not have been greasy haired suntanned charmers, these guys were certainly not idiots. They were very good, super swift, and worked as a team brilliantly.

Karen reminded Ham and William about the telephone calls Michael had made to the garage in France, two days before his death. It was Karen's belief he must have set the deal up with Jacques then and organised the concealment of the cash in the horsebox before his murder. It was unlikely the garage in France would have sat on Michael's drugs for six months, so it looked as if the garage could be a central hub, probably for countless drug smugglers, from all over Europe. This could be a massive operation, which had to be linked to Alfonso back in the United Kingdom.

William continued. "I could not see the denominations of the euros extracted from the horsebox, but there were lots of them, this was a big commercial transaction. The team was highly organised and every one of them knew what they were doing. The deal to purchase these drugs, could have been as much as one hundred thousand euros, perhaps even more. That is big money!"

Karen announced, "We must get back to the garage and collect the horsebox. Time is getting on."

Ham cut in, "Are you serious? We must not have any further

involvement with that thing. This is a serious crime. I do not want any more to do with it and neither should you two."

Silence followed a meeting of minds. Karen did not want to publicly admit it, however she was quietly excited about converting the drugs back home into lovely spendable money. Forget for one moment the unsavoury consequences of getting caught in Dover by Her Majesty's finest.

Ham clearly did not want any more to do with the horsebox, his moral standpoint and strict religious code had a significant bearing on his outlook. As did the hole wearing through Ham's trousers where the horsebox keys were currently residing.

William was the undisputed influential referee on this one. He had experience of crossing the line, keeping the good, dabbling with the bad, and more importantly always coming out on top without being caught or being shot at.

William mulled the situation over in his mind, being very careful what he was about to say.

William commenced. "As I see it, we have two options. Option one, we can walk away now. Option two, we throw the dice and take a gamble. If we get the booty back to England and on to Alfonso, we can trade with him, and pay off Collard. Karen gets to sleep better!"

There was very little protest coming from Karen. This windfall of a task had its benefits. Ham was clearly very concerned about this predicament, he remained silent, looked distant, and wore a face which personified the expression seriously pissed off.

Karen asked William, "What are our chances of getting caught by Customs in Dover when we return?"

William went on to state he thought the chances of them getting caught were slim. Even if the vehicle got tugged in a line up, it would take some serious digging, from a super vigilant officer, to find the hidden treasure. William also reminded them that Michael must have pulled the trip off several times before, without a hitch. The omens surely were good.

Ham, sensing he was swimming against the tide, with a ball chained to his leg, asked a perfectly reasonable question to the both of them. "Remind me, what sentence do drug smugglers get these days?"

William retorted nonchalantly, "Ten years, assuming this cargo has a street value of one million quid plus, which is totally possible. Within five years you could be out on good behaviour and living in Spain."

With the thought of ten years in prison running through their thoughts, the sobering sensation of reality draped them in silence. Eye contact between all three of them bounced uncomfortably around the table.

William, whilst still wearing his accountant's badge and slipping at will into high street villain, offered, "Think about this you two. We have not done anything wrong. We have not bought any drugs, or whatever those packets concealed in the horsebox are. It was not our money that paid for them. All we have done is get a horsebox serviced in France, and asked a service manager a few questions about a murder. As far as I am aware, that is not an illegal activity."

It was quite clear to the three of them that circumstance had dealt them a highly unusual situation. Did they have the balls to proceed and overstep the mark, or were they about to fold and walk away?

Swerving around a prison sentence was one thing, dabbling with ruthless drug dealers was another, however Ham was just about to bring the whole scenario into sharp perspective.

"Think about the children who get hold of this stuff on street corners, William. Do you really want to be part of the supply chain regarding this junk. Do you, Karen?"

Ham continued, "It is not just the money, and our selfish consequences we need to consider, it is other people's lives you could be playing with here. Young lives. If we do this, we do it for the right reasons, and we have got to think of a way to ensure Alfonso's network suffers."

Sensing the conversation had moved forward, when in fact it had probably moved backwards, Ham started having a laugh and a giggle with himself. "Can you imagine the field day the press would have if we got caught. A vicar, a chartered accountant, and the highly respected lady of the manor with a horsebox full of drugs. We do not exactly fit the profile of international drug pedlars, do we."

The three of them were almost giving themselves a pat on the back, after all they were the archetypal pillars of the community. The problem was pillars can crumble and when that happens, lives suffer.

Ham pointed his index finger at himself, then at William, and finally at Karen, then declared, "This venture has got the potential to be a high-end pants down moment. If the shit hits the fan with this, all three of us will be facing the music. Remember that, and it will not be Swan Lake."

William keen to get things moving, raised his beer bottle and stated, "I am in. It has got to be worth a chance, hasn't it."

Ham then raised his coffee cup. "Against my better judgement, I am in. I am not happy, however I am in."

Karen agreed, however she had one final condition. "I will do this, however I want to be sitting next to Ham in the horsebox. It is not fair for him to pass through customs alone." She also reminded William that, whilst he might be sitting in his sports car, detached from the action, he was still very much a part of this intricate gamble. They were taking the plunge together.

As Ham clinked his coffee cup with the others, he stated the immortal words, "For better, for worse." Only a vicar could come up with a rubbish send-off line such as that one.

Ham, William and Karen settled the bill and left the restaurant.

As bold as when she had arrived, Karen entered the garage, and was greeted by the same smart service attendant as before. She paid her service bill, got her invoice, collected the spare keys, and went back to the horsebox..

Ham was already in the driver's seat, while William was ready and waiting in his trusty Maserati backup car.

Karen looked to Ham, "Thanks for doing this."

Ham smiled, looked up at the heavens, and said softly, "Lord, please forgive me."

As Ham pulled the horsebox round from the garage parking area, the horsebox mysteriously stalled. There was an uncharacteristic pop from the exhaust, then mechanical silence. Karen and Ham exchanged concerned glances with one another; this was not the time for the horsebox to breakdown. Ham attempted to start the vehicle again, there was nothing. Ham paused for a few seconds then tried again. Suddenly the glorious six-cylinder diesel power plant burst into life, leaving a trail of smoke until the engine warmed and settled down. Ham and Karen had never been so pleased to see smoke lifting in their rear view mirrors.

Ham enquired, "You sure these guys serviced this truck?"

Karen responded, "Probably not. They might have got distracted doing something else! They still charged me four hundred euros for the privilege though."

Ham wondered, "Perhaps they put sand in the fuel tank, in retaliation for losing the battle at Agincourt. The French have long memories, you know."

The five-hour drive back to Calais was quite punishing on the mind, however the horsebox fortuitously performed without any further hitch. There was no danger of Ham nodding off to sleep however, he had so much adrenalin pumping through his veins, and enough prickles in his nerve endings to keep him awake for days. It is amazing what breaking the law does to a man.

Soon enough the large road signs announced their arrival at Calais, the French ferry port. As the clocks approached midnight, the booking clerks took their tickets and dispatched them to their waiting ferry.

Once comfortably on board, the three of them, led by Karen, enjoyed a strong coffee. Reminiscent of three captives sitting on a time bomb, conversation was not brisk, and humour, unusually for these three, was not flowing between them. The weight of deception was bearing down on all of them.

The ferry's distinctive chime and recorded announcement, indicated the request for all passengers to return to their vehicles. The Ferry docked timely at Dover port and embarkation was typically swift and efficient.

Heartbeats raced as engines sprung into life and traffic started to flow from the ferries. William was home and dry, he followed the other cars through HM Customs and Excise nothing to declare lanes. William had nothing to hide, only a slightly smug conscience. Ham and Karen were carrying the baby, their horsebox traversed the intricate internal Eastern Dock roadways, obligated to follow the freight lanes with other trucks and lorries. Progress for them was painfully slow at times.

Ham up until that point had been perfectly calm and collected. As his thoughts played games, he suddenly freaked out. "My god, we forgot the horse!" he yelled.

Ham advised Karen, "Who in their right mind, takes an empty horsebox to France, then brings it back again, empty?" The Dover Customs men were sure to pick up on this and smell a rat. Ham was convinced HM Customs must have access to shipment intelligence, such as which vehicles left the port previously empty, and which returned empty. Perhaps they even had access to the gross vehicle weights too? Their only hope, Ham reasoned to himself, was that something more interesting for the border protection officers to investigate stood out from the ships manifest, hopefully leaving their path reasonably clear.

Michael's success with this ploy previously was probably due to his ability to get a return trip loaded with livestock. That was the whole point or maybe he was just good at arriving in the UK, when the border patrol was undergoing a shift change! Ham's hands were beginning to shake and he began to perspire as his resolve was starting to crumble.

As their horsebox nudged ever closer to the front of the immigration queue, Karen told Ham, "Relax, I have this covered, let me answer any questions."

Karen's total control and cool composure was an annoyance to Ham. Why wasn't she fidgeting and tearing her fingernails out? The airbrakes hissed and the engine's revs rose, headlamps bobbed in the darkness as first gear was engaged, and the trucks in all four lanes moved forward. Ham and Karen were now at the front of the queue.

As a port officer holding a clipboard approached the cab, Ham wound his window down.

"You loaded or empty?" asked the young officer.

"Empty," replied Ham.

The officer instructed Ham to move forward and drop the ramp at the back so they could see inside. Karen got out to open the ramp at the rear. Once the ramp was lowered, Karen intentionally tried to look as unconcerned as possible, by wearing one of her tired and bored faces.

"Where have you been?"

"Reims," Karen replied.

"So where's your horse?"

Karen explained they had been hired to collect a horse from a stable in Reims, and bring it back for covering at a local stud. Karen vented her frustration at the horse being unwell, it had developed colic, it was unfit for us to load. "The owner will still be getting my bill for the transport along with the two-hundred euro invoice for my fuel," she mused.

The officer then walked inside the load area and had a nose around, tapping the wooden sides and waving a large portable torch around. Karen again tried to look uninterested and did not show any concern regarding what the officer was doing, intentionally looking away, deflecting any internal curiosity.

"You had any fresh work carried out in here recently?" shouted the officer, inspecting the inside sections with his penetrating bright light.

"No," replied Karen.

"I can smell fresh paint back here. Why do you think that is?" asked an ever-inquisitive officer.

Karen shrugged and replied calmly, "I don't know. I have not painted anything. You can probably smell the rear brakes binding; they could use a service."

The officer stood still and remained in eye contact, then after a brief pause. "Okay," came the reply. "Best you get those brakes looked at. On your way now."

The officer stamped their port control slip, and they were free to leave the Eastern Docks. With the rear doors secured and the entrance ramp back in situ, Ham engaged first gear again, and they were on their way to the final exit control barrier within the port.

William could hardly contain his excitement, witnessing the exit barrier rising, and the horsebox being given the approval to leave the restricted area.

Karen looked at Ham smiling, waving her triumphant fist in the air. "We bloody did it. We made it work."

Ham responded, "You were brilliant. How many lies can you tell in one conversation! You handled the Customs officer fantastically."

This was a textbook operation if ever there was one, and all concerned were justifiably proud of their performance. Perhaps things had gone too smoothly!

# 12

The journey from the Eastern Docks in Dover to Karen's home in the village of Hawkswold was only a thirty-minute drive. Ham steered the horsebox sharp left out of the Docks and made the slow journey up the steep hill, leading away from the port. Ham was relieved he could breathe properly again. Passing through Customs without a crisis was a major weight lifted from his shoulders, especially as Ham was the one holding the steering wheel. It was likely to be a momentous occasion when all three of them got the horsebox back to the barn. All of them were likely to share big hugs, and mutually give a well-deserved sigh of a relief all round.

William had been slowed leaving the port car park where he had waited to witness the horsebox leaving the port. A careless holidaymaker had parked their car behind William, blocking his exit from his selected parking bay. No damage was done, William left as swiftly as he could, chasing Ham at the helm of the horsebox playfully up the hill. Ham had a good two-minute start, and there was no way William was going to give Ham the satisfaction of beating him up the torturous hill from the port, not with his stylish Italian Maserati at his disposal.

The hill out of Dover was just over a mile long, and was a

challenge for all but the most powerful of vehicles. William, at long last, was able to really put his car through its paces, having been constrained and tethered for so long playing chaperone to the lumbering wreck of a horsebox. He loved every minute of his newfound vigour, really pushing his car through each gear ratio and extending into the rev range with enthusiasm. Ham's progress in the horsebox may have been less energetic, but it was valuable headway all the same.

Ham became increasingly aware of a car sitting on his back bumper, as he began to reach the top of the mighty hill. At first, Ham believed the car behind to be William, he soon realised however, this was not the case, the light clusters behind giving a totally different headlamp beam footprint than the one he had become familiar with from William's Maserati.

As Ham approached the brow of the hill, the car behind started flashing its lights aggressively, and then began to swerve alarmingly from side to side of the horsebox in a very frightening fashion. Ham advised Karen to hold on tight as he straddled both lanes of the duel carriageway to prevent the driver behind getting past. Regrettably, when you are going uphill in an aging truck you cannot put your foot down and pull away. The best you can hope for is to employ defensive blocking tactics, and leave your braking until the very last minute.

Ham's driving was about to get very busy, fast. Ham was now on top of the major roundabout at the top of the hill and had to make a decision on which exit was best. Distracted by looking in his rear mirrors, he approached the roundabout with far too much speed. Fortunately, given it was the early hours of the morning, there were very few other vehicles on the road network, which was just as well as Ham could not stop the horsebox at the junction on the entry into the roundabout. Ham cornered hard left, sweeping the horsebox almost on two wheels, tyres squealing in protest as he took the roundabout with excessive speed, only just staying on the road glancing the inside kerb of the roundabout. William, in a vehicle better suited to enthusiastic driving, was closing in on the unfolding drama fast.

The car training on the horsebox was still right behind him, so Ham decided to serve up a dummy and make the driver think behind he was about to take the second exit. At the last minute, Ham yanked the steering wheel round to the right and just missed the barrier defining this escape route. The horsebox was so cumbersome to manoeuvre that the chasing driver was not fooled. The swaying sides of the horsebox could not defy the laws of physics, or the chasing driver behind.

William by now was also on the large awkward-shaped roundabout and was closing swiftly on the mystery car behind the horsebox. Ham made a split-second decision and decided to exit the roundabout at the third exit, following the coastal road above the famous white cliffs. This was not the road of choice to get to Karen's house – Ham was improvising with the route as he went along, ultimately aiming to avoid a seemingly inevitable disaster.

William, pre-programmed to drive to Karen's village by taking the second exit, was surprised with Ham's choice of route, and nearly hit the barrier Ham had done so well to avoid. The coastal road they found themselves on was a very quick single lane road, with only minor kinks, joining up the sweeping straight bits in between. The road was heavily banked on both sides, making this in many ways an ideal course for Ham, as it meant it was easier to keep the chasing car behind him. The lack of severe bends would not test the chassis or the horsebox's aging springs too much, which not only helped the forward-motion dynamics, this also helped Karen retain her sanity as she clung on to the cabin's grab handles for dear life.

After plenty of swerving, more obligatory tyre squeal, and arm twirling from Ham, in no time at all another two miles of tarmac had been dispatched. William seeing Ham was well under control, not only with the villainous type chasing him, but also secretly impressed with his driving control, decided to hang back, ever so slightly. William was sure this chase was going to end in tears, and he wanted to be well placed to launch a one-man offensive on the chasing bandits, when the opportunity presented itself. William was also keen not to get tangled up with the almighty mess, which was sure to unfold when the wheels stop turning before his very eyes any time soon.

Ham and Karen were now fast approaching a crossroad's junction, the natural flow of the road for them was to keep going straight ahead. Ham had other ideas. Oncoming traffic presented an additional opportunity, which Ham was keen to seize. By a stroke of luck, the oncoming traffic would hit the centre of the crossroads, at precisely the moment Ham would arrive with the horsebox.

Ham told Karen to brace herself as they entered the crossroad's junction zone, Ham hit the brakes hard at sixty miles per hour. All four wheels of the horsebox lit up and clouds of tyre smoke stirred the night air as speed was scrubbed off and their momentum waned. Ham knew the car which was close behind would likely fail to stop, and would have nowhere to go accept hit the horsebox hard from the rear. The plan worked to perfection; the chasing car smashed into the back of the horsebox, assisting it into a forced ninety-degree spin, missing oncoming traffic by inches. Ham quickly dropped the gear-lever into first gear and hit his accelerator hard, steering right into the spin, executing a perfect power slide up a surprising large country lane, now heading towards the sea across the cliff top.

Ham was rather hoping the tactic would immobilise the chasing car, however this was not the case. The car did look crumpled, from what Ham could see in his limited vision rear view mirror. The most notable damage being the offside headlamp was not lit. Ham had a plan, he knew the road he was now on would lead to a small village. In the middle of the village was a seldom-used road which would take them to a series of tight challenging bends. Some locals referred to this piece of road as the Alpine section. Ham recalled it was great fun in the right car, Ham however, was not driving the right car that night, so knew he had to be on his guard and be prepared to improvise.

William was still bringing up the rear and could hardly wait to see what trick manoeuvre Ham had up his sleeve next. This was surely the drive of Ham's life. William just hoped the elderly horsebox held itself together in the face of such glorious punishment.

It was evident initially that the villains had pulled back a little, realising their car was no match for the horsebox's robust construction and considerable girth. The chasing outlaws were clearly concerned with the manic qualities of the unpredictable wheel-smith tearing up the tarmac from the horsebox's cockpit. Having been outwitted by Ham once, they were undoubtedly keen not to replicate this mistake twice. For sure they were licking their wounds and checking their vital systems were still working, their lack of one headlamp must have had a severe impact on their ability to see on these unlit country roads.

Ham turned right in the village, into the narrower lane which led to the famed Alpine route, and pushed the horsebox as hard as he dare. The connecting road to this section was a long two-mile straight which was bumpy and very easy to get out of shape along, especially if the vehicle you were driving had severely worn suspension and questionable road-holding qualities. Ham was more than up to the task with this, and his plan initially was to block the road at speed, forcing the chasing duo into a hedge, where Ham and William could then overpower them and get some well-needed answers. *Reality may work out differently*, Ham thought.

The chase was now likely into its final stage. Ham, ready to throw the gauntlet down, entered the Alpine section with renewed enthusiasm. First up was a sharp left hander, overlooking a sheer drop. Ham planned to take the corner wide, driving the horsebox on the wrong side of the road to give extra cornering speed. Ham was a brave man. The villains demonstrated renewed pace and got their vehicle up the inside of Ham's horsebox, forcing Ham ever wider. As Ham's box was forced to hug up against the barriers, bright sparks and the sound of shrieking metal filled the night air in spectacular fashion.

Gravity and the physics of moving mass played their part and assisted Ham's amazing slingshot acceleration out of the curve down the hill to a waiting right-hand hairpin bend. Neck and neck, Ham used his considerable width of the horsebox to crush the chasing car into the bank which defined the twisty road, running alongside him into the ever-looming embankment.

The villains, sensing what was happening, felt the squeeze and hit the brakes, causing Ham to swerve to the other side of the road, momentarily losing control, overshooting the hairpin bend which was now on top of them. Ham to his credit, prevented the horsebox from leaving the road, took the hairpin wide, scrabbled for a gear, found some grip, and looked in horror as the villains had pulled round on the inside and tried to overtake them.

It was clear the villains' car was suffering, and did not have the performance advantage it should have had. Ham's battered horsebox was also limping with battle scars, the engine sounding increasingly strained, and the tyres lacking useful grip. The smell of a well-used clutch, hot brakes and burning gearbox oil filled the cabin with a delightful aroma. Karen felt sick and was sure she could not take much more.

Ham was not about to be beaten, and as the villains' car nudged in front, Ham powered up and controlled the snaking horsebox directing it into the passing flank of the rogues' vehicle, side swiping it into a spin. As both vehicles accelerated, desperate to regain the upper hand, the chasing car slapped into one side of a bank and then across the road into another. The speed of the impact acted like a rocket on a launch pad, the car disappearing over one of the numerous cliff sides, down a one hundred and fifty-foot drop into the wooded area below. There was no question, at that speed and with that trajectory over a sheer drop, surviving that kind of accident was not possible.

Ham hardly had time to compose himself, he was now hurtling towards the final sequence of bends leading to a bridge with excessive speed. In distressed composure, Ham realised his brakes had been cooked, they were not working, worse still is accelerator pedal was stuck on. If only Ham had time to panic, his face would have been a picture!

Ham's only option was to take the left-hand bend wide, and nudge up against the barrier, letting this robust piece of engineering help steer his horsebox around the oncoming corner and not straight on, over the edge of the bridge which was soon to come into view. The plan was working well until a rock concealed in the verge, snapped the steering column, forcing the front wheels to steer the horsebox hard left, which forced the truck to turn away from the guiding steel barrier, sending the horsebox across the road, mounting the kerb and hitting the barrier on the other side of the road head on. The horsebox immediately toppled over and slid on its side for what appeared to be ages, eventually stopping on its side, blocking the road completely. Karen's screams were barely audible over the din of the out-of-control chaos she was reluctantly party to.

William arrived behind the horsebox, witnessing a cloud of dust, smoke, sparks, and debris being thrown across the full width of the road. The force of the accident complimented the disarray by showering the area with fragmented wreckage. William stopped his car in the middle of the road and shook his head in disbelief. His headlamps lit a path through the slowly clearing dense smoke and dust cloud. This was a serious high-speed impact. William's fear was Ham and Karen could be seriously hurt or even killed. He was reluctant to approach the horsebox cab for fear of what he might find, remaining seated in his car for the first thirty seconds or so, literally waiting for the dust to settle.

The picture of destruction and knowledge of friends inside

the wreckage stunned William momentarily into shock. The horsebox was resting, sitting on its side, driver's side down in the road. William climbed on top of the horsebox and peered down inside, through the smashed passenger side window. Visibility was poor, however Karen was groaning, and she was found in a pile on top of a motionless Ham.

William reached in and grabbed Karen's arm. "Are you hurt, Karen? Are you okay?"

Karen responded, "My head aches and I have a pain in my pelvis. Help me out of here."

William asked, "How is Ham?"

Ham was silent. Deadly silent.

William could now smell leaking diesel. "Karen, come on, give me your hand."

William assisted a dazed Karen. She climbed up from the cab of the horsebox and he helped her down to road level. Karen then walked over to the barrier and sat down on the pavement. Head in hands, she sat motionless, understandably mesmerised by the collision.

William frantically shouted at Ham. "Ham, talk to me! Are you okay? Talk to me, you bastard."

Ham remained still and silent. William cleared some glass from the broken passenger window and was trying to look for the best way to climb in and see Ham when suddenly Ham started making incoherent noises as his senses grappling with reality, jostled back into life.

"Ham, it's me, Will. Give me your hand."

Ham started to come round, coughing and groaning, then slowly but surely Ham was able to move and reach for William, who helped him climb out of the wreck.

"Ham, are you wounded?" William asked.

Ham replied, "It is just my back, My head, my arms, my foot, my leg, and my arse. Bugger, I have never had such a pain in my arse before. I never realised it was possible!" Ham groaned again.

Ham eventually extricated himself from his hole with William's help. He limped over to Karen sitting on the floor and sat down next to her. His hands were beginning to shake and he needed to sit down before he fell down, and settle his thoughts. Karen, shaking her head, addressed Ham as they both looked back towards the steaming, smoking wreckage. "And you wanted to transport a live horse back to the country in the horsebox, driving like that!"

William was amazed Ham and Karen had got out the horsebox with what appeared to be only minor injuries. He was quite taken by the cracked windscreen and the huge indentation that had been left in the glass, as Karen's head had obviously hit it. The barriers the horsebox had hit did not fare much better either, however at least they stopped the vehicle going over the edge, onto the drop below. The outcome was sure to be a lot different had the horsebox taken a plunge.

William turned round to face Ham and Karen. Ham asked the question, "Who were those idiots who tried to run us off the road?"

William offered, "If I was a gambling man, I would put money on Collard's crew. We need to look closer at them tomorrow – they will not bother us any more tonight."

The dust, smoke and sparks which had defined the crash scene had now lifted. It was a beautiful clear night and the moonlight provided the smallest inkling of visual assistance in enabling William to survey the wider trail of destruction. The footprint remaining, began in the wake of the first impact on the other side of the road leaving an almighty scatter, stretching across the double-width twin-lane road. Total carnage would have been a very good summary.

It was then William noticed what appeared to be hundreds of small packages strewn across the road, lying between chunks of torn off bodywork, smashed glass and kerbside debris tossed in the road as a result of the double impact.

"Oh, my god!" shouted William, pointing. "Look!"

It was evident their precious cargo had been sprung from the truck during their epic accident. The under-truck seam welds, provided courtesy of their French friends were clearly not as robust as their precision transaction handling would have you believe. The mystery cargo needed to be recovered quickly, before any onlookers arrived or before the local wildlife snatched it, and started hopping and popping in the cliff top grasslands.

William opened the boot of his car and started collecting up the eight aluminium cases, and strewn merchandise. When the load was packed, there were twelve neat plastic wrapped packages in each aluminium case. The cases were smaller than holiday-bound suitcases, however bigger than conventional holdalls. William knew he would struggle to get all eight inside the boot of his car, but he was definitely up for the challenge.

Progress was predictably very slow to start with. The initial scurry and blind panic lacked co-ordination, resulting in more than a few Keystone Kop moments. If the situation had not been more serious, William was sure to have had a laugh at Karen and Ham's predicament. Clearly impact trauma has many different forms of manifestation. Fighting an unstable equilibrium, challenging the laws of gravity and lacking simple manual dexterity skills were all qualities William witnessed in abundance during this latest impromptu episode.

Once their heart rates came back to the right side of normal, Ham and Karen assisted William as best they could; all the cases and cargo were soon collected and placed in William's boot of his Maserati. William got five of the aluminium cases in his car, and dumped the remaining three cases over the bridge, to be forever concealed within the plentiful wild shrubbery below. The remaining merchandise was placed loosely on top of the cases and the boot firmly closed with a quality-reassuring thud.

Ham reached into his jacket pocket, pulled out his mobile phone and called his friend Mark. His friend was on standby with a recovery truck, in case the horsebox developed mechanical problems whilst on the jaunt to France. Ham made the call, knowing Mark also had a friend who had a four-wheel-drive car with a winch to assist in the horsebox's recovery. Whilst the horsebox had not suffered a breakdown in the traditional sense, it was party to a catastrophic failure all the same. The recovery of the horsebox was going to be costly, however, given the circumstances, the three of them could not afford not to have the vehicle righted and recovered.

Fortunately, where the accident had happened was on a little-used road at night. The road was popular during the day, especially in the summer with sightseeing tourists and locals alike, but thankfully after midnight the road was deserted. They could not have picked a better stretch of road with which to have staged their accident.

In no time at all, Ham's friend had arrived with a recovery truck, to commence retrieving the forlorn horsebox. The trusty trio climbed inside William's car and then left the recovery to the professionals. William was keen to get moving, feeling terribly uncomfortable with a boot full of a substance that would require a lot of explaining should they get caught. Ham and Karen were equally keen to get moving as they were desperate for a clean-up, fresh clothes, and had plenty of minor wounds which needed attention. Assuming the excitement of the evening did not kill them first, some sleep would be good too.

Poor timing, William's low-fuel warning light came on as he set off on the final trek home. This was not a major issue as the route he was taking took them past a local twenty-four-hour fuel station. William was being extra vigilant with his driving that night, watching his speed and using his indicators with extra diligence, his road manners really were impeccable for obvious reasons, as he did not want to attract the attention of any roaming officers.

William stopped at the fuel station and as a matter of routine, went about his normal business and filled his car up with petrol. William's stress levels were at an all-time high. He was tired, he had experienced the euphoria of feeling like he had got away with what he thought felt like, getting away with the crime of the century. He then seemed destined to lose his collective ill-gotten gains, as the result of a quirky accident. To cap it all, he felt the harrowing emotions of deep concern, knowing he came very close that night to losing two dear friends.

The rollercoaster ride of the night just got a lot worse for them; a police car appeared in his rear view mirror, lights flashing and sirens squealing. William had no option but to stop.

Stopping at a conveniently placed layby off the main road, William lowered his window in anticipation of the police officer's sermon.

"Shit, I forgot to pay for the fuel," William said in a frustrated tone. "I never forget to pay for my fuel."

Karen remained wide-eyed with concern and Ham threw his hands in the air quietly in disbelief.

William waited the short period for the police car to pull up behind, and for the officer to get out of his car and approach his driver's window.

"Good morning, sir. Can you guess why I have stopped you?" asked the traffic officer, shining a torch around inside William's car.

William responded, "I suspect it is because I forgot to pay for my fuel back there. I am really sorry, I was distracted and tired, that is all. It is late, I am nearly home and I need some sleep. I can go back and pay the fuel, it is not a problem."

The policemen paused with his delivery for the next part, as he was sure there was more to this stop than just a theft of some fuel. He shined his torch at Karen, who was sitting in the front passenger seat, and then to Ham who was sitting in the back, albeit long ways across the back seat as his leg was hurting and the room in the back of William's car was not super spacious.

William, Karen and Ham's thoughts were all racing. This was the sharp end of a worst case scenario, and whatever question was coming next from the officer, the answer if they were not careful was likely to start unravelling a night of drama, which none of them wanted unwinding.

The policeman looked squarely at Karen, and asked her in a tone of concern if she was all right. Karen, for her part, looked distressed and was a bloody mess. You could imagine the police officer thinking, *You have got an expensive sharp car here, a well-dressed guy at the wheel. A woman who looks distressed, who has make up on, which has been smudged and had run where she had been crying. She has dirt on one of her cheeks, glass glistening in her hair.*

Her hair was a mess, bedraggled and roughed up, and topped off with a blood-stained creased and torn white blouse, also marked with dirt and grease. Ham in the back looked equally rough, without any make up, with a jacket with holes in it and a facial expression which told the world in all innocence, he had had one hell of a night of it.

Karen calmly told the policeman she was fine, and like her driver, just needed some rest and some sleep.

The policeman then pointed the torch at Ham in the back, and asked him if he was all right.

Ham replied. "I am fine, just a few aches."

Surprisingly, the officer did not ask what they had been up to. Instead he looked back at William, and asked him to step out of the car.

The predictable line of questioning followed, typically, "Was this your car?", which it was, and "What is your name and address?" which William duly gave.

"Could you open your boot for me please, sir."

William got back in the driver's seat and swallowed hard, and looked sorrowfully at Karen, their eye contact with a tinge of pissed off sadness said it all. He could not believe they had been through all this, and then get tripped up by a small hurdle at the end of their run. A hurdle which should not even have been a hurdle!

William made a decision, to not open the boot remotely, this made the boot pop up automatically, instead he decided to use his master key. He got out the car again and walked to the back of his car. At that point, he was aware the police officer had been beckoned back to his patrol car.

The police officer returned. "Sir, we have to go, there has been a bad accident on the London-bound motorway. I suggest you go back to the garage straight away and pay for your fuel. We have a log of your registration number etc., but I suggest you clear this issue up with the fuel station directly."

With that, the police officer jumped back in his patrol car, and sped off at speed to sort out his newly unfolding event. As the police car turned around and left the lay by, relief overwhelmed the trio.

"Fucking hell, I need a drink," William said as he kissed the night air. "We came so close to the brink of disaster, and we got away with it. Wow."

He got back in his car, and decided against his better judgement, to go back to greet the cashier in the garage, make his apologies, and pay the bill. Some people!

# 13

The next morning, the three bears with sore heads were fumbling around in Karen's house, drinking lots of coffee trying to grasp some sense of the events of the previous day. Karen wanted the benefit of quality time alone, and chose to soak nicely in the comfort of her own bath, filled to the brim with hot water and topped off with lots and lots of bubbles.

Ham and William were freshly dressed, very pleased with themselves at being able to co-ordinate and consume a mammoth fried breakfast, and were now busy removing their hoard of drugs from William's car and concealing them temporarily in Karen's loft.

Ham enquired, "How much do you think this lot is worth?"

William answered, "I am not sure. I am not certain what the hell this stuff is, aside from a guaranteed lengthy prison sentence if we get caught with it."

As the two men had finished moving the cache, Karen joined them downstairs.

She advised Ham and William that if she had read the play right yesterday, the two guys who tried to run them off the road, were most likely to be connected with Collard. If for no other reason, it was the sort of aggressive stunt she thought Collard would pull and it certainly seemed within his capability.

The question was, if this were the case, why do it. If Collard wanted the drugs, and was hell bent on getting them, he could have contacted Karen, arranged to have bought them, and ruthlessly killed all three of them when they made the drop. A chase through the Kent countryside was too much of a risk; if Ham had lost control of the horsebox, and it had toppled over the cliff, nobody would have got the drugs. It did not make sense to any of them, why did they do it?

Karen also highlighted the fact, she was unsure how tightly knit Collard and Alfonso were. It seemed clear Alfonso ruled the roost, and for sure later that day, Karen wanted to be speaking to Alfonso again. She was well aware this carried risk, however she had very little option.

First things first, Karen wanted to go back to the crash site, and see if she could get any clues from the guys in the car who went over the edge of the embankment. She needed to know for sure who wanted them dead the previous night.

William interjected, "Are you sure that is wise, Karen? I think it is safe to assume their accident last night killed them – they will not be pretty."

Karen responded, purposefully and slowly, "I know, regardless I want to see them."

William looked at Ham, making firm eye contact with him, raising his eyebrows without saying a word.

Ham stood up. "I know, I know. I will babysit the cargo here whilst you two go off playing detective. I will nurse my bruises, and reminisce to myself about my last enthusiastic drive in the horsebox. You know, some racing drivers would have been impressed with some of those tail slides and last of the late brakers' tight cornering manoeuvres."

William acknowledged Ham had done well, and offered him a gentleman's nod with a knowing smile.

William, being ever resourceful, gave Ham a handgun, pushing it into his hand, reminded him to keep his gun near him, and be prepared to use it, if he had to. For a chartered accountant he did very well, seemingly having an endless supply of armoury equipment.

Karen reminded Ham to keep his mobile phone on and to call them should he have any issues.

"Anything else?" Ham enquired, comments ringing with sarcasm. "No late night parties, no high end call girls or testing our very own mystery product upstairs!"

"I can't believe you are leaving me on my own," challenged Ham mischievously.

"I can't believe you used to be a vicar," retorted William with a smile.

William grabbed Karen's stiff bristled yard broom as they both left her house. They then set off for the tricky road section that had proved so hard for them to negotiate the previous night.

After a brisk twenty-minute drive, they were both at the scene of the previous night's accident. William approached the accident spot, in the opposite direction to how the events had unfolded. William momentarily parked his car on the bridge section, and both of them got out to survey the scene where the horsebox had met its demise.

The first thing they saw was some broken glass and some small bits of bumper in the road where the horsebox had sided the barrier as it came round the corner, and the massive indentation in the barrier on the other side of the road where the horsebox had hit the barrier head on. It was evident on closer inspection that the barrier would not have taken much more force, to have completely broken and snapped in two. The difference in the quality of the barrier and the damage it sustained was the difference between two people having cuts and bruises and complaining of a sore head that morning, as opposed to two extra fatalities the previous night.

Whilst Karen stood still, almost in shock of the speed of

the events of the previous night, William went to work with the broom. Clearly anyone could see there had been an accident here, the barriers told their own tale. William nevertheless, was keen to ensure that any loose debris was removed and concealed as best it could be. After ten minutes of vigorous brushing. The road looked a lot clearer, and put greater distance between when the accident had happened and when it eventually got discovered.

Karen and William jumped back in the car and travelled the short distance up the hill to where the chasing car had left the road. Again William paused briefly on the verge and got to work with his broom. It was clear, looking at the grass and soil and bank damage, that something had hit one bank, and crossed the road into the other. Whilst William could not cover up the dent in the bank, or freshly exposed brown earth, he could sweep up the debris and soil, which diverted attention away from the severity of the accident.

After another fifteen minutes' brushing, William put the broom back in his car, and then drove a further three hundred yards to a parking area higher up the hill.

Karen and William, convinced they were less conspicuous, proceeded to walk back down the hill, and followed the crashed car's path as it bounced off one bank, and got catapulted off the other bank which had acted as a launch pad as it shot off the road into the woodland below.

Karen and William climbed carefully down an increasingly abrupt sheer sided edge of what could only be described as a steep-sided valley. The area was rich in vegetation and heavily wooded. The natural camouflage for such an accident provided fantastic cover, however proved a treacherous obstacle to walk down.

Given the terrain, it was one of the few areas not popular with ramblers in the area. Quite frankly it was too much hard work to make progress; if you managed to get down the bank, without spearing yourself on a strong outreaching branch, you did very well. Climbing back up was likely to be a generous quest too.

After twenty-five minutes of brushing through hedges, all sorts of undergrowth and tiresome vegetation, William and Karen came across the car that had chased them and met an ugly end in the woodland.

The car in question was a Volkswagen Golf GTI. It had left the road at speed, bounced from one bank to another, and on landing down the slope bounced nose to tail, and rotated onto its roof, taking small trees and bushes as it scrabbled to slow down, fighting the ferocious incline. Eventually it had come to rest nose down, its back end forty-five degrees upright in the air, having lost its final duel with a strong old elm tree, finally killing its momentum and slaughtering its hapless occupants.

Laid to rest in the woodland below, William looked up and tried to work out how long it had been airborne. It could have been flying for forty metres or greater, it was a difficult call to make. The final few impacts were massive. William regarded the Volkswagen as a strong car, and yet its chassis had been split and its back had been broken, such had been the force of its various vigorous collisions. No amount of airbags or clever electronic trickery was going to help the unfortunate occupants.

Karen peered inside the car, from the driver's side. The driver was still in situ, the front passenger had been thrown clear. The steering wheel had been bent, probably as a consequence of the driver's head smashing into it. In fact when Karen looked again she noted the whole dashboard had been contorted and half of it had been pushed into the cabin area of the car.

Karen put her hand inside the dead man's suit jacket, and found to her horror, the pockets were all squidgy and wet. When she pulled her hand out, she found blood all over her hand. It felt like this guy's ribs had pierced his chest, as they had been forced to spring outwards. What a mess.

Unperturbed, Karen reached into the other inside breast

pocket of the driver, and this time found success in the form of his wallet. She then tried his other pockets, seeking out his mobile phone. There was no joy, she would need to look further afield.

Looking deeper in the car, Karen saw that the glovebox lid had been torn off, the interior was full of leaves, bits of trees, soil, glass and other unmentionable debris.

Suddenly she hit the jackpot; in the foot well on the passenger side was a mobile phone. She reached in, stretched herself and then grabbed it. Good, she got what she wanted and had something to work with.

Karen then went over to where William was crouching down.

William said, "This guy is a little grizzly, Karen. He has been impaled on a stump from a tree, and decapitated for good measure.

Karen could not resist looking. "Oh God, that is disgusting."

She turned away. William was right; for one moment she thought she was going to vomit. She soon recovered when she had a flashback to how scared she was, the previous night, when the two guys were using bullyboy tactics to get herself and Ham off the road. If the tables had been turned, then the blood spilt and body parts strewn around this woodland could easily have been theirs.

William passed the dead man's wallet and mobile phone over to Karen.

William noted the dead guy missing his head had a redeeming feature. The guy had a holster, holding a very rare Remington R1 classic handgun. William would have liked to have discussed his personal armoury with this guy. This was not a normal weapon of choice for a conventional villain, this guy had some class, even if his table manners and etiquette were questionable.

Karen and William started making the uncomfortably steep uphill journey back to the main road. They needed to find out who the two guys were and who wanted the horsebox off the road so badly.

As William drove back to Karen's house, Karen flipped

through the dead duo's wallets, to see what facts she could salvage from the bloodstained pocketbooks. Aside from the obligatory loose change, the odd ten and twenty pound notes, fuel receipts, credit cards, and driving licences, their wallets were very simple affairs with nothing too informative being revealed. The driving licences revealed one of the men to be named Eric Harvey, originating from East London, the other victim was Victor Gates from Newcastle.

Next, Karen interrogated both men's mobile phones. She looked closely at the call log history, and bingo, both men had a history of talking to Collard, and three hours after Karen, Ham and William had departed from the garage in France, Collard's frequency of calls to the man named Eric went into overdrive. Karen's hunch was right, however the reasoning why was still a puzzling mystery.

Since the previous night's escapade, Eric's phone had five missed calls, Victor's phone had three missed calls. With timing you would struggle to replicate, Eric's phone burst into life in Karen's hands, it was another incoming call. The caller ID identified the caller as Collard.

Karen looked at William and said playfully, "Shall I answer it, and tell the man what a scheming arsehole he is?"

William turned to Karen and said, "I do not think that comment will come as a surprise to him."

Karen let the phone ring, then tossed it out the car's window in disgust.

When William and Karen returned back home, they filled Ham in on their morning ramble. Ham had prepared some lunch for the three of them, actually it was more of a banquet. The food was very welcome, more so following the physical exertion of climbing up and down a very steep embankment, which had kept William and Karen busy all morning.

Karen enquired, "Have we had any visitors or phone calls, whilst we have been out, Ham?"

Ham replied, "No, guard duty has been very quiet."

Karen, William and Ham discussed their next move and the options open to them. It was clear they had to offload the drugs soon, and get them away from Karen's house. They could not continue with one of them babysitting them all the time. They all had lives to lead. All three of them were looking at one another, raising eyebrows as if talking without actually saying a word.

It quickly became clear that they did not have any option other than to contact Alfonso again and to try and broker a deal with him. He was the master link. The only concern was if Collard was working on Alfonso's instruction. That would make the meeting very difficult. Karen's hunch was that he was not, however they could not be sure. They were not expecting to find themselves in possession of such a tricky commodity, and knew they did not have a long list of brokers queuing up to buy the drugs. Where would they start?

It was dangerous, however both Ham and William were behind Karen in her decision to contact Alfonso. After lunch, Karen made a short telephone call to Alfonso, and they agreed a meeting later that afternoon back at Alfonso's house.

William made the point he thought it would make sense for all three of them to go to meet Alfonso this time. Even at the expense of leaving the drug stash in the loft unattended, it was a necessary evil and a risk worth taking. If the meeting with Alfonso got strained, and things turned ugly, they needed a show of strength, and three of them stood a better chance of success than just two and if nothing else, three targets were harder to hit than just a couple.

The three of them climbed into William's beloved Maserati and spent the next two hours on the road, until eventually they were back in Alfonso's leafy expensive avenue.

William asked Karen, "How much are you going to ask Alfonso for, for our consignment?"

Karen responded, "The more I think about it, the more I just want the drugs sold and off our hands. I will ask him to make us an offer."

William remained silent, however he could not conceal his look of disapproval, fearing Karen would cave in and the mystery commodity would be sold to him too cheaply. It was not lost on any of them that they did not know precisely what their merchandise was, what it's value was likely to be and what tariff would be reasonable to ask. Alfonso did not only have the potential to be very dangerous and a pain in the arse, he was also a very shrewd operator and held the upper hand when it came to negotiating this trio's product.

William pulled into Alfonso's drive, noting the gates were already open, and another car, an Aston Martin Coupe, was parked at the front. Was this Alfonso's car or was this a visitor? William wondered.

Ham, William and Karen extricated themselves from William's Italian thoroughbred, and walked up the steps to Alfonso's impressive home. Once again they found themselves outside the super large double white front doors. Before they had time to ring the door chime, they were greeted by one of Alfonso's staff who explained Alfonso was just finishing off a meeting and hopefully would not keep them long. They were escorted through the house and asked to take a seat, whilst they waited, in a small room next to Alfonso's home office.

Ham asked, "Who is Alfonso in a meeting with currently?"

Alfonso's member of staff, a pretty young lady, looked a little uncomfortable and paused slightly before spurting out, "Mr Collard is with Alfonso. Mr Collard is not a very happy man. Please do not let on I told you this."

Raised voices could be heard coming from Alfonso's office. It was clear Alfonso was laying down the law, and Collard was being his normal charming antagonistic self.

There were then sharp purposeful footsteps heard and the office door opened swiftly, followed by Collard walking out briskly without eye contact or an acknowledgement towards Alfonso's waiting guests. Just like a scalded cat, marching off loudly down the wooden hall floor and then off into the distance, Collard was typically purposeful, and hopefully suitably irritated, thought William.

Alfonso's decorating was moving on, however he still did not have much in the way of furniture in place. The house was still very bare, it was bright and freshly painted, perhaps Alfonso had spent all his money on expensive rugs!

Shortly after Collard's departure from Alfonso's office, Karen, William and Ham were beckoned inside. After the typical introductions and shaking of hands, Ham and Karen took the two guest chairs the other side of Alfonso's impressive desk. William declared he was happy to stand by the door, leaning up against the wall.

When all of them were comfortable, business commenced.

Alfonso, whilst confident and polite, was very cautious and measured with his approach to his visitors, more so than on their first visit to him. It was immediately evident to them all that the tone of the meeting had a serious side and appeared to be on more of a formal business footing. Alfonso was keen to see his guests as he sniffed a deal with Karen's cargo. However, Alfonso was very unhappy with his prior meeting with Collard as he was concerned Collard's intervention with his drivers' antics the previous night could make negotiations prickly between them all. Time would tell.

Alfonso, keen to find out how the land was lying between them, asked inquisitively in his typical agreeable Italian accent, "You wanted to see me, Karen. What is up?"

"I have some cargo and I want a buyer, and I wondered if you would be interested in bidding to buy?" Karen asked in a seductively playful manner, flirting with her eyes.

Alfonso, aware he was being watched closely by Ham and William, was not about to start caving in to Karen's charms. There was too much money at stake, besides he had seen it all before and never allowed himself to get distracted when talking money. With Alfonso it was always business first and fun later.

"What have you got to sell, Karen?" enquired Alfonso.

Karen bent slightly towards the desk, enough to reveal a teasing glimpse of her ample bosom, having carelessly let her top buttons of her blouse fall open.

"You know full well what I have to sell, Alfonso. The question is, are you interested in buying?" Karen continued to make teasing eye contact with Alfonso and remained silent. Karen knew to her advantage, successful men could be very hard in business to negotiate with, however a flash of the flesh normally worked wonders to offer a lady dominance with a deal. Unless of course the man in question is gay. Alfonso, by the way, was most definitely not gay.

Alfonso cleared his throat, and was very careful where to let his eyes wonder, pausing slightly, regrouping his thoughts for his next move.

Ham was super impressed with Karen's strategy, she was more than holding her own, demonstrating she was a woman not to be messed with. Ham, however, wanted to get his own question directly speared across the desk to Alfonso. "What is your relationship with Collard, Alfonso?"

Alfonso was keen not to fall out with his sparing partners, and was also keen to demonstrate warmth by offering honest information.

Alfonso held everyone's attention. "With Collard, I have no relationship. I can tell you I spoke to Collard this morning, and I was not at all happy with what he told me. I think he has handled things very badly, and his actions were of his own doing. I had no party to them. His actions and the actions of his men last night were deeply regrettable."

Alfonso then went on to make them all aware he was happy to discuss certain elements of his business however before he answered any further questions, and hopefully put their minds at rest regarding his integrity as a trading partner, he would like his own question answering.

Looking Karen squarely in her eyes. "What prompted you to go to France, Karen, with the horsebox? How did you set the deal up?"

Karen knew she had to be careful with her answer here as she knew if she admitted she never knew about the money concealed in the horsebox that would undermine her position to negotiate. If the money used to buy the consignment of drugs was not her money, what right did she have to sell the drugs for a sizable profit?

William, whilst not willing to steal Karen's thunder, could not help himself. "We set the deal up with Jacques following the correspondence trail left by Michael. We thought our dexterity might impress you, and hopefully rekindle your thoughts regarding Karen's first visit when she enquired who you may have thought killed Michael and his wife Helen?"

Karen added, "We thought a lucrative import deal might assist you in helping us find Michael and Helen's murderer. That is all."

Alfonso had heard what he hoped he was going to hear and told them all a little more about his history and how he worked. He made them all aware he imported various goods, most of which were illegal or stolen. Typically he was offered goods, from sellers all over the world. Alfonso would buy the goods directly, via various online bank accounts he had in operation. He was proud to advise Karen he had significant global connections, which generated vast amounts of wealth for all trading partners.

Alfonso went on to explain, he kept cash purchases to an absolute minimum, as unsurprisingly, when sending these with mules to collect merchandise, especially abroad, the money went missing, either by foul means or fair, or on rare occasions with Customs and Excise intervention. Losing large sums of money was not desirable. Electronic cash flow was best for security of the transaction, but worst for electronic trail detection. Being careful and always being in control were key elements of success, Alfonso reminded all present with a passion.

With Alfonso's drug dealing empire, he imported vast amounts of goods from several hubs he had established over the years spread across Europe and further afield. One of those hubs was operated by Jacques, with his garage in France. Michael had organised the drug deal, directly with Jacques, shortly before his death. Jacques was pleased he got the visit from Karen and the horsebox and the deal went ahead, with cash payment fulfilled as agreed. The time delay was not ideal, however, with death some things do tend to take a more leisurely pace.

Jacques notified Alfonso what was happening, as he suspected he would get asked to purchase, and would naturally like to hear from the horse's mouth, exactly what the consignment contained, to avoid any misunderstandings or suffer a short-shipped deal. The other reason for Jacques notifying Alfonso about the transaction was to enable him to put measures in place to monitor the consignment's movements when it came back to England.

The act of monitoring was to ensure these drugs did not fall into the wrong hands or get sold to a rival dealer without Alfonso's knowledge. At the very least, Alfonso expected first refusal, the bottom line was he wanted to be in the loop with this deal and he expected to win the business. He reminded his gathered friends it was him who had laid the foundations of the relationship between Michael and Jacques, again demonstrating his ability to be distant, however still very much involved.

Alfonso assured his assembled party, no heavy-handed tactics were employed, asked for or intended. Alfonso confirmed he contacted Collard, a decision he later regretted, to monitor the horsebox's route, after the vehicle was back on English soil.

In fact, Alfonso said, "I must congratulate you all on a well-executed transaction and masterful creative importation. The only fly in the ointment being the lack of a horse being brought back, which would have acted as perfect cover for you all. That said, any issue you encountered with HM Customs was handled exceptionally well. Well done."

"So how much would you be prepared to offer for the cargo?" enquired Karen.

Alfonso, chancing his arm, said, "I am willing to offer you two hundred thousand pounds."

Karen fired back immediately. "I need four hundred thousand pounds minimum, these goods are worth it."

Alfonso paused, then smiled. "Given the issues Collard caused you, I will increase my offer on a goodwill basis, to two hundred and fifty thousand pounds. That is my final offer. It is a generous offer." Alfonso then pushed himself back from the table on his wheeled chair in a confident gesture. He remained silent and looked at all the eyes in the room.

Karen looked at Ham, who nodded gently in agreement, then she looked round behind her, to face William. He nodded in agreement too. For a moment, she was tempted to ask for a higher amount, however getting the cargo sold and out of her loft was massively appealing.

So after a brief silence, the deal was done, and Alfonso walked around the room and shook each of their hands, thanking them for the deal.

Alfonso then added, "I can arrange to forward funds directly to your account electronically, if that is agreeable to you. You will need to create an invoice for me, for consultancy fees. That is my business card."

Karen quickly scribbled her account details down, enquiring, "When can I expect the money?"

Alfonso replied, "I will log into my bank account and I will send the money to you within the hour."

Karen enquired, "Would you like us to bring the consignment to you here tomorrow?"

Alfonso was quite firm. "No, you must never bring consignments to my house, that is forbidden. I will arrange for one of my contacts to collect the goods from you tomorrow morning."

Ham rather playfully suggested to Alfonso, "What would happen if we received the money, then disappeared with the cargo you had bought?"

Alfonso replied, smiling as he spoke in characteristic Italian style, "Then I would be forced to kill you."

Ham's face dropped to a more serious level, thinking to himself, hoping the cargo did not go missing that night.

Alfonso, pleased the deal had been done, asked, "What happened to Collard's men, are they bound and gagged in a remote barn somewhere."

William replied with authority, standing in the doorway facing Alfonso. "They became boisterous and unruly, and tried to take us off the road with their car. So we rammed them and ran them off the road. Their bodies are in the mangled wreckage, or very near to it. They went over an embankment, through the air at speed, and down a very steep slope to their deaths. The impact would have killed them instantly."

Alfonso responded still smiling. "Seriously, tell me what happened to them?"

Karen supported William's statement with a passionate glare underlining her serious response. "Collard's men tried to stop the horsebox, they tried to cause us serious harm and almost destroyed the cargo in the process. Collard's men were unruly and dangerous. We had no other option."

Alfonso unhappy with this level of coercion demonstrated by Collard's men, enquired, "Did anyone else see what you did?"

Ham confirmed, "No."

Alfonso gave a word of caution. "Collard will not like that; you outfoxed two of his top men. Well done to you, please be careful. Collard often requires special handling, challenge him by all means, just do not expect to have a pulse at the end of your squabble. That man is high risk!"

It was evident from Alfonso's comments that there was more respect between them now. The task Karen and her team had performed was a very difficult one. They had shown all the qualities needed to inspire confidence and to build on the relationship with Alfonso, a relationship which would hopefully lead to answers into Karen's sister's death.

Now the deal had been brokered regarding the cargo, William pushed Alfonso for assistance with the murders. "We would be grateful for any information that can assist us, we desperately need leads. Somebody knows something. Michael's murder trail is going colder by the day."

Before they left, Alfonso made it clear he genuinely did not know who would have killed Michael and his wife. However, he would make a concerted effort to do some digging with Michael's mutual contacts, to see if he could uncover something useful. He confirmed should something turn up, he would willingly let them know.

With the deal done, Karen, Ham and William made their way through the house to the front door. As they said their goodbyes, Karen embraced Alfonso in a parting hug. There was a strong sense they would all see each other again.

The three of them then climbed into William's car and returned directly to Karen's house.

The morale in the car on the way back was buoyant. All three of them were pleased the deal with Alfonso had been struck, and the weight was lifted from their minds as to what to do with the precious cargo. It would also be a relief to see the back of it, so they would not have to babysit the damn stuff anymore or worry about the police arriving for some obscure reason.

The next morning could not come soon enough, and all of them would take comfort waving the goods up the road goodbye.

# 14

The next morning, Karen logged onto her bank account online and was able to confirm to William and Ham two hundred and fifty thousand pounds had been transferred by Alfonso into her account. *My god*, Karen thought, *How easy was that!* This was a useful injection of funds by anyone's standards.

At eleven hundred hours, two men appeared at Karen's front door sent courtesy of Alfonso, ready to collect the cargo. Ham and William got the goods down from the loft, the cargo was packed into the van, and was sent on its way.

This was definitely a champagne moment, or at least it would have been if it were a little later in the day. Once the couriers had left, the three of them enjoyed a group hug, and remaining in situ for what appeared to be a few minutes. All were amazed they had pulled off quite a surprising feat with their health intact and money in the bank. All they had to do now was look out for Collard's next appearance, keep the police at bay, and solve the murder of Karen's sister.

Karen wanted to go back to Helen's house that morning, so decided to take a stroll. Ham, wanting to check the adjoining churchyard was being cared for properly, went with her. William decided to leave them to it, fired up his laptop and checked his emails.

As Ham and Karen walked down the village lane, Karen put her arm around him, cuddled up and asked, "Ham, are you mad we got tangled up with this drug deal?"

Ham thought for a moment and replied, "I am not mad. I think in the great scheme of things we had very little option. Best we do not make a habit of it." Ham smiled to the heavens and winked to the sky, hoping to attain the authority of higher approval.

Ham, beaming, turned to Karen, and he let her continue up the lane to Helen's house. Ham walked up the churchyard path, inspecting his old stomping ground. He loved this churchyard and although he was only just fresh into retirement, he struggled to keep away. Now he had retired, he realised one of the big attractions he had to the church and the surroundings was the peace and quiet, the solemn order, it was a positive place to be with a quality hidden depth. *It is interesting*, Ham thought. Those same qualities drove him away. That is the paradox of life, when you have not got something, you want it and when you have something dear to you, you want to try something else.

Karen unlocked Helen's cottage and walked inside. Karen always felt sad when she came back to the cottage, all the lovely memories came flooding back of course and the world was a better place. The cottage always felt cold now and without sound, without the fun and cheer people bring to a property, it just highlighted to her things are never the same when a loved one has gone. Murder has a devastatingly profound effect on everyone.

Karen quickly despatched a dozen letters on the doormat. Most were junk mail, one was from a solicitor regarding a progress report on Helen's estate and another mystery letter was post marked from London. Karen opened it revealing a rental invoice for a lock-up garage in South London from a leasing company there. Karen had no knowledge of the lock-up, Helen and Michael had never mentioned it. She decided to check the key box in the kitchen for a key for it, however nothing was obvious.

Karen thought, *This is interesting, this is quite exciting.* She wondered what was in the lock-up. Even if it were empty there might be a few clues to uncover.

Karen called the property leasing company, made her apologies for the late payment, and explained the situation regarding Michael's death. It was agreed she would collect a spare key from the office later that day, and then make a decision over whether to keep the lock-up garage lease ongoing within the next seven days.

Karen gave the cottage a quick once over to ensure everything was well, then locked up and walked back up the village lane to her home.

Karen pondered the likely interior of Michael's lock-up, it was sure to be an Aladdin's cave of clues, or would it? What would he want with a lock-up, sixty miles away from home? Karen licked her lips with the delicious thought; he must have been up to no good. This had to be good news, there must be a significant find within.

Karen was eager to share her news with Ham and William. Ham was still out parading around the local churchyard, tormenting the spirits, and William was sitting in the lounge, enjoying a strong Italian-branded coffee. As soon as Karen walked in, she was aware William was not his normal upbeat self. He was bothered by something, probably something important.

Sensing the shudder of an emotional surge, Karen enquired, "What's up, William?"

"I am fine, however you have had another letter delivered."

William passed Karen another hand-crafted note. It had been dropped from the letterbox when Ham and Karen had left the house that morning. Karen initially thought that was odd, as she thought she would have seen it, sticking through the letterbox as they left, anyway.

Karen opened it to reveal another threat. it read

*I want my money.*
*Pay me.*
*My patience is running out.*

C

The note left nothing to the imagination as far as Karen was concerned. This was Collard putting the pressure on, turning the thumbscrews just a little bit harder. Karen passed the note to William for his thoughts.

William was not sure what to make of it, only that he believed Collard was not the sort of villain to send notes. He would send two henchmen, or gun-wielding maniacs to your front door to put the frighteners on, he was a more hands on, in your face kind of guy. He was a few more rungs up the ladder in the mobster league to bother about sinister blackmail notes. Karen, rightly or wrongly was not convinced, Collard was her man and the pressure was starting to tear her apart inside. Cracks were starting to show in her armour.

Karen declared, "What next, that is the bloody issue here, what will he try next?" She stormed through into the kitchen, hurrying to collect her thoughts.

William followed her and tried to offer her support, stating he thought they should set up a meeting with him and talk things through. Karen was not convinced with this and needed more time to consider her options. In a bizarre twist, when she never had the money, she hoped things would change so she could offer Collard a pay off, he was obviously still sore about the drug deal which was not up to scratch handled by Michael. Those thoughts to one side, now Karen had the money and could easily pay Collard off the seventy-five grand he was shouting about, she was not prepared to let it go. They had all worked really hard, and took a great deal of risk bringing the drugs back into the country. No, Karen was adamant she was not going back to Collard with a cash-in-hand offer. He was a pain in the arse, good-for-nothing scumbag, and he could swivel.

With bad timing honed to a tee, Ham came through the front door happy as you like, full of the joys of a bright summer's day and fresh from a jovial jaunt down the village country lane.

Karen and William were silent, their facial expressions told a story, they looked like two school children who had just been caught by Mum, doing something disgusting. Silence was golden, even if it did have an edge to it. Ham sat down and grabbed the daily paper, he thought it best to keep his head down and await further comment.

Karen alerted her two men the news she had learned about Michael having a lock-up, and she felt it was well worth a visit. It might be something, it might be nothing – regardless, they had to check.

"Okay, let's go," William said as he tossed the keys to his beloved Maserati in the air, and all three of them jumped into his car, destination the letting agent in Bexley, South London.

After a ninety-minute drive, they pulled into Bexley High Street, and slowly counted down the shop numbers until the letting agent came into view. William parked up on the other side of the road, and Karen set off to meet the agent, and grab a spare set of keys. Once she had the keys and details of where the lock-up garage was they were off and en-route.

Karen made Ham and William aware the lock-up garage was costing three hundred and fifty pounds per month. Michael obviously had a purposeful need for its use.

The garage was situated just off a very nice residential area, only a two-minute drive from their current position. They made good progress through the traffic and were closing in fast. They turned left into a small residential road, then at the end turned right into the narrow road the lock-up garages were located in.

When they found their destination, William pulled over and

all three of them got out. The agent had warned them power was connected to the garage, however it was fed via a coin-operated meter. Ham's stash of loose change were clinking in his pocket in anticipation.

Karen surveyed the area and made sure the lock-up she was about to attempt to open was the correct one. The external number tags used were not terribly clear. She put the key in the lock, and nothing happened. She tried forcing it, to the point of finger pain, again nothing happened. She then tried wiggling it, and after a shove the handle moved and the garage door sprung open from the bottom.

Ham and William assisted in putting the door into its highest position, maximising the light flow from this 1970's up and over entrance door. Inside was a car concealed under a bright red car cover. Ham and William looked at each other knowingly with an excited nod of approval between them. They did not know what the car was at this stage, however they knew it was an older car, an interesting car, something worth discovering. As both men tugged at the red cover, they slid it down off the car revealing a nineteen sixties Jaguar E-Type finished in a glorious sixties period colour; gunmetal grey.

"Wow," said Ham. "This is stunning."

Karen put her finger on the light switch and the garage light flickered into life, revealing a very well-ordered storage facility measuring approximately ten feet by fourteen feet.

Space either side of the car in the confines of its storage was not great, they really needed to remove the car from the garage to see what else had been left within the garage. William managed to slide inside the car and soaked up the nostalgic atmosphere from the driver's seat, the keys were already in the ignition, so he gave them a turn with the snap of his wrist. Nothing happened – the battery had to be flat. William unlatched the bonnet from inside and Ham moved round and lifted the bonnet forward. The battery on this car was situated low down in the wing on the near side, it could not have been any worse to get to, however contortionist Ham worked his magic and was able to confirm the battery terminals were connected.

Typical of stored enthusiast motorcars, Ham's eagle eyes detected a battery isolator switch, to prevent the battery from discharging from prolonged non-use. What he needed to get the car started was a circular circuit key, Karen looked on the bench at the far end of the garage and offered up to Ham all manner of different inappropriate tools. She really did not have a clue.

Ham stretching over to the bench saw something which might do the job. Clicking his fingers to get Karen's attention, he received from Karen a bolt-type tool with a green plastic top. This fitted into the isolator a treat, and Ham signalled to William to try the E-Type one more time.

William turned the key, this time carefully and slowly eagerly watching the Jaguar's instrument binnacle for life. Firstly the oil light and battery light illuminated, as you would expect, then the key was cranked one more notch and the engine turned over, very slow and sluggishly at first, then with more enthusiasm until eventually the six-cylinder thoroughbred roared into life with a thunderous sound. The idle initially was very rough with a pronounced clatter. However, with every second of running, the idle became stronger, more purposeful and smoother. The strong whiff of petrol and plumes of blue smoke announced to the world, the beast had once again sprung into life and was just begging for an enthusiastic spat down some well-chosen A roads.

William gingerly extricated the Jaguar from its resting place, and let the rays of sunshine dance on the gloriously sexy bodywork. What a wonderful place the nineteen sixties must have been.

Ham enquired enthusiastically, "What do you think this is worth, William?"

William ran his fingers across the bonnet and down the off side front wing. "This could be eighty thousand pounds' worth, could be ninety. It is gorgeous, what a find."

Karen was getting slightly agitated by the pair of them. Here stood a lock-up, with probably countless clues, with a world of opportunities, and the two men were focussing more on an old car. Granted, a pretty old car, but an old car nevertheless.

Ham, trying to justify the time the pair of them had spent sitting in the car, listening to the engine, playing with the period tactile intoxicating switches, rummaged in the glovebox and under the seats to try and find some clues. Nothing was forthcoming.

The lock-up was of course a traditional garage, a natural haven for a classic car. However, why store a car so far away from home? Why keep a car that close family or friends knew nothing about? Why the secrecy and why the location?

Other finds within the lock-up were typical car related items. There were two battery chargers, a jump starter, numerous car tools, some out-of-date insurance paperwork, and a selection of miss matched spanners. Oil cans and a few maintenance books littered two walled shelves.

William moved out a small old table in the far right-hand corner, and sitting underneath, all on its own was an old-style combination-dial safe. Probably a collector's item now. William crouched down and joyfully freely rotated the dial, and tugged at the handle. The safe was locked. William thought afterwards, he should have pulled the handle first, as he may have inadvertently locked the safe, and made the situation more challenging than it needed to be.

Ham purposefully put his fingers on William's shoulder, with an action that said 'get out of my way'. Without saying a word, he muscled in on the safe, crouching down and making himself comfortable. William sheepishly let him have the space. Ham looked focussed and unusually confident. He felt like a rugby player being given the free kick. The world was watching, and Ham tickled the dial. He spun the dial first backwards, then forwards, then backwards, and again slowly forwards.

Karen and William stood over him as he pulled the lever, then nothing. The safe door remained closed.

Ham amused with himself, turned back to face them both and smiled. "This safe is a cheeky one," he exclaimed.

Karen and William looked at each other in bemused disbelief, not sure whether Ham was being serious or not. Well, have you ever seen a vicar trying to crack open a safe?

Again, Ham started the process, gently caressing the dial and rotating it one way and then the other. The witnesses heard non-meaningful clicks, and Ham was clearly in tune with something.

After a few minutes of rotating the dial with quiet endeavours, Ham took a final tug at the large safe door lever. This time there was a satisfying clunk as the mechanism engaged and the multi-point lock released. Ham was in, and the safe door sprung open.

Karen gave Ham an excitedly passionate kiss and a hug, William gave Ham a slightly more restrained pat on the back.

William enquired, "Ham, that was fantastic. How an earth did you learn to do that?"

Ham joyfully explained, "Many years ago I worked closely with a bishop who enjoyed too much a tipple with the demon drink. He could never remember the combination to the church funds safe, and to save embarrassment I learnt the fine art of working out the combination, from listening to the ratchet mechanism as I turned the dial. It was the ultimate lock manipulation for good causes. It worked for me then and it worked for me now."

Focussing back on the contents of the safe, Ham pulled out a ring binder full of paperwork: various maps featuring France and Italy, the Jaguar's service history and a pouch with approximately three thousand euros inside. What a catch!

Ham teased what appeared to be a false back to the rear section of the aging safe. Interestingly this action also revealed there were some Italian vehicle number plates, Italian registration papers for the Jaguar, and continental parking permits. It appeared the Jaguar was probably another smugglers' tool and definitely required further investigation.

William asked Karen, "Were you ever aware Michael owned a classic sports car?"

Karen replied, "I was aware Michael purchased cars abroad erratically. These were always moved on quickly, which I assume was his sideline for extra income. His dealings with classic cars were very low key. I certainly was not aware he was a long-term owner of any."

Following a further hour searching and sifting through the contents of the garage, it was decided to make an impromptu stay at a local hotel for one night. This would give Karen a good opportunity to look closely at the contents from the safe, and would give William the chance to call on an old friend, a small garage owner who would be able to give the E-Type a once over and reveal if the car had been played around with.

William escorted Karen in his beloved Maserati, off for their rendezvous with a local hotel. Ham followed. He got behind the wheel of the Jaguar E-Type, and fulfilled a lifelong ambition to drive one of these iconic cars. It was a shame the hotel they were staying at was only five minutes up the road.

That evening, Karen looked closely at the paperwork and the contents of the ring binder retrieved from Michael's lock-up garage. Ham and William made tracks to the hotel bar whilst Karen searched for facts.

Karen made a few intriguing observations: the Jaguar was registered on a UK number plate, with a UK registration document. One of the previous owners was a titled fellow with an impressive address. Old ferry tickets retrieved from the garage showed the car had left Dover at least five times in the last five years. However there were no return tickets evident. Tickets were found however detailing the Jaguar had travelled back into Dover, typically ten days after departure, this time on an Italian registration number with full supporting Italian registration documents! Why?

There were receipts from a prestigious-looking car auction brokerage firm based in Monte Carlo, detailing the sale of the same car, several times over the previous five-year period. Karen smelled a rat.

The registered owner in Italy was a Luca Peroni, who resided in Positano, on the Amalfi coast in Italy. So who was Luca? Was he a fictitious figment or dangerous reality and another piece of the jigsaw yet to be unearthed? It was time to do some digging.

Karen joined her two favourite men for drinks in the hotel bar. She relayed her thoughts and findings to William and Ham.

William was of the opinion the E-Type must have been a mule vehicle, used for the illegal importation of drugs, or at least something, however a few things did not make sense.

If you were using a Jaguar E-Type to import drugs, why use something which was likely to attract attention, rather than blend in with the masses? Why use a car with very little storage space? It really did not make any sense. There were better methods to use out there – you really had to question the wisdom.

Karen carried out an internet search on the Italian's address, and it all checked out, so the obvious next step was to check the address out in person.

Ham felt the straps on his black leather driving gloves tighten with anticipation, and getting carried away with the romance of the moment, suggested he would drive the E-Type to Italy to check out the address.

"Luca, the mysterious Italian, could be an important figure in one of Michael Stansfeld's business interests. Why don't we all meet him?" Ham reasoned.

Karen and William looked at each other, offering a glimmer of a smile.

Before commitments and travel arrangements could be made, William reminded them that the first step was to get the Jaguar checked over first thing in the morning. Karen did playfully accept there could a whole bunch of good reasons to visit Italy, and they were bound to have some fun along the way. Would the visit provide answers? Time would tell. However, Karen reminded the group the last time they all got carried away with a vehicle jaunt abroad, it almost ended in disaster with skid marks and fatalities as side dressing! Did the three of them really need a punishing journey to Italy to ask a few questions? What could possibly go wrong?

# 15

Karen stood up and asked for William's keys; she had left her notebook inside his front passenger door pocket. It was approaching ten o'clock in the evening, and there had been an unexpected shower of rain outside.

Karen walked snappily outside and went straight over to William's car to retrieve her notebook. As Karen closed William's car door and locked the vehicle, she was aware of movement in the far corner of her eye. The car park, whilst well lit, had a number of well-concealed blind spots. Perhaps she had seen something, perhaps she had seen nothing. After a brief pause, she did not witness a repeat of the distracting movement, so she continued.

She turned and made the short walk back to the hotel entrance foyer. Her route took her along the back of the hotel complex, between the dining room and the meet-and-greet visitor turning area and drop off point. Between the main hotel and the dining area was what appeared to be a poorly lit alleyway. In all probability this was likely to be a discrete hotel service access point or emergency exit.

As Karen made her way to the entrance a figure appeared from the dark alleyway and she felt her momentum brought to an abrupt halt. Collard was blocking her path, and rudely forced

Karen up into the alley where she was pushed hard up against the wall facing her protagonist.

Karen felt the grip of Collard's hand, surround her throat and she watched in terror as his eyes moved, snake like, monitoring his surroundings, without once moving his head.

Karen instinctively made counter actions to Collard's stronghold. Her first action was to hold her left hand out, to protect herself from the wall she was squeezed and turned against. Her second instinctive action was to slide her right hand inside her handbag, and to see what she could feel, to act as a weapon.

She finger-felt the contents of her bag, digging deeper and deeper. She felt her lipstick, then her purse and some keys, until her fingers finally came to rest, perfectly surrounding the grip of her gun. The trigger was poised, however even given this terrible stressful ordeal, in her own mind she never planned to fire the gun, her vision was to use the gun like a hammer, bashing Collard over the head, in the hope he would lessen the grip and she could free herself.

From what Karen knew, Collard was apparently well versed in roughing up his victims, he was clearly a successful man who was not used to receiving much in the way of resilient retaliation.

In judging Karen, Collard thought he had the measure of her. After all, she was the woman, the weaker opponent, the less successful of the duo and easy prey for his despicable character. Collard revelled in the fact he had won and controlled more skirmishes with tougher guys, proper hard men, during his unsavoury career. Collard raised his hand and fingered Karen's face, smudging her immaculate make up, belittling her graceful presence.

Collard then ran his finger over her lips and down her chin, tugging off three buttons from her blouse as he made a move towards one of Karen's breasts. Her heartbeat raced as she tried to control the struggle, as her anger boiled within.

157

Collard pushed his head towards Karen's and whispered in her ear in a gritty no nonsense tone, "Karen, I want my money, and I am getting tired of asking."

In a further despicable act, he gently kissed her ear and allowed his tongue to follow down her neck, holding her tight as her struggling movements continued.

This scuffle only lasted seconds, however it seemed an age for Karen. Her thoughts once again raced with possibilities. What would Collard do next? Was his plan to seriously hurt her? Did Collard plan to rape her? Did he have a concealed knife, and was he about to inflict more acute harm on her?

"Giving you more time is not an option," whispered Collard as he moved his head away from her, and released his grip, pushing Karen away, putting distance between them.

Although for the moment, the torment seemed a little more relaxed, Karen knew her torture was not over. Collard noted for the first time, Karen's right hand moving inside her handbag, and the handbag itself starting to point towards him. Collard, for once in his life, looked slightly concerned with the situation he created.

Collard repeatedly looked feverously at her handbag, then at Karen's face. Karen expected Collard to speak, he never did.

For what seemed like an eternity, Karen exchanged piercing eye contact with a man she loathed with a passion. She tried to make sense of it all, she tried to look deeper into the mind of a man who was a heartless killer. Her reaction was cold, nothing could recover the depths of hatred consumed within her. She loathed his style, his mannerisms and his bullyboy tactics. Her eye contact revealed nothing, nothing worth saving.

Karen felt inner strength from her adrenalin-fuelled predicament. She was, however, alarmingly controlled, she looked Collard squarely in the eyes and without further hesitation, she pressed the trigger and discharged her firearm in Collard's direction. For a brief second, Karen observed the whites of

Collard's eyes enlarge and briefly sparkle, frozen in disbelief. He clearly could not believe what he was witnessing, or the pain he was enduring, albeit briefly.

Karen's concern when she fired the gun was, could she miss? Fortunately, on this occasion, she hit her target, bang on. Once the brutal echo of the gunshot had faded, silence prevailed. Serious silence.

Karen had never really thought about the physics of killing anyone before. However she was genuinely stunned at the speed at which a lifeless human body dropped to the floor when shot. She will certainly never forget the distinctive thud as Collard's body hit the ground.

Her fingers buzzed with the tactile experience of squeezing the trigger for the first time in anger. The energy released from the gun, made the bones tingle from her hand, all the way up her arm. She felt her whole body beginning to shake, with the shock of the enormity of her actions now beginning to take hold.

Karen stepped over Collard's body, as it lay there motionless. She inquisitively kicked her victim's leg to see if she got a reaction. There was no reaction, just a lifeless pile.

It was now time for Karen to leave the scene and resume her evening with Ham and William at the hotel bar. She needed a strong drink followed later by a long bath. First a visit to the ladies cloakroom was in order, as she needed to inspect the damage to her expensive designer handbag, now it had a hole in it. Oh and her makeup was smudged, badly needing refining. Tough work for a lady whose life was getting more complicated by the hour!

Before leaving the ladies to return to the bar, she took one final look in the communal mirror at the woman she saw in the reflection. For the first time in her life, she saw a killer looking back at her. For one brief moment, she admired her own composure as she knew she had taken her act of survival to another treacherous level. At the risk of being vulgar, she grappled with the raw awareness that she found pulling her guns trigger in anger, gave her a delicious buzz. It was time for Karen to go back to the hotel bar – she had been alone far too long.

A confident stride and head held high did not fool Ham and William as Karen returned to their table. As she passed William's keys back to him, Ham and William looked at each other with slight concern as Karen clearly had an edge of distress about her. Men being men, they often found it difficult to read a woman with any accuracy, so was there a detectable problem? Regardless they both felt Karen looked different, she had blossomed in a funny sort of way. The only danger being was she about to flounder? The bottom line was she did not appear to be her normal self, which was a concern. Whatever the issue with Karen was they found it hard to put their finger on it. The conversation between the three of them for the next thirty minutes or so was pretty limp. William and Ham never had the courage or the inclination to ask Karen what the problem was as they were both fearful they may not like the public answer.

As the evening drew to a close, all three of them made the trek upstairs to their respective rooms. Ham disappeared into his hotel room first, then Karen came to her room and stood pensively outside her door. William put his arm around Karen whilst they stood in the corridor and asked the question, "What is wrong, Karen?"

Karen turned her head to face William. Her eyes sparkled, filling increasingly with emotion. William assisted Karen into her room, put the lights on, and sat with her on the edge of her bed, offering her a reassuring hug.

As they sat next to each other alone, there was a contrived pause, tinged with a flicker of submission. Were they about to step over the awkward boundary from being just good friends?

Karen turned away and went on to tell William in full detail the intricacies of her evening ordeal. Given her face was full of drama, it was then quite an achievement for her to take her expressions to another level, this time to a vision of shocked. She explained she was dazed, not at what had happened to her, although this was clearly jarring. She was disturbed at the impact her actions had on William's reaction, after she had conveyed to him her course of events.

William went on to clarify his thoughts and anxiety. It was not good to commit a crime, especially one as severe as murder, and to remain any longer than necessary at the crime scene. His concern was as soon as the police were alerted, and Collard's body discovered, the whole hotel would become one big crime scene. Questions would be asked.

William started firing queries at Karen, in his typical self-styled accountant manner, tinged with mild-toned annoyance. "Did anyone see you?"

"I do not think so."

"Did anyone hear the shot?"

"I am not sure."

"Are you certain you killed him?"

"I think so. I kicked him afterwards and he never moaned."

"Did anyone witness you coming back into the entrance of the hotel from where the body was left."

"I cannot recall anyone seeing me."

"Bloody hell!" exclaimed William with increasing frustration.

Karen, feeling the urge to explain herself, went on to state the hotel car park appeared quiet, and she could not recollect anyone else walking around in the hotel grounds. She recalled a rowdy group in the hotel restaurant which were sure to drown out most of the noise of the struggle and the gunshot.

Karen then flipped. "Forgive me for not taking notes, William. A dangerous man forced me up against a wall in a dark alley and assaulted me. He could have knifed me, raped me, strangled me! I never knew what he was going to do next. What I did was self-defence, it was bloody scary."

Karen continued. "Before you start giving me a lecture on

161

how to behave in public, remember it was you who gave me the bloody gun in the first place."

"I did not expect you to use it," retorted William. He instantly regretted those comments, as he realised how stupid they sounded.

Karen then sighed in amazement, verging on bafflement, shaking her head in disgust.

Not wishing to retaliate, after a short break and a few deep breaths, William walked to the window on the other side of the hotel room and he reminded Karen that whilst she may have thought she acted in self-defence, it was still illegal to kill someone in this country, let alone explain to the police why you were walking around with a loaded unlicensed firearm in public!

His frustration was not about to get him anywhere fast and he knew it. William declared it would be best for all three of them to stay the night as agreed and try and get some sleep. Leaving the hotel early would be sure to arouse suspicion and was an option best avoided. The most desirable course of action would be to stay the full night at the hotel as arranged, and for all three of them to check out first thing in the morning after breakfast.

Their best assessment would be for the police to be alerted to the murder in the morning. Knowing how busy the hotel was sure to be during this peak period, events would be certain to add to the chaos of the normal hotel proceedings. Cornering guests for questioning in a large hotel such as this would be extremely difficult. Game on.

William would fill Ham in on the detail in the morning. It would be helpful, William thought, if at least one of their group got a good night's sleep.

# 16

Karen awoke to the sharp clarity from her recurring memory of her attacker's actions the night before. Her mind was once again full of ifs and buts, regrets and maybes. Feeling her heart was still beating a little racy, she searched long and hard for personal justification for what she had done. This was a tough one for her, however, all things considered, she felt she had done the right thing. It was time to move on, before her past caught up with her.

A brief spritely breakfast followed downstairs in the main hotel restaurant where Karen joined William and Ham's table. There was not much talking between the three of them – what could they discuss within such a public open forum?

That morning's programme was simple: have some food, eat well and quickly, check-out from the hotel before the police got too involved, and take the Jaguar over to one of William's friends to give it a once-over.

Ham had been filled in with an update to the past evenings events by William, courtesy of an early morning visit to his room.

Ham could not resist. "You well, Karen?"

"I am fine," said Karen bravely if not totally convincingly. "My handbag is a write-off!"

Ham did not really understand the point of that remark, so carried on sipping his morning glow orange juice, keeping a look out.

Breakfast over and brandishing credit cards, the three of them were very soon joining a small queue at reception to hand over their keys and check out from the hotel.

In the background outside, police cars were evident in attendance, and a large unmarked van had pulled up in front of the small alleyway, Karen knew all too well. The police were in the process or cordoning off an area adjacent to the hotel entrance. The timing was impeccable and in many ways could not have been better. As fresh officers arrived on the scene, scratching their heads, soaking up the ambiance, now was an opportune time to be leaving the building.

William led Ham to the exit, with Karen bringing up the rear. Their progress was swift, with Karen holding her breath as she passed the growing thong of policemen and women clearly putting some form of strategic plan in place in the foyer.

Right at the last minute, as Karen was about to walk over the hotel threshold to the outside, a young policewoman stopped Karen, pointing to her designer handbag and the damage.

"Oh dear, that hole looks expensive. How did that happen?" asked an inquisitively young observant, servant of the realm.

Karen smiled and stood still briefly. "Oh, I caught it on a fence."

Whether that was plausible or believable, Karen continued on her way, clutching her handbag for dear life. That pretty young policewoman came very close to making a name for herself. She was sure to go far, perhaps.

As they made it to the hotel car park, Karen jumped in the Maserati with William, and Ham got to jostle with the fabled E-Type's keys. Karen took one lasting glance at the crime scene acknowledging to herself she could have been very easily, the one on the floor soaked in blood. The two cars then set off to

William's acquaintance who ran a small garage a few minutes down the road.

William and Ham were both like excited little schoolboys again, and they were keen to find out how mechanically strong the old Jaguar was. Karen could not care less about the car; she was struggling to keep her emotions in check.

The garage William led them to was effectively an old converted barn affair, painted white. The core business there for the owners was servicing classic cars, welding, and MOTs. It was a proper cottage industry, run by classic car enthusiasts for enthusiasts. It was a dream destination for both Ham and William to visit as there were plenty of old cars in various states of repair parked in and around the bespoke premises. Karen was bored stiff, tired from a restless night, and her enthusiasm for life was fading fast.

The owner of the garage took the keys to the E-Type and put it up in the air on one of the typical ramps used in modern garages to inspect and report on customers' vehicles. William never gave the mechanic a remit, he just gave him the keys and would await an honest appraisal for his seventy-five pound inspection fee.

The news, which came back in the form of a detailed checklist, was generally very positive. The car had been well cared for, which made sense given it had completed a few runs to the south of France and back. There was slight rusting to the lower part of some of the panel work, but nothing structural or serious. The front tyres were passed their best and some minor oil leaks were noticed around the engine.

There was one other thing, pointed out the mechanic. "There have been some trays connected to the underside of the car. The bizarre thing is they are very small, very slight, and not welded in place. They measure approximately nineteen inches long and no taller than two and a half inches in height. They are held together by a Velcro-like substance and not sealed. Very odd!"

William said his goodbyes to the mechanic and the three of

them headed back to Karen's house for further thought diagnosis. The journey back was interspersed with the odd stop for petrol, the purchase of a case of wine and the procurement of a joint of lamb and fresh vegetable's, as William wanted to demonstrate his culinary flair by cooking the crew a memorable evening meal.

The three of them sat down for their evening dinner, and the white wine flowed generously. They all had a lot of ground to cover that evening, with each of them having pent up remarks and feelings to be aired.

Karen was cool, immaculately presented, and back to her normal measured confident self. William was totally in control as normal and could not wait to throw his detailed analysis of the past twenty-four hours into the pot. Ham was loving the wine, and was likely to be the first to be cracking jokes and fully endorsing the need to travel to Italy in the Jaguar E-Type anytime soon.

Once the food had been digested, the plates were cleaned and numerous bottles of white wine emptied, the comments began to flow.

Karen made the men aware she knew killing Collard was risky, however, in the heat of the moment, at the sharp end of an attack, alone and vulnerable, she felt she had little choice. He was clearly a nasty piece of work, who should have been gunned down by arch villains years earlier.

William keen to throw his perspective and experience into the mix asked, "Why do you think Collard was not killed by one of his rivals sooner, Karen?"

All three of them knew Collard was a despicable character, certainly not liked in the underworld smuggling community. This country is full of people who are not nice, like Collard. These people live their lives by a different set of rules to the rest of us.

William continued airing his view, before Karen had any chance to answer. "With villains such as Collard, come a long line of foot soldiers eager to take over in their place. That is the problem, Karen; Collard vanishes, before long another leader will appear, and inflict the same threats and corruption inducing strategy to get what they want. You can never square the circle, that is the concern. The pressure you endured to pull the trigger never lifts. It will live with you always."

Ham offered, "Sobering thoughts, William. The man is dead. The world is a better place now Collard is not part of it."

William's point was enough to make your nerves tingle. You may have removed the man, however you may not have removed the problem. What was certain, however, was that Karen had now distanced herself from Collard. As Collard's men re-grouped and planned their next move, would they continue their quest to track Karen down with the same enthusiasm demonstrated by Collard. Time would tell, however William suspected they would find bigger fish to fry and in the great scheme of things their energies would be better placed chasing softer targets and bigger wins.

Karen of course never let on, however she had worked this all out herself. She was a smart cookie. Whilst the tears and rollercoaster feelings she had experienced were quite genuine, what she never let on and what William had never mentioned, was the tremendous satisfaction and spirited feeling of euphoria she felt, which was quite unexpected. Not quite like having an orgasm, however in some ways, committing murder the way she did, felt very close. Dare she admit it, given the right circumstances, she actually enjoyed the thrill of the kill. With pain sometimes comes enhanced pleasure, she thought quietly.

Karen held her right hand out, glass tightly gripped, and with firm eye contact requested, "Fill my glass, William."

The next topical subject round the table was the police investigating Collard's murder. Were they likely to come knocking on Karen's door? There was an outside possibility, clearly for a murder to be committed at the hotel, you could not rule out one of the patrons committing the deed. There were a couple of observations with this. Firstly, the hotel had 350 rooms. Even if the hotel was only half full, that would be a lot of door-to-door knocking for detectives to follow up leads and to interview all suspects residing at the hotel during the night of the murder.

Were any traces of evidence left at the murder scene? Only a non-descript unmarked standard 9mm calibre bullet remained. William took the handgun from Karen, now they were at her home, and replaced it with another one of similar origin but without the violent history. William's plan was to discard forever the firearm Karen had used, and he knew exactly how he was going to do it. Clearly secrecy was the key, as William was not forthcoming with any likely following call to action.

William's view regarding the police investigation was interesting. He felt the police were unlikely to push the case too hard. Whilst senior officers disliked unsolved murders, ruthless men such as Collard being gunned down acted like a community cleansing procedure. In the long term, it did more good than harm.

The police were more likely to focus on a respectful member of societies murder, than the death of an ugly lowlife such as Collard. Besides, William reasoned the police were always fearful with a high-ranking villain, one undesirable murderer could lead to another. Put simply the personal risk for a police officer to get embezzled on a gunman's hit list was not worth the wasted pension fund. Policemen and women were normal people with families, and feel the pain too, after all.

The next subject matter round the table was the mysterious Luca, the man detailed on the Jaguar E-Type's registration document. Who was he? If indeed he did exist, or was he merely a fictitious bit-part player in an extravagant smuggling operation. Karen had no recollection of the man being mentioned by her sister Helen. There were no telephone call listings made on the statements Karen had reviewed so the likelihood of the guy being genuine appeared remote.

Ham predictably spoke up with a gem of a suggestion. "Why don't we go to Italy, let us take the E-Type, see if we can stir up some emotions down the Amalfi coast road. Besides, Karen, with your recent ordeal, I think a little splash of Mediterranean sun and a fun trip for a few days would do you the power of good. What do you think?"

Karen smiled. "Why not? Let's do it. After all, I will be picking up the tab."

William, never short on having the last word, suggested with a downcast delivery, "What is the point?"

William's view was that, now Karen had killed Collard, who was the number one suspect between them all for killing Karen's sister Helen, what was the point of looking for clues which may not lead anywhere? What more was there to uncover?

Karen was enthused by the fact they found the Jaguar, and the few thousand euros in a lock-up garage the family never knew anything about. Perhaps it was a long shot, however there might be further revelations waiting to be uncovered when they followed the trail to the lovely coastal town of Positano in Italy.

If Michael could keep these elements of his life secret before his murder, what else was there waiting to be discovered. Imagine if Luca really existed, that may or may not be significant too.

"Who knows?" responded Karen. "All I know is I have not come this far to not take another step chasing the clues. I owe that much to my sister. Come with Ham and I, William, we need you."

William responded, "I think you are making a mistake, however I will follow you and Ham. You will need a fast car as backup anyway for when the E-Type fails to start, the electrical system sets fire to itself, or the clutch cable snaps."

Karen suddenly looked slightly less enthusiastic.

Was Ham concerned about squeezing his generous frame into the small cockpit of the Jaguar, for a challenging three-day drive? Not a bit of it. Ham opened another bottle of wine, he was beside himself and could not wait to be clutching his passport and chasing the high life in Italy.

# 17

A day later, all three of them were back on a ferry, crossing the channel from Dover to Calais. Ahead of them was a punishing seventy-two hour drive and stopover's planned in a prominent hotel in Colmar, France and then Portofino, Italy.

Whilst enjoying a coffee on the ferry mid channel, the discussion centred around Luca and is relationship with Michael. Whether he existed or not, the trio would find out soon enough, however there had to be an angle here. The assumption drawn from the evidence thus far indicated Michael drove the E-Type to Italy, met up with Luca or another contact, and then travelled back to the UK in the same car. The trick, however, was to put Italian registration plates on the car, prior to it being driven back to England.

If he were challenged by Customs and Excise when he returned to Dover, his story would be he bought the Italian-registered car at an auction in Monte Carlo, and was bringing the car back to the UK. He had a mock-up of an auction house's sales receipt, and an Italian registration document.

Ham asked the question, "Is the Italian registration document genuine?

Karen added, "It might be, it might not be. The point is it looks genuine enough. Who would know?"

It was evident given there was no central European registration office for motor vehicles, each country did their own thing. It would be very challenging to highlight any discrepancies at the port of entry, especially when some of the paperwork was Italian, from a French seller. How much confusion and head scratching could one transaction generate? The smoke screen seemed perfect.

So it was agreed the likely scenario was the car was registered in both countries, without either licensing agency in either country being any the wiser to the other country's interest or current registration status.

Michael would then attach the original number plates when back home in the UK, drive it back out again, and repeat the cycle. It looked like he only made the trip once a year so it would not be frequent enough to arouse the authorities' suspicion. Clever.

Karen seemed to remember Michael importing the odd classic car before his horsebox smuggling racket took off. So perhaps the poor security trays under the Jaguar were used for drug samples or similar. Clearly Michael's techniques had developed with the horsebox into a more elaborate process, with tidier and better-protected welded sections concealed underneath. Robust enough to withstand most challenges, however not enough to survive Ham's driving or head-on impacts.

Ham made an astute observation, indicating that contrary to what they may have thought, using the E-Type to smuggle things made a lot of sense, even if the quantities concerned were small.

Ham explained, "Remember when we first set eyes on the Jaguar E-Type in the lock-up. We could hardly take our eyes off it. With retrospect, we were confronted with an Aladdin's cave in that lock-up. With the possible exception of the old safe, we never looked twice at anything else. What we have here is the automotive equivalent of me!"

Karen looked baffled.

Ham provided his answer. "A sexy distraction!"

William laughed as Ham rocked his twenty-stone-plus frame, reminding the others that when they were on the ramp waiting to board their ship, not one of the crew checked the boarding cards properly, all eyes were on the car. Ham had a point. Sexy indeed.

With three days of hard driving behind them, arriving at Positano, on the Amalfi Coast, Italy was a welcome destination. A perfect stop, that part of the world really was gorgeous. Karen had decided the guys could use a quality rest, and to thank them for their supportive actions, following her sister's murder, their treat was to spend four nights in the swankiest hotel Positano had to offer. All courtesy of Karen or Alfonso, depending on your viewpoint on where the money came from!

The hotel was a highly polished, large plate glass entrance affair overlooking the cliffs of the gloriously picturesque valley sides of Positano Bay. Warm frothy waves lapped the silky sand as the beautiful bodies came out to play in the millionaires' playground.

Having had a well-deserved good night sleep following their epic journey from Blighty, the three of them were on tenterhooks, itching to get their maps out to check out the address of a certain Luca Peroni residence.

Breakfast was sharp and tasty, and by nine-thirty in the morning, our three would-be detectives were pacing up the main road getting to grips with the local navigation pointers, and with map at the ready, they were off exploring.

Positano was a busy little place, full of charming Italian architecture with an added dash of bustle. The brisk main Amalfi coast road clung to the cliffs overhead, and the feeder road which served all the residents houses in Positano was based on an extremely narrow one-way system, with sharp corners ready to catch out the unwary. With delivery drivers blocking the cramped road, impatient locals sounding their horns, and enthusiastic Latin types on mopeds buzzing every which way, this small corner of Italy was witness to unrivalled beauty and delightful chaos in equal measure. Karen, Ham and William loved Positano.

From the pointers they had on their map, they were soon walking down the street of Luca's residence. A light blue door with number forty-three came into view. Their fantastic journey had brought them to the house of Luca.

Karen knocked at the door, silence followed. Karen knocked again, there was nothing. There was no apparent noise inside, and no answer. The house of Luca was a relatively small three-level house at the right end of a terrace block. The property was finished externally in white, as most of the properties seemed to be there, and it was very quaint. Not the sort of property you would immediately think of for a base for an international drug smuggler, or a smuggler of any description.

Whilst Karen and Ham stayed at the front, William explored the rear. The back entrance revealed a slope which accommodated a garage bay effectively under the house, in a typically continental, attractively muddled fashion.

William noticed one of the mid-tier windows was open. Given the street where Luca lived was relatively quiet, William was in favour of chancing his arm and getting a foot inside and seeing what he could discover. He ran round to the front of the property to tell Karen and Ham what he was planning to do, and he told them to ring him on his mobile if they witnessed anyone coming back.

William climbed a small trellis to get onto a small sun balcony, which housed the external window to the rear of Luca's abode. With a sharp flick, the window was open, wide enough for William to get his arm in, to unlatch the bigger window underneath. Within seconds, William had the larger window open, and he had climbed inside.

William immediately broke the silence of entry by stepping on an empty container which crinkled up loudly. He then knocked some items off a small table just under the window, breaking something which sounded like glass. So much for the element of surprise. It was a good job nobody was at home. Clearly breaking and entering was not one of William's fortes.

"Bloody hell," William said to himself under his breath as he realised he was in a very small bedroom, doubling as a stock room. Inside were piles and piles of designer watches and what appeared to be quality jewellery and necklaces. The main pile, a masterpiece of clutter, was approximately three-feet tall, with other items on cabinets and shelving left in some disarray. If all the merchandise were genuine, it would be worth a small fortune, or even a large fortune. Some of the items had their respective de rigueur boxes, and some did not. Without exception they all appeared to be big brand items, all well weighted and desirable. The question was, what was Luca doing with this hoard and what was Michael's connection?

William opened the bedroom door and moved into the next room, which appeared to be the main living quarters. The room was clean, comfortable, and fairly simply furnished. The absence of any photographs was noticeable, as was the lack of feminine touches such as decorative objects or any evidence of ladies clothing. If ever there was a bachelors' pad, Luca's place was it, albeit with a dash of warm Italian style.

There were no surprises in the washroom – only male deodorant, fashionable aftershave, and other male shaving products were in evidence.

Moving into the small hall, the table by the door had a few items of mail, which had been opened and left in a neat pile. William noted the name and addresses on all items of mail of the occupant matched the registration document of Michael's E-Type exactly. William was surprised by this and had expected Luca to be fictional, or at the very least to be a creative alias.

Climbing the flight of stairs to the top floor, the hall led into the master bedroom. This was again very tidy, with the main

174

element of focus being the very large double bed, with very little else in the room worth mentioning. Amazingly beautiful view from the bedroom window though.

As William went down the stairs, he approached the front door to leave the premises, this time in the conventional fashion without the assistance of an open window. He was careful to leave the house how he found it. His final distraction prior to leaving the house was a door which must have led to the basement garage. Predictably this was locked, and despite a few drawers being pulled, and a general search in all the obvious places, no key could be found. William thought better of forcing the door. He did not want to alert Luca to his presence, especially in view of the fact he had not got the measure of the man yet and was not totally sure what the three of them were dealing with.

William could not help but feel slightly surprised by the bedroom-cum-stockroom; it was unusual he thought to find one room in someone's house in what appeared to be total chaos, totally incongruous to the rest of the house which was commendably tidy. William then got a grip on his thought process priorities. What he should have been concerned about was why had this guy got a stockpile of desirable jewellery and watches in his house that could be worth five times more than the house they were located in. All this without any visible signs of security and a window left open. This Luca character had to be crazy. Anyway, with those thoughts, William opened the front door to leave, being sure to close the front door quietly behind him.

Ham and Karen walked across the road to greet William as he appeared from the house. As the three of them met, a neighbour of Luca's appeared briefly, putting out some rubbish. Karen immediately went over to her, and introduced herself and asked about Luca. She explained she was a friend from England and wanted to meet him.

Fortunately the lady neighbour spoke reasonable English and

advised her that Luca was frequently away from home. He was a partner in a small nightclub and would often spend the nights away from home working, perhaps sometimes never returning home for days on end.

"You need to be careful with that one," said the neighbour. "He likes the ladies, especially pretty curvy ones like you!"

Karen smiled, thanked the lady and went back to Ham and William with details of a club where the neighbour thought Luca could be found. Apparently he had short cropped hair and designer stubble and nearly always wore a black suit with a fresh white shirt. He was tall, tanned and handsome. Karen could hardly wait.

William remained open-minded and cautious, Ham hated Luca already. Karen had a glint in her eye as they went back to the hotel to collect the car.

William fired up his Maserati and the three of them set off for the area where Luca's bar was claimed to be situated, some fifteen kilometres from their hotel.

The Amalfi coast road is one of the great drivers roads of all time, and William ticked his life box with vigour as he raced other road users on this notorious stretch of road, a genuine Italian masterpiece.

Soon enough they were at the next town and once William had found a safe place to park, our heroes were back on foot, walking down to the bay in search of the bar.

It was now eleven-thirty in the morning, and they had found the bar they believed was the one which would lead them to Luca. Being a semi nightclub, it was no surprise to find the establishment closed, however it was surprising not to find anyone on the premises preparing for the opening later in the evening.

Ham decided that given their trail had gone cold until opening time, he would offer to treat Karen and William to some fresh quality food on the beautiful island of Capri. It was only a short hop via jet boat from the bay from whence they overlooked, and would add some fun and culture to the Italian experience.

Karen enjoyed the attention as an extremely sexy Italian, fitting Luca's description, albeit wearing a flannel beige suit rather than black, held out his hand to assist her on-board the boat. Her arrival on the jet boat was greeted by her suitor in typical theatrical fashion, making the obligatory Italian comment "Bella" as she came aboard.

Karen loved it and laughed as she realised the comments made by Luca's neighbour, describing his appearance, could equally apply to well over half the Italian male population. She might as well be looking for the archetypal needle in a haystack, but wow, what a haystack! The joy of Italy.

William raised his eyebrows in approval; he knew exactly what was going on in Karen's mind. More to the point, Karen knew exactly what was going on in William's mind as another scantily clad Italian lady came aboard the same boat, probably on her way home, poor love. Ham by contrast was vague and detached from the surroundings of the moment, or he certainly gave the impression as such, that was Ham's way. Ham was contented with his inner self. Unless he was confronted with a shiny piece of engineering or exposed pipework, he took everything in his stride, without the obvious need for flirting and mutual eyeball dancing.

Alfresco lunch followed from a glorious cliff top location, overlooking Marina Grande, Capri. Whilst the three of them enjoyed the ambiance of the surroundings, William reviewed his findings from his morning escapade at Luca's house. The general feeling was Luca had to be stealing his goods from local, or not so local, boutiques and designer outlets from along the coast. He was clearly very good at what he did, looking at the size of his stockholding.

With numerous questions still needing to be answered, the trio frittered away some time by taking a walk following lunch, around the supremely picturesque gem within our world. With shops, scenery and a climate to die for, eight hours passed in a blink of an eye, and it was time to head back to the mainland and pay a visit to the bar in the bay. Could Luca be found?

Ham was first to the entrance of the bar, pushing open the strangely small door, which provided a very welcome and refreshing mild wave of cool air-conditioned atmosphere to kiss their sun-soaked faces. Whilst Ham was ordering the drinks, William checked the club out by giving the interior and its patrons a fleeting once-over. The premises was busy and lively and probably about half full. Karen leant over the bar gently, and enquired with the barman regarding the whereabouts of a certain Luca.

The barman's eyes scoured the interior until his sight of vision centred on a young man reading a newspaper at a table by the entrance door they just come through. His eye contact was held, until the man at the table nodded seemingly in agreement. The barman indicated Luca was the well-dressed gentlemen sitting at the table.

Karen went over to see the Italian alone. "Excuse me, are you Luca, an acquaintance of Michael Stansfeld?"

"Yes, I am Luca," the man responded, introducing himself.

Karen sat down at the table and went on to explain that she was Michael's sister-in-law and she had been tasked to sort his personal affairs out now he had died. She mentioned she had been given Luca's details in a confidential folder with instructions to meet him. Hence she was now in Italy with friends to try and piece some fragments of history together.

Luca seemed very young and quite a happy soul, and he appeared genuinely pleased to meet Karen. He suggested it would be better if they met later that night, at ten o'clock at his home. It would be a lot more private there. Karen agreed, shook Luca's hand, said goodbye, and went back to the bar to re-join Ham and William. They enjoyed their drinks then decided to continue their tour.

"Well, that was easy," said Ham, referring to how quickly

they had located Luca. The three of them walked around the bay, stopping off at the odd fashionable and typically stylish wine bar for top-ups.

"I would not be too trusting of that one," came William's predictable words of caution.

Karen said of Luca, "He is lovely, just what the doctor ordered." Giggling to herself, wrapping herself round William's arm in an impromptu snuggle as they walked along by the sea, Karen teased her two chaperones with her playful heady flippancy.

"Cannot wait to meet him properly later!" came Karen's spirited declaration.

Ham and William looked at each other, sensing Karen was going to be a nightmare that night. Women!

# 18

At ten o'clock, Karen, accompanied by Ham and William, stood in front of Luca's front door once again and tapped the knocker gently to announce their arrival. Luca welcomed them in with warmth and a cheeky grin, inviting them to sit down with a strong coffee and the offer of liquors later if they would like them.

Interestingly, as they made themselves comfortable, they all sat upright on the edge of their seats – this was a very different meeting to the individuals they had met previously. The curious element here was that Luca was a youthful man, he was twenty-five years old, however in some ways he appeared younger. All three of them were keener than ever to hear what they would learn from Luca's story.

Ham immediately liked Luca. Whilst Ham was inclined to take people at face value, he was no idiot and would make a judgement call once all the facts were dialled into the complicated equation of life. Whilst Ham had a circumspect approach, he did have the odd habit of going off on a tangent. His downfall was that he believed everything that everyone told him, within reason, and was probably the least challenging of the three when questions were being asked. He did have a leaning to forget people did sometimes tell him lies, either that or he let detailed comments rise over his head with gay abandon.

William, by contrast, was not fazed or impressed by Luca's cheeky grins and flashing eyes with accompanying smiles. He had seen it all before. William was up for giving him a rough ride that evening, assuming the information did not flow as freely as the quality coffee.

Karen, oh dear, she was starting to slip into her own little world. She was falling in love with Luca, albeit only superficially. She had succumbed to his charms totally. The question was, did she have the resolve to pull it all together, to get the all-important answers they critically craved? It was sure to be a stimulating evening.

William viewed Luca as a self-styled playboy, a man who fancied himself with life, fancied himself with the ladies, ultimately he just fancied himself. Luca displayed an all-year-round bronzed tan on his toned physique and was likely to be able to water ski perfectly, flashing the cash when needed. He was likely to always wear suits, immaculate shirts, and was probably never seen wearing a tie.

He was the sort of guy some women found sexy, then as they got to know more about him, they tried to steer clear of him, however some women are more successful at this than others. In short, Luca's interpretation of a lasting romance was likely for him to stay with a lady for the whole night. The likely conclusion with this was if you are after a one-night stand, he might be your man, however do not be fooled into thinking you could keep him to yourself. He had the potential to be a nightmare, laced with a free spirit that had no intention of making a commitment to a long-term mortgage.

Karen made Luca aware that Michael, and her sister Helen, had been murdered back in England, and that she, Ham and William had travelled to Italy to try and patch some clues together, to find out more about Michael's life out there. Luca sat still, nodding his head in approval and acknowledgment – he loved being the centre of attention. It was clear he was not surprised regarding the news of Michael's death.

Karen firstly opened up a little bit, she made him aware that as she was Helen's sister she was keen to find out more behind the reasoning of her sister's brutal death. Michael's lifestyle and the people he was acquainted with was of secondary importance to her. She really wanted to know who had killed her sister, and why. It was Karen's belief that the murderer's target was Michael and not Helen. She looked Luca squarely in the eyes and made him aware she would be sincerely grateful for any information he could provide. Her flashing eyelashes and charm offensive went into overdrive.

So the questioning began. Karen started by asking Luca how had he become acquainted with Michael and how did the pairing work?

Luca replied, "If you want the full story, I will tell you everything. But I warn you now you may not like some of the content of my account."

Karen, contrary to what William was thinking, was fascinated with Luca as a person, and she started to take a more focused view on what he was about as an individual. He was not only his toned physique, all over tan and bulging groin she was interested in, she wanted to tickle his brain too.

She indicated by offering her hand and eyebrows upwards for Luca to continue.

His story started fourteen years earlier when he was eleven years old. He briefly got mixed up with some bad kids at school and started pickpocketing tourists who were generally easy prey. Their approach was generally one of careless enthusiasm, with splashes of aggression. They would often bump into tourists, almost knocking them over, then run off with their purses, handbags, or wallets with speed. There was little skill in this activity, their ability not to get caught was mainly down to the pace of their getaway on foot, capitalising on local knowledge and utilising group decoy techniques.

Luca favoured a more clinical, focussed approach, targeting wealthy tourists, not just any tourist. His execution was more skilful as he developed a genuinely masterful approach to lifting wallets from passers-by undetected. Firstly, he developed a sense for spotting wealthy visitors to his locale as he focussed on the richer pickings available. He analysed hundreds of people who walked past him daily and he could always spot the wealthy target. There was an element of wealthy tourists who wore expensive watches, top-branded sunglasses or big-brand designer clothes. The big factor which set people apart, however, was the way they walked. This was Luca's key to getting a juicy target. Wealthy people always walked in a confident style, they walked the walk. This activity sets them apart, that was his theory anyway, and it appeared to be a successful recipe for strong results for him.

At fourteen getting on fifteen years of age, he had left his fellow schoolkids behind and was earning a comfortable living as an independent pickpocket. It was around this time he became more interested in girls and especially women. Luca always enjoyed the company of older women, especially those aged between thirty and forty years. They were always annoyingly out of reach, however their company was very appealing.

His distraction with the female form was shortly to be his downfall. He had clocked a wealthy guy who had just visited the ATM machine in the high street and had made a useful withdrawal. Luca acted quickly and positioned himself directly behind the target, walking down the street in unison. He carefully positioned his hand on his prey's wallet in his back pocket and began the artful movement of removing it without the target knowing. At this critical point, Luca could not resist playful eye contact with a stunning lady who had caught his interest walking in the opposite direction towards him. Uncharacteristically, in this rare moment of distraction Luca was thrown off balance and his juicy victim turned and caught him red-handed.

The target did not respond kindly to what he had witnessed. He grabbed Luca by the scruff of his neck and threw him up an alleyway, pushing him up against a wall with one of his arms firmly and painfully thrust up behind his back.

"Give me one good reason why I should not give you a good hiding and then go to the police?" shouted the victim loudly in Luca's right ear, pushing the left side of his face painfully into the wall.

Luca responded tearfully, shaking with eyes wide open. "I am sorry. I am just a kid, I apologise, you have got your wallet back, Please do not hurt me, do not call the police. I am really sorry."

Luca was genuinely scared and apologetic, he had learned a valuable lesson. The man, who two minutes earlier had been his prey, agreed he would not call the police if he never tried this trick again. "If you are going to steal from people, you must be focussed and sharp. Today you were clumsy." Luca speedily agreed and was somewhat bemused as to why he had not got a sermon on moral behaviour and a chapter on knowing what was right from wrong. Strange!

The man requested Luca's full name, address and telephone number. In return, the victim handed over one of his business cards and confirmed he would not take the matter further with the authorities.

The business card came with a mischievous verbal request, "Do not lose my card, and if ever you come into contact with something you want to move on, give me a ring, I might be interested."

The man he had tried to steal from, and the man detailed on the card, was a guy called Alfonso.

Luca kept the card safe. He was not sure whether he would ever have the need to ring him as he seemed to only deal in cash, which he could dispose of himself easily, without complications.

Afterwards, Luca reflected and took some comfort from the fact that in three to four years of street working, he had never been caught by the police or one of his victims, although he had had the odd hairy moment. Interaction with Alfonso on this day was sure to change his outlook and precision, and most definitely, his quality of life for the better.

Alfonso was a shrewd character, although he was not pleased to be the victim of crime that day, in the great scheme of things it was only a minor skirmish. He liked Luca's style and his approach, although being critical, his execution that day had been flawed, as after all he had been rumbled and was lucky to get away with a few harsh words and a thick ear.

Alfonso was always on the lookout for fresh talent, and although his challenger still had some growing up to do, his brief snapshot analysis indicated he offered tremendous potential for the future. Whilst cheeky Luca was only pickpocketing that day, he was sure to develop his career and get involved with more interesting commodities as he got older.

Alfonso's unorthodox form of networking had brought him a star that day, for later commercial opportunities. Alfonso was sure Luca would move on to bigger things at some point in the future, and that was when a beautiful relationship could be forged. As Alfonso walked away from the scene of the accident, he smiled to himself knowingly, as in a youthful Luca, he had witnessed himself, that was exactly the way he had started out in life as a younger man. From humble beginnings as a pickpocket, his flair entwined with a covert ability developed him into a major player within a distribution network. Alfonso revelled in handling all kinds of merchandise, dealing in the sort of stock which always came with a story and reaped the benefits of the associated inflated supervision premium. *Welcome to my world*, Alfonso thought, as he walked on by with Luca's fond memory and more importantly, his contact details firmly in his possession.

# 19

Another round of fresh strong coffee was poured, recharging his guests' vessels as Luca relayed his story of how he had started out in a life of petty crime, and met his influential mentor, fellow Italian Alfonso.

Karen was intrigued by how such a bright young man, with clearly several positive qualities, had chosen to take such a dishonest route through life at such an early age. This form of career was certain to end badly, surely.

Luca continued telling his story. Shortly after his failed attempt at stealing Alfonso's wallet, on that fateful summer's day, he took things easy for a while. He had amassed a hoard of cash and did not need to take risks for the foreseeable future, so kept a low-key presence. A legal low-key presence. One thing that did not sit well with him was the fact other thieves were having a field day, taking money from targeted tourists he should have been lifting. Still, a rest to re-focus and recharge one's inner self was not to be missed.

It was quite noticeable over the next eighteen months or so that the police presence within the built-up area of his haunting ground had increased tremendously, making an income from crime-fuelled snatchings and pick-pocketing increasingly difficult. Long term job prospects were gloomy.

After a break from crime for nearly two years, Luca was now eighteen years old and he was ready to start earning an income again. His lifestyle dictated he needed the money so he prepared himself to pounce on the unsuspecting public once again.

Quite by chance, his next opportunity took the form of a middle-aged woman who met him in the bar of the local club as he was enjoying a chilled beer one evening. They first made eye contact as she entered the bar. The lady then went on to order a drink for herself and spent fifteen to twenty minutes on her own, apparently waiting to meet someone.

As the mystery other party never arrived, the lady, named Francesca, honed in on Luca and made his acquaintance. She claimed one of her girlfriends had not materialised for a night out and she was at a loose end.

"You could buy me a drink and break the ice. That would be a good start," said a sexy and assertive Francesca, her glossy red lipstick doing its best to entice him.

Luca duly obliged, and honoured her request for a glass of white wine of her choosing. It is worth pointing out, whilst only eighteen, Luca looked older than his age may suggest. Women liked his rugged tanned good looks and designer stubble, and he was seldom without a partner, even if his relationships only lasted a few short hours.

From what he remembered, Francesca was good fun to be with and they made each other laugh. She was quite a little bit older than him, approximately forty years old, she had a stunning curvy figure and she knew how to work it. All eyes in the bar were on her. Clearly wealthy from the way she wore her hair, her expensive jewellery glistened, and her teeth gleamed pearly white, leading a path all the way to her nearby bedroom.

Their resting place for that evening was Francesca's five-star hotel room. Francesca, an Italian too, was away from her husband for a few nights as she was a property developer and was in the area conducting market research. Luca predictably had plans to conduct his own market research later, however firstly her sexual desires needed satisfying.

This was quite a landmark night for him for a number of reasons; firstly he loved the thought of being with an older woman. This really was a rare treat, he found middle-aged women took control brilliantly in the bedroom and naughty pillow talk was of the highest order. The fact that Francesca was married, flirty, and was definitely steering the ship that evening ticked a lot of life boxes for Luca, all at the same time! Few things could snap knicker elastic quicker between strangers than an enthusiastic fumble, a well-formed lady's thigh and an energetic tumble, guaranteed to make your world fuzzy.

Following their vigorous work out which they had both relished, the pair of them laid on the bed smiling and stroking each other, cuddling, then slipping off into a well-needed snooze to recover their composure and lower their beating heart rates.

Luca awoke at five minutes past five in the morning. He looked over to Francesca's fantastic naked body lying on her back next to him. It was hard for him to resist one final intimate touch. Francesca was in a deep sleep, and dead to the world and it was not worth the risk waking her. The mornings after were best avoided as far as he was concerned. Flattering comments, false promises for a future rendezvous, uncomfortable exchanges of telephone numbers and further contact details were painful at best. He disliked commitment and avoided anything steering towards another meeting. A stolen night together or worse still, a long-term furtive relationship turned his heart and hunger for passion cold.

As Luca put his jacket on to leave, his attention was drawn to Francesca's purse, perched on the dressing table, which was bulging with ample fresh folding currency. He opened the purse and helped himself to the contents, taking five or six hundred euros, leaving fifty behind. He also lifted all but one of the well-used exclusive credit cards and then focussed on the jewellery scattered around the room, helping himself to various items of bright work, a gorgeous watch and some chic expensive-looking ladies rings.

His attention was then turned to the hotel room safe which had been left open. He relieved his new partner of some delicate, well-cut, highly polished diamond earrings, a stunning diamond necklace, and numerous designer watches. This was all bankable stuff and although Luca was not sure what these items were worth, their value was likely to be very useful to him indeed.

With all pockets brimming, he blew a kiss goodbye to Francesca and left the room a very happy man.

His next activity, once he got safely home, would be to research the items in more detail, with the assistance of the internet. He would then make contact with Alfonso, who would arrange for a courier to collect the items and covertly import them into the United Kingdom. It was a well-known fact once items had been stolen, it made perfect sense to dispose of them in another country. Communication from one country's police force to another did not filter well if at all, which assisted in swift unencumbered disposal.

The United Kingdom also had a massive appetite for precious stones and bespoke designer jewellery of all types. Once the goods were in the England, liquidating stock became a matter of routine to well-informed and well-connected fencers, such as the ever-resourceful Alfonso.

Karen by now, had heard enough of Luca's ramblings, she was fuming and could not contain her feelings any further. Having heard his distasteful story in his own words, she could not contain her silence, her anger was plain for all to witness.

"You're despicable, Luca. How can you lead your life like this? To sleep with a married woman is bad enough, however to steal from her afterwards, following an intimate moment, is tasteless beyond belief. What you are doing is hurtful and wrong. Have you no scruples? Why don't you appear to care?"

Luca went on to explain, the women he slept with used him and he used them. The women he slept with were all wealthy, all their goods were likely heavily insured, they could get any items he stole replaced through an insurance claim, or they simply got a rich lover to buy them for them all over again. "I always leave them some money and at least one credit card in their purse." He claimed he was not totally heartless, and many men out there were even worse!

Luca was quite defiant in his actions, stating, "It is a business, Karen, that is all. It is a cold transaction. Women I spend time with know how the game is played and they know the risks. I repeat, it is a cold transaction. Nothing more."

Karen's vision of a sexy Italian with a cheeky smile had been transformed instantly. Any lusting thoughts she secretly harboured for this well-toned source of entertainment had vanished. She was so annoyed on so many levels from what she had heard. She could not believe what he did, the fact he did it and could see nothing wrong, and that he did these things and seemed to be proud of it. His ability to also freely discuss these things confidently without even a hint of personal embarrassment further heightened her annoyance. This lifestyle was just totally unbelievable. Her mind was in a violent spin, dazed with disbelief.

Karen stormed off to the kitchen, having released her pent-up steam. William followed close behind to offer her support and to try and get her to keep her cool.

Karen continued with her unhappy thoughts, ranting at William. "The man is a menace, a parasite and a rat. He is an arsehole and he deserves punishment. I cannot cope listening to any more of this drivel."

William stood directly in front of Karen and put both his hands, outstretched, onto her shoulder blades and looked into her eyes and said strongly in a tone which left no doubt he did not want to be messed with. "Karen, calm down. You're getting too personal with this. Just bite your lip, listen to the facts, take stock of it, smile, and move on."

Ham enquired, whilst he was alone with Luca, "If you have got something stronger than the coffee to offer us, now would be a good time!"

Whilst William and Karen were in the confines of the kitchen, William reiterated to Karen the fact Luca was giving them his story, which might assist them in understanding Michael's illegal activities, which in turn might assist them in finding Michael, and her sister Helen's killer. Which may or may not have meant Collard was the right man to shoot!

"Without wishing to state the obvious, you are no angel, Karen. It is just your wavelength for assessing right from wrong which may need a little fine tuning," said William in the hope he had strung a chord which would bring her blood pressure and her moral barometer back somewhere near normal again.

Group session now over, Karen and William returned to Luca's front room, to commence the next exciting instalment.

Now alcohol was in attendance, courtesy of some fruity Italian liquor, Luca continued his story with a not-so-convincing smile.

Luca admitted that meeting Francesca had been a real eye opener for him for many reasons. He never thought in a million years he could seduce a beautiful middle-aged woman, have an evening of fun accompanied with great sex, and take rich pickings so easily from his prey. All elements of the provocative heist were magical and highly recommended. Once he had sampled the taste of a delicious stolen evening, such as the one with Francesca, he knew he had to experience that again, whatever the risk or cost.

He soon developed a night owl mentality and his stomping ground included areas wealthy ladies frequented. He would often visit the bars of luxury hotels or clubs situated adjacent to quality marinas, and wait to see if women on a ladies' night out would say their goodbyes and leave him the opportunity to seize a piece of exciting evening game.

Whilst the hotel room scenario would offer a real temptation, there were also an increasing number of lonely ladies who might be on their luxury yachts or motorboats in the harbour, who might also seek the unique Luca experience. He would often tour some very exclusive port areas and get acquainted with wealthy ladies and spend many a night in unchartered waters, finding the booty available to be endless, stunning quality, and worth a small fortune. His nocturnal habits had made him a very wealthy man. It was just a shame his actions, by contrast, made him unpopular, annoying and promoted anger inducing thoughts from his well-connected victims.

Alfonso was only too pleased to get the call in England to collect some precious cargo of questionable origin. That was where Michael Stansfeld came in. Michael was the courier appointed by Alfonso and he devised this plan where he would come over from England in a classic car, his Jaguar. Once in Italy, the car would be fitted with Italian number plates and sent back to England as a personal import. Michael had cleverly fabricated some auction sale papers from Monte Carlo, indicating to the world that the car had been bought privately, ready for importation into England.

Concealed under the car were storage trays, which were something a mechanic friend of Michael's had fitted to the car one weekend. Externally they looked like chassis support beams. It was all a bit crude, and rough and ready, however it worked a treat. Although the trays were quite small, a little bigger than a desktop computer keyboard, they were plenty big enough to conceal ample jewels, watches and diamonds. Whatever they had to sell.

The importation thing was just a perfect smoke screen. It never occurred to the authorities that this car was currently already registered in the United Kingdom, Why would they, it was travelling on false Italian registration plates. The French purchase paperwork just added to the confusion of the transaction. With Michael driving the car, the whole thing worked brilliantly.

William enquired, "Did Michael ever get stopped by customs in Dover?"

"Only once," replied Luca. "They checked the papers, and spent most of the time lost in the beauty of the Jaguar E-Type design. That was it, the scheme was laughably easy. Naturally we made sure Michael arrived on one of the bigger ferries, with greater passenger traffic at approximately five in the morning. Customs and Excise are a little more sleepy at this time, eagerly looking forward to their shift ending at seven o'clock. Besides, Customs & Excise were becoming increasingly focussed on discovering people-trafficking and chasing hard-core drugs cartels rather than to worry about a few watches, some diamonds and a broach coming home to roost."

William was very cautious with Luca's behaviour. Whilst his demeanour was very polite, upbeat and helpful, William could not help but ask himself why he was so helpful. Criminals did not give up their secrets easily, especially to foreign strangers.

Luca carried on talking fluidly, he secretly made the assumption that Karen, Ham and William knew all the operational aspects of the smuggling racket in fine detail, and felt that their visit to Italy had a hidden agenda. He went through the motions regardless as he got a real buzz from telling his story, and enjoyed telling people how successful he had become.

William suspected that Luca would have been tipped off by Alfonso regarding Karen's visit. They were not expecting to surprise anyone, however it was them who were to be surprised with Luca's effervescent patter and unadulterated delivery.

Ham enquired, "Tell us about Michael."

Luca went on to explain he had met Michael, via Alfonso, approximately five years earlier. Michael was the courier, the carrier, the man in many ways who took more risk than anyone else in the organisation. It was his responsibility to get the goods from one country to another, without attracting undue attention. The facts were if the police came knocking on your door, anyone could be obstructive or swerve questions and defend their innocence. However, when you are stopped in a car or carrying a case fill of drugs, gems or other stolen goods even contraband, no amount of words can save you from jail. It is fair to say Michael had nerves of steel and bravery of the highest order. The risk element took on another dimension when you considered the open-ended risk of the transport arrangements being hijacked by another smuggling gang. People often forget that in times of hardship, when the global economy is not doing well, this impacts the underworld market too.

People of all origins become desperate and take risks, the scope for drama is a very real, personal one. Luca reminded his assembled audience, "If the goods did not reach their destination, payment would not be honoured. Imagine how you would feel if you took on a job and did not get paid? Michael lived with that hazard on every trip. He endangered his life, and as we all know, regrettably he paid the ultimate price."

Karen was quietly stunned by these revelations. She knew in her heart of hearts what Michael had been doing, particularly after the horsebox import scenario. However, when a stranger tells you what was going on, it somehow hits the point home harder and tangles with your emotions with greater impact, especially when you discover these things were going on long before close family or friends knew.

Karen wondered, did Michael's wife Helen have a clue what was going on? She kept telling herself she must have done, however she could not be sure and could Helen have kept a secret like that so close to her chest, on her own? Karen believed her relationship with her sister Helen was a close one. It then occurred to her, what if Michael had made Helen aware, and she felt for her own life. Did fear prevent her from talking? If she knew, she must have been churning inside, the pain of not being able to tell anyone else must have been horrific. She must have felt so isolated, so alone. The consequences of that thought when considering a close loved one did not bear thinking about. This was not a nice experience for Karen and she was starting to feel drained and nauseous.

Ham asked Luca, "What did you think of Michael, as a person?"

Luca paused, thought to himself, then said, "I thought he was a very focussed and a very nice man, a quiet man. He was probably the least likely villain of any of the smuggling community I came into contact with. He had balls and was a pleasure to work with and was typically English if you know what I mean. I miss him. I never forgot his generosity and concern when I racked up some gambling debts a few years ago, and he let me stay at his house here for as long as I wanted."

Karen rolled her eyes in wonder, and thought silently, clearly emotional and doing her utmost to hold herself together. She was doing well, albeit wobbling slightly.

By contrast, Luca swiftly went on to explain working with Alfonso was a different animal; he was a no-nonsense individual with a hard-core edge. You would never mess with Alfonso.

William asked, "Who told you Michael was dead?"

Luca replied, "Alfonso, of course. It was very sad. I knew you would be in contact at some point to collect the other car and Michael's goods!"

Karen was slightly bemused, "What goods? What car?"

Luca explained Michael had made his payment to him a few days before he died for the latest consignment ready to be shipped back to England. The goods were upstairs in the spare bedroom.

All four of them walked upstairs and entered the spare bedroom. This was the room William had accessed the day earlier when breaking into the same property. All three of them touched and fingered the bounty as Luca looked on, and were divided with their emotions.

William made the remark there was a lot of value there. It was all good-quality pickings, highly desirable merchandise. Ham made very little comment; he disliked any involvement and was not happy about the whole thing at all.

Karen was even colder. All she could think about was the distress and pain individuals experienced once they had learned their personal effects had been stolen. There was too much trauma attached to the shipment – she did not want to be any part of it. It was not a good way to earn an income.

Ham asked quite passionately, making eye contact with Luca, aiming to make a connection, "Some of these things may have had sentimental value to some of these owners. How do you feel about that? Some of these items may have beautiful memories attached to them. History and feelings which cannot be replaced."

Luca held his head down, collecting his thoughts carefully before making a statement with a smile and hanging on every word with his enticing Italian accent underpinned with his typical arrogant confidence. "Of course you may be correct. This side of things does not please me, however I believe many of these people are very foolish with their security and take an unnecessary risk. Do not forget, many ladies I sleep with are cheating on their partners with me, their morals are not as high as their panty line. Your concern with my activity may be misplaced! I sleep with myself very easily."

William, whilst not condoning Luca's occupation, liked his answer and enjoyed a brief wry smile to himself. "It takes one to know one, eh!"

Karen broke her silence, her thoughts trying to catch up with the world wind of information she had learnt that evening. "What did you mean, Luca, when you said Michael allowed you to stay in his house when you got into debt?"

Luca replied, "This house, this is Michael's house. I thought you would have known that! When I first met Michael, I played the casinos. I got carried away, lost lots of money and needed a roof. Michael helped me. I now have an apartment in another town along the coast, however I do stay here occasionally, and I like the local bars and use the nearby beach. Michael has always been approving of this as he liked the house to look lived in when he was away."

Karen looked at Luca, and then rolled her eyes, glancing at the walls. "So this is Michael's house?"

"Yes," came the reply, quite conclusively, with a disbelieving laugh. He did not believe they did not know about Michael's house in Italy. Luca thought it was somehow amusing.

Karen was shocked, the kind of nice shock you get when you realise you have just received an inheritance of a several thousand euros' worth of Italian bricks and mortar. Whilst it was not a massive house, it was a useful retreat, and Karen was sure her sister Helen never knew anything about this property tucked away overseas.

Ham asked, "What other car were you referring to? You mentioned Michael owns this house and another car?"

Luca presented Karen with two sets of keys for the house, and a set of keys for the classic car in the garage below. He explained the Austin Healey was part of the duo classic car import scam Michael used as a ruse to bring the stolen goods back into the United Kingdom without detection.

Luca took his guests downstairs, and led the way to the internal garage access door William had failed to open when he gained entry previously. To William's annoyance, the door was not locked, as he had thought, it was just very stubborn and needed a good shove to get open. Once opened, it revealed inside a reasonable useful, if cramped, garage. Under a large white dustsheet was a glorious sky-blue metallic and white Austin Healey convertible sports car. William and Ham's eyes immediately lit up with enthusiasm and knowledgeable acceptance of another great British classic car icon which sat quietly before them.

*Bloody hell*, Karen thought, *and Michael kept this quiet too*, running her fingers along the lovely exposed front wing.

William and Ham carefully put back the white dustsheet over the classic car and ensured it was fully covered again.

As William turned, he faced Luca, he asked, "One thing does not add up; why did you keep the stolen items upstairs? You could have sold these things on locally and nobody would have been any the wiser. Was your loyalty really that strong to Michael? You would not have kept these items indefinitely, would you?"

The explanation from the master of bed-hopping and thieving was a complex one. "I am an honest thief; when someone pays for a consignment, I always honour the deal. In my line of work, if you double cross an associate, you expect to get a knife in your back or a bullet in your head. I did not want that. That is why my loyalty is sealed. No question."

William replied, "Bollocks. What is going on?"

Luca continued, "My loyalty is with Alfonso and Michael, of course. Michael has paid for this consignment, the details of which have been sent to Alfonso. When the goods get back to England, he will pay the carrier two hundred and seventy-five thousand pounds. It is easy money for you all."

Karen, William, and Ham looked at each other in curious silence. Eye contact between them said a lot for the next minute or so of eyebrow movements, twitching and clashing thoughts.

"Who killed Michael, Luca?" asked an increasingly tired Karen.

"I do not know."

Karen looked quite stern. Trying to get a reaction, she poked, "Was it Alfonso? You said yourself he was not to be messed with."

Luca was not troubled by the question, answering, "Alfonso was becoming increasingly frustrated with Michael. I was aware he was trying to cut better deals for himself and sold some items without using the Alfonso channels. Whilst Alfonso was unhappy, their partnership was not yet that bad that it warranted him to kill him. Remember, Michael had useful skills, he was knowledgeable, mostly reliable, and provided Alfonso with a valuable income, even if he did present some minor difficulties. Why would he want Michael dead? It makes no sense."

William fired his suggestion. "Did Collard kill Michael?"

"I only met Collard two or three times at Alfonso's parties. I did not warm to him, I found him to be over assertive and arrogant. He was an arsehole. Did he have the capacity to kill Michael? Possibly. Perhaps this is a more likely candidate for his murderer. The same remains however, why would Collard kill Michael? It would be like him severing a major artery. My understanding is Collard was more needy of Michael than Alfonso, so I would be surprised. Like I said, I never knew him that well and all things are possible, even if some scenarios are unlikely."

It was getting late and it was time for Luca to leave and say goodnight. As it turned out, the guests of the evening were now saying goodbye to their host, their guest!

Luca gave Karen a final smile, placed his business card in Karen's hand, and said his goodbyes.

With Luca gone, Ham, Karen and William stepped outside Karen's new house, and closed the front door with a reassuring thud.

As Karen took a few strides, she looked round briefly to face the front door. She looked at the key in wonder and held the moment. What had Michael done? What did Helen know? How many more surprises were there and how many more questions were there that they needed to try and find answers for?

William, Karen and Ham chatted small talk as they walked back up the undulating road, the short distance to their hotel. They were exhausted, however following another productive day, a proposal was about to be tabled that could solve their newly exposed problems.

# 20

Breakfast does not get any better than when it is a tasty delight served with friends, at a grand hotel overlooking a stunning Italian coastal view. Blue skies with the warm continental air circulating your body and the bright Mediterranean sun bearing down, topping up your tan, there really is no better way to start your day.

Predictably, Ham and William were polishing off a traditional cooked breakfast and enjoying cup after cup of strong Italian coffee. Karen was eating croissants and drinking fresh fruit juice and water. The conversation round the table was numerous and of a typical normal morning banter, mostly commenting on the other guests' wardrobe malfunctions and other people's senses of style or lack of it. Nobody discussed the previous day's events, they all waited with anticipation for someone else to start with an opening.

Ham asked William what he thought of Luca. "He is a crafty, cheeky little sod who has done well, doing the unspeakable. You could never trust him. He needs to change his ways, however I doubt he ever will. He needs to find himself a good woman, and settle down. It's obviously not from want of trying."

Karen, feeling it appropriate to make her views known following the previous day's findings, made Ham and William aware that having discovered the house, the other classic car, and the small point of a quarter of a million pounds' worth of stylish stolen stock in a spare room, gave her a lot to think about the previous night.

Ham and William remained silent, sipping coffee and pretending to be more interested in the local surroundings, other people, and sea views than Karen's next remark.

Karen commented, "Personally, I think the best option is for me to contact Luca and to ask him to get rid of the stolen stock. I do not want any involvement with it and I do not want the risk of smuggling it back into England."

Ham replied, "I agree, I think that is the best option, I think a lot of people have felt pain with these thefts and I believe your suggestion is the right thing to do."

William not totally convinced he had just heard what his ears had told him, offered, "I think we were very lucky when we took the horsebox job on, and we got away with it, that was a very close call. We should not tempt fate by trying this kind of risky importation again. I am with you on this one, Karen."

Karen teasingly played with her fruit juice glass, and looked on into Ham and William's eyes. Karen saw contentment and stillness, however they lacked a certain something; they lacked a charge-fuelled passion. They lacked jeopardy.

Karen thought carefully then made another playful statement to her two trusted colleagues. She was upright in her chair in a commanding position, then declared slowly, "I thought about the hoard sitting in the spare room and I thought what a waste. The worst part of the crime had been committed, all that had to be done was to carry out the easy part and bring the goods back to England. Who could do that, I wonder? Then I thought, we could do that, couldn't we?"

Karen sat back in her chair, intentionally drawing her eyes away, focusing on other distractions. Italian waiters immaculately presented were a good distraction that morning. Karen remained quiet, sitting very relaxed without a care in the world. The submissive move enhanced her comments, which were sure to provoke an answer from her men.

William smiled and played the delay game too. After his brief pause, appreciating her playful delivery, he spoke. "You better drive my Maserati back home then, Karen. It is an animal, however it is a lesser evil than the other two classic drives on offer."

Ham wasted no time in tossing the keys to the Jaguar E-Type to William, and requested the keys to the Austin Healey from Karen.

Karen laughed at the pair of them. "You have no backbone, do you. You two would do anything I suggested. You change your mind at the drop of a hat, anything to please me!"

William responded, "We like to think in some small way we will get rewarded for our stamina and unstinting support."

"We will see." Karen smiled at them both, stood up, and walked off back to her room, with a little extra bum wiggle, just for good measure. She knew both men would be watching.

Car swaps organised, the plan was to get back to the house to sort the stolen goods into manageable bundles which could easily be concealed in the hidden storage compartment trays placed under both classic cars. Whilst Ham and William sorted the booty, Karen wanted the opportunity to search the house for any tasty documents or for any other clues Michael may have left behind. It was much better done without Luca's prying eyes in attendance. She knew she would be unlikely to find anything of interest as Luca was sure to have concealed or destroyed anything too useful. Regardless, it was something she needed to do as part of her inheritance and crime-solving therapy.

As the trio went back to their respective hotel rooms briefly after breakfast, William had a quiet word with Karen. He was intrigued regarding her change of heart with the stolen consignment. Karen explained that in her heart of hearts, she did not believe she really had much of an option. Did she need to wait until things turned nasty, before she agreed to take the stolen items back to Alfonso? No, much better to make an informed choice, be in control, and complete the deed one last time.

In the context of other traumas in her life, Karen could definitely conceal a few diamonds, watches and rings, and smile as she passed through Customs and Excise in Dover port. William reassured Karen that she had their full support and would make sure they pulled this latest challenge off successfully.

Later at Michael's Italian residence, Ham could once again hardly contain himself at the thought of getting behind the wheel of another classic British icon of the road. Ham, standing in the garage, removed the white dust sheet. As it was pulled off, Ham revealing a very tidy example of the Austin Healey experience. Inside the car the interior was a little dusty, however it all appeared to be complete and looked to be in good working order with a lovely timeless natural patina.

With the garage door opened, the classic roadster was encouraged into life with a turn of the key, a bark, a deep growl, and a slight splutter from the exhaust indicated the car was eager for its wheels to get turning again. Ham disconnected the trickle charger from the battery and needed no encouragement to give the Healey a blast up the road and back again with a generous dose of accelerator and de rigueur opposite lock accompanied with ample tyre squeal.

His thoughts were, Wow, you had to work at this car, but what a driving experience, well worth inputting your energies. That is before you start dribbling over the glorious retro styling and unique road presence wrapped up in generous old English charm.

After a fifteen-minute blast along the coast road, Ham reversed the Austin Healey back into the garage, leaving the bonnet exposed to the sunlight. This afforded Ham and William more room to carefully conceal their special cargo into its new home for the journey.

Shuffling under the car, Ham was able to release the obscured partitions and fill them with carefully bundled items.

After less than an hour, the job was done. The car was now fitted with Italian number plates, found in the garage storage cupboard. Blank classic car auction house bill of sale documents were located and fresh sale details entered for both the E-Type Jaguar and the Austin Healey. The subterfuge of a successful visit to an auction house was all in place should documents be requested for the customs authorities to substantiate their story of a recent overseas shopped spree.

The fully authentic Italian registration document was located, detailing the ever-mischievous Luca as its rightful owner.

If only the polizia really knew.

Ham wondered to himself, how many road traffic regulations and cross country vehicle laws was it possible for one person to break in one journey? Ham was certainly not going to Heaven, however he might just gain entry acceptance to a lower authority on a vigorous appeal.

William brought the Jaguar E-Type round to the garage and the pair of them carried out the same exercise loading up the cars' storage trays with all manner of concealed glitz and glamour. Fortunately, the end of terrace house backed onto a sleepy small residential area, it was like a select mews arrangement and their activity was broadly masked from the wider world.

With both cars laden and ready for the journey back to England, the Jaguar E-Type was driven back to the hotel car park, and the Austin Healey was snugly put back in its safe haven garage, eagerly awaiting the starting flag to be dropped the following morning.

The owner of the luxury hotel had something of a soft spot for British sports cars, and welcomed William to park the car in the privileged VIP parking at the front of the hotel. Whilst this raised the profile of the car and its occupants, this action assured them of improved security over the following night. Who would dare break into or try and steal such a highly visible vehicle in full gaze of hotel reception staff, concierges, and the obligatory inquisitive passing tourists?

Ham, having finished his work in the garage, put the Austin Healey to bed, being careful to cover all its glorious bodywork under the white car cover.

Karen watched how carefully Ham had covered the bodywork for its last night in Italy. "Have you put her to bed then?"

Ham replied, "A car like that is like a fine woman; look after them at bedtime, and they look after you in the morning!"

Karen smiled. "Would love to see the car cook you breakfast in the morning."

Ham returned the comment with a cheeky smile and a predictable retort. "It was not breakfast I was referring to."

Karen, clutching lots of documents found around the house, put them all into a folder and closed the front door for the night.

"Find anything interesting?" Ham asked as he left the house with Karen.

"Only documents regarding the ownership of the house and various legal paperwork, that is all. Nothing juicy, nothing that links a smoking gun to Michael," claimed Karen courteously.

The pair of them walked arm in arm, slowly up the familiar winding hill back to the hotel. Karen expressed her view that she felt she would never find Michael and Helen's murderer. Collard was still the firm favourite, and obviously he was now out of the equation as far as being a nuisance was concerned. Karen confided in Ham that she felt now was the time to stop looking as she had learned more about her sister's life with her husband than she had the right to know. Delivering the precious cargo back to England and contacting Alfonso was likely to be the last chapter, as far as she was concerned.

Ham comforted Karen, praising her efforts, highlighting she should be proud she found out more about Michael's lifestyle and questionable socially entwined business associates than their local police had uncovered.

# 21

By eight o'clock in the morning on their final day in Italy, Ham and William had beaten Karen downstairs into the hotel restaurant, despatched breakfast, and were outside Karen's latest Italian residence to be added to her property portfolio. Allowing their childish side to be exposed briefly, Ham and William teased the locals by enthusiastically revving the engines of the Jaguar E-Type and Austin Healey 3000 in anticipation of an amateur road race back to England. Big boys think this practice makes the cars run smoother, and prepares them for launch, when in fact it only massages their minds and makes their ears buzz with joy. Boys will be boys.

With all the cars loaded with luggage, it just remained for Karen to settle the hotel bill and get acquainted with William's pride and joy, his trusty Maserati.

A note left on the dashboard said it all:

*Karen, use the brakes as a last resort and do not hit anything, enjoy, kisses, William.*

Karen drove the Maserati to meet up with the other two, being careful as she adjusted herself to the dimensions of her new powerful steed.

Karen eyed up her opposition, the swanky new modern Maserati against the stylish Austin Healey and timeless Jaguar. Fifty years separated the technology under their respective right feet, and there was as much difference in the variable power deliveries and output as there was with the braking performance and confidence inspiring stopping ability.

With endless twisty bits, undulating peaks, and hairpin bends, the coastal mountain road served up before them was sure to be a fun, draining, and unique driving experience. The unavoidable scenic route taking them on their first leg of their adventure back home.

Snaking north up the western coastal road of Italy gave all concerned the opportunity to lead for a while, hang back, overtake, and dice with death, approaching blind bends outrageously fast, leaving their braking until the very last moment. The British had certainly left their mark on these roads, black rubber skid marks trailed from excessive power slides and awkward angled acute corner approaches were taking their toll with the little remaining rubber left on the tyres.

All cars and drivers got one hell of a workout, thrashing their chosen metal on roads which encouraged hard use, exploiting their respective talents to the limit.

All good things come to an end, and after a long hard day driving, they were back in the Alps and ready for a brief overnight stop at a cheap and cheerful, however very pretty, hotel.

The following day was more of the same, this time with a more relaxed motorway cruise as the auto routes took the strain, allowing the punished suspension systems to at least take things relatively easier.

The journey, even with plenty of fuel stoppages and regulation breaks for coffee, was a one hell of task. After two days buzzing in an aging Jaguar E-Type, William had pretty much had enough. His arms, knees and ears could hardly cope with any more abuse, as his romance with this vehicle was well and truly over. Karen, driving the modern Maserati, had a much easier drive, however it was still painfully draining and the fatigue from driving was taking its toll on her. Pleasure and pain in not so perfect harmony perhaps! Ham, felt ruffled and battered by the experience, however he was never going to admit to any exposure to trauma. Life was too short and he loved classic cars too much to offer any resistance to an epic drive, even after travelling one thousand three hundred and eighty miles in an open-top, fifty-year-old motorcar. This was two months' driving for some people in two glorious days. What an opportunity! Ham was the only driver who appeared to love every minute of it.

Road signs for Calais and the popular ferry port were a very welcome addition to the horizon.


After an hour in port waiting to disembark in the obligatory queues, the ferry was loaded providing valuable opportunity for the travellers to grab refreshments and a well-needed snooze.

In what seemed no time at all, the cross-channel ferry journey was over and it was time to disembark in Dover and enjoy the run down the passenger car exit ramp, savouring the relatively cooler night air. Firstly, Immigration were despatched without drama, passports shown with no issues and only a cursory glance from officials into the back seats of the cars.

Karen wondered, Why did immigration staff always look so bored and uninterested?

Released from passport control, our three heroes followed the disciplined route through the port straight into the clutches of Her Majesty's Customs and Excise at the arrivals hall.

The passengers in their cars from the ferry crossing all queued, awaiting their turn to be beckoned into the hall. This was the final link in the chain to freedom. Soon enough, Karen was called first, and drove slowly passed the assembled security crew. In a line of five bays it looked like she was going to pass without a challenge. Finally, at the final inspection crew she was selected, and asked into an inspection bay.

The questions were relatively easy going, and presented no problems. Karen always found the close scrutiny of customs and excise disconcerting, even when she was innocent and had nothing to hide. Her thoughts were magnified, especially when one member of staff did the talking, and two others remained in the background, pointing and whispering to each other inspiring annoyance. The subterfuge of clarity of the facts was a powerful one, she thought. Being called for an inspection, in the great scheme of things, presented little conflict for Karen, as she was not carrying a significant amount of smuggled or stolen jewels. What she did have wrapped in her hand luggage could pass off comfortably as her own, given the smaller quantity and the other genuine ladies paraphernalia she had masking her hoard.

With a brief impromptu inspection inside the boot of her car, she was free to go, and roared off to the nearby customer waiting car park, on the right side of the security barrier.

William was next into the hall, making a typical grand entrance as the beating heart of the Jaguar made a stunning noise popping and barking, awaking all but the most stubborn of residential roof-hugging seagulls.

Predictably, William was directed straight into an inspection bay, with an enthusiastic story and false paperwork at the ready. The banter between the officers and body language was very amusing to watch. For a brief moment in time, the Customs crew appeared to forget what they were employed to do, allowing the impact of the beauty of the classic car to work wonders. Everyone seemed to have a favourite classic car, and most people seemed to choose the Jaguar as theirs.

William could not believe how easy this was, and was soon encouraged to leave the inspection bays and was on his way. Brilliant, he thought.

Ham was next into the lion's den, and in many ways received

a very similar welcome to William. The strange thing with Ham was that he looked more like a villain than some villains, and immediately aroused suspicion, just by being present when it was dark outside wearing a beanie type hat. Ham's ability to look like he had been involved in a drama, chased and shot at whilst actually being totally innocent and only slightly removed from a man of the cloth, was most commendable. Perhaps it was the lack of sleep, the long-distance drive or the rough cut of his jacket that got prying eyes twitching.

Ham was invited to leave the comfort of his snug cockpit and stand next to the car as the crew Ham had met went to town looking under seats and allowing a resident sniffer dog to give the interior a once over.

Things were not looking good, and whilst Ham tried to look relaxed and unperturbed, his clammy hands, shifty eyes, and awkward stance told the assembled inspection crew a lot more than words ever could.

Just when it was thought things could not get any more demanding, another inspection team descended on Ham's car. The new team in attendance had with them an odd device, a mirror on a long pole which was used to put underneath suspicious cars to check for concealed packages. Upon checking Ham's car, one side appeared to be fine. They then walked around the other side and paused, looking at each other cautiously. It looked likely they had found something that required further investigation under the Austin Healey. Both officers crouched down for a closer inspection, one outstretching his hand underneath for a closer feel. Had their plan been rumbled?

At about the same time, a buzz of activity broke out at the other side of the inspection hall. It looked like something had been found concealed in another motorist's car as the driver had been hand cuffed and marched off into a nearby office, under heavy guard.

The team inspecting Ham's car were now needed to attend

this newly developing distraction, and with no senior members of staff looking into Ham's situation, he was waved to go through by a junior member of staff, free to join his colleagues in the port car park, sitting the right side of freedom.

With all three of them now passed the goal post, with fresh enthusiasm and a blast of power, William, Ham and Karen took off up the hill, leading out of Dover port with speed and lashings of relief. They had done it, and without a tail, any unexpected bandit chasing or rogue gunshots hurtling towards them.

Within half an hour, they were back safely on Karen's drive, it was hugs all round as they had pulled yet another white rabbit out of the hat and returned home in one piece with goods intact and no prying eyes in evidence.

Ham and William quickly released the container pods from underneath the classic cars, and put all the valuables into a large sports holdall Karen had fished out of a storage cupboard. With the hoard now safely inside Karen's home, it was time for some well-needed sleep.

First of all though, Ham had to remove his shoes, and given his driving style, and the stresses of the moment passing through customs, he was likely to need surgical assistance, or at least a very strong air freshener as the results of his sock removal were likely to be upsetting. William was not pleased to be sharing the same room with Ham that evening.

# 22

Karen tossed and turned in her bed that night, her mind playing with thoughts and scenarios as she thought quite a lot about talking to Alfonso regarding the cargo they had brought back into England. Were they going to get a friendly welcome? Would the financial exchange be as easy and as straightforward as Luca had suggested? More to the point, would the amount mentioned to her be the amount she would receive? Anticipation, wrapped in worry, was the order of the day for Karen. She was certainly not able to relax fully until all the loose ends had been tied. There was only one way to find out, and she needed to ring Alfonso in the morning to complete the transaction.

Pressing issues needed to be attended to first and the best she could offer Ham and William as guests was a strong black coffee and an omelette. The great thing about entertaining men, she thought, was that they were not always bothered about the finery of hotels or exotic origins of the cuisine. So long as the delivery was timely and the food hit the spot, happiness could often come at a very cheap price. Oh, and with the proviso the men did not have to create the food themselves, of course.

A knock at the door was guaranteed to send Karen's heartbeat into overdrive, and the robust knock she heard from her front door was no exception. Karen knew she had a very slim window of opportunity to intercept a parcel from a delivery company before they drove off so she was always one step away from panic when post and delivery men called.

Karen opened her door and was stunned to see Alfonso standing facing her, immaculately presented in an expensive looking dark blue suit, greeting her with his cheeky Italian grin. "Hello, Karen. You are back."

"Alfonso, hello. Please come in. What a surprise."

The warmness of her welcome was less assured than the one she had received; she hated unannounced arrivals. The genuine surprise and a feeling she was not as well dressed as she would like to have been slowed her response. Her hair had not been styled to a standard she would have liked, she worried to herself, as she gave Alfonso a hug as he entered her house. Her thoughts raced as she wondered why Alfonso had chosen to call without an appointment and why so soon after her arrival back in England.

Karen had wanted to remain in control and make the call to Alfonso herself. She did not enjoy being on the back foot. As Alfonso walked into Karen's house, he was accompanied with a gentleman he introduced as his personal assistant, Spike.

Spike performed guard duty inside the lounge, standing by the doorframe. He remained static and looked straight ahead without deflection. His stance was sculptured in true nightclub-bouncer-cum-bodyguard style. His message was a simple one: I am here to intimidate you. Enjoy. At least he appeared house-trained, William thought, as Spike remained totally silent.

In an attempt to regain control, Karen invited Alfonso to take a seat in her lounge and offered refreshments. The room was to remain dry as Alfonso declined – he was clearly only interested in one thing.

Karen brought over to Alfonso the sports holdall with all the valuables inside which had been brought back from Luca in Italy. Alfonso fingered the contents of the bag, and spent a lot of time checking each item, some more carefully than others. The collection of diamonds and some of the designer watches were excellent quality and very rare pieces, and Alfonso was visibly pleased with his catch, smiling and nodding his head in knowledgeable approval.

Karen should have kept quiet and let Alfonso make the first comment regarding payment, however she could not resist getting in with the first word. "We discussed the valuation for the items with Luca, and we agreed two hundred and seventy-five thousand pounds for delivery in England."

Alfonso remained silent, glancing at Karen briefly, smiling and then returning his attention to the catch. Alfonso, a very shrewd man, replied, "Luca has over estimated the quality here. They are good, however some scratches and missing details do negatively impact the value."

Karen remained silent, thinking to herself how surreal the meeting and transaction seemed, ready for a fiscal kicking.

Alfonso was now ready to discuss business. "I have two hundred and fifty thousand pounds for these goods. I have cash."

William, annoyed at Alfonso's game, suggested to Karen in a firm tongue, "We should try another buyer, I think we can get three hundred thousand with the right buyer!"

Alfonso responded swiftly and with urgency in his voice. "You will deal with me. Two hundred and fifty thousand pounds is a good trade for a consignment you knew nothing about until you stumbled upon it with Luca. Do not get greedy, greedy people can come to harm."

Spike the doorman woke up and opened his suit jacket briefly, just enough to flash his gun he had tucked away in his military styled carrier, strapped firmly to his upper body.

Karen did really well to remain silent and to keep eye contact with Alfonso. She was not fazed, she just kept her head and did not agree or disagree, she remained calm and neutral.

Alfonso eager to keep the upper hand, looked in turn at

Karen, William and then Ham, and spoke again. "You made a big mistake by killing Collard. Please remember I know this fact, when you finally make a decision."

Karen looked at William, her thoughts tussling with indifference. She then turned and faced Alfonso, speaking very controlled and purposefully. "Okay, I agree. I accept your offer."

Spike the charismatic doorman disappeared, then came back into the house after a brief visit to the waiting black Range Rover on Karen's drive. Spike returned carrying a large briefcase, put it on the coffee table and flipped the locks, opening the top of the case, revealing inside two hundred and fifty thousand pounds sterling, in neat bundles, smelling gorgeous, ready to be spent.

As Alfonso did the zip up on his newly purchased sports holdall, he looked at Karen and said, "Your team did well with this job. Well done. If you want to do the run again in six months' time, ring me or stay in contact with Luca. That is, if you think you can handle it!"

As Alfonso got up out of his chair to leave, he proceeded to lean over to Karen, and went to kiss her cheek in a traditional goodbye gesture. Karen did not respond initially and then moved her head away in the opposite direction, in a signal of disgust.

Alfonso moved his head away, laughed to himself, and walked away, the transaction was complete with no flying bullets or smudged lipstick in evidence.

Karen had developed a soft spot for Italian men, however if she learned anything fast, it was striking men with dangerous tendencies had an edge which was a serious turn-off. *Why are so many men either arrogant or ignorant bastards?* she thought.

She turned, holding that thought to see William catching her glance in a smug way he did so well, and a playful Ham, quite content just sitting down minding his own business, acting nonchalantly detached. *Men, they go from one extreme to the other. Arrrrrrggggggghhhhhh...*

# 23

The next day, Karen was keen to do something to raise her spirits. Karen missed her late sister Helen terribly and whilst her recent adventures had mostly worked out well, she felt strangely unfulfilled. She had experienced some thrilling times and had enjoyed excitement, fun and mystery, perhaps doing deeds and finding out things she had not done in her life previously. She was grateful she had taken new risks, and she had regretfully got involved with some illegal practices. Putting a line under her encounters, she had no plans to repeat these events or continue associating with people who were fundamentally ruthless criminals.

It was time for her to thank her trusty colleagues, William and Ham, for their support and what better way to do this than to give them a super treat for lunch. The plan was for Karen to take her two favourite men to a plush eatery in central London. The way to a man's heart, as all women know, was generally accepted as being through their stomachs.

Ham had been marvellous, in many ways he never did anything that was his strength, he never interfered. The important thing with Ham was that he was available if needed and always by one's side. He was like a lump of ballast you could

216

tie yourself too on the coast in rough seas, and when the storm of the moment eased, Ham threw you the slack back, and off you went on your journey. He was solid and generous of heart.

William was capable, however he appeared distant. Not in mind, but in application. This was his strength, as it was Karen's family issue and she wanted to deal with it her way. She did not want to be burdened with an assistant who was too assertive or dominant. Nothing phased William, he was hugely experienced, very controlled in approach. He was a colder animal, and Karen sensed he never let anyone get too close to him. In that respect she had two very different, perfect partners to help her over the last few weeks. She was very grateful to both of them.

Karen wanted to ask William how he felt, knowing he had killed before. He had killed many more times than Karen, in quite different circumstances. Yet he remained silent, he never discussed it. You had to prod him to get a response. Karen was fine with her feelings until she thought about it, and she could not escape the constant pressure from the guilt of committing a murder. She had committed a crime in killing Collard, and the memory of the crime was not dissipating at anything like the pace she wanted and hoped it would. The weight of guilt was crushing her, it was dragging her down, and she could not switch it off.

Karen kept telling herself, self-defence, it was self-defence. Her emotions were tangled and they never heard her internal cries. Peace and contentment were not in her life. They were in another place, and she wanted her old life back, she wanted her sister back, however she knew that was never going to happen. That was a raw fact of life.

It was time for Karen to move on. She had, after all, inherited a small house in Italy and her bank balance had swelled enormously. She wanted to do something different to perk her spirits up from the normal retail therapy splurge or a girls-who-do-lunch get together. She decided it would be appropriate to escort Ham and William to a top London venue to have a classy dinner, a kind of thank you meal and last supper all wrapped into one.

Karen laughed out loud as she gathered her thoughts in the plush central London restaurant of her choosing. The three of them sat at one table, Karen next to William, and Ham sitting opposite.

Ham enquired, "What is so funny, Karen?"

Karen replied, "It is you two. You do not fit in here."

William replied, looking around, wearing a playful smirk and a frown, "You implying we are not good enough to eat in here?"

Karen was sophisticated and a lady, she could mix it anywhere and carried herself well. Ham looked like he had just travelled nearly two thousand miles in an open-topped sports car, chasing destination unknown across Europe. William looked like a hitman, who had just been caught running.

They were typical fun-loving blokes; they did not care. Dinner after all was dinner. Did it really matter where it was served or how they looked?

Karen, soul searching, wondered what she needed to do in her life to be happy. She had found good friendship in both Ham and William. She now saw William in a very different light. No matter what the stress, whoever he had to deal with, he never appeared to waiver. Karen saw great strength in William and it was a quality she liked, and perhaps the feelings she felt, there was a need to make William aware. The only failing with William being the fact you sometimes needed to dig a little deeper to discover his warmth and charm. But it was worth the digging, Karen thought.

Ham was a nice guy, odd, but nice. Very caring and massive fun. Soaked up all the troubles in the world and always left a situation with a positive twist, even if he did cause an element of chaos and left the scene of the accident, having often caused it.

Karen was extremely grateful for all elements of support

Ham and William had displayed whilst assisting her in her quest to find her sister's killer. Her outlook on life was now very different, given the associates she had met since getting involved with Michael's business dealings and low-life connections. She realised with stark gravity what William meant by people out there who lived their lives by a different set of rules. Who would have thought on reflection, it was Karen who had turned into a killer, albeit only with severe provocation.

Karen acknowledged her appreciation to both Ham and William by sliding a bulging envelope across the table to both of them. She gave each of them a cheque for twenty-five thousand pounds, Ham the keys to the trusty Austin Healey roadster and William the keys to the Jaguar E-Type coupe.

Karen stood up and decided it was now a good time to leave, she hated goodbyes, and this one was one of the saddest of all. "Goodbye, boys. Collect the cars when you can. Thank you for everything. Stay good."

A kiss on the cheek to both of them, and Karen walked out the restaurant. All eyes were on her; she certainly had presence. It was an emotional farewell. William stood up, wanting Karen to stay. Ham's eye contact suggested it was best to let her walk, let her find herself. She needed her own space.

As Karen walked outside, tears to one side, the only saving grace, adding a cheeky smile, was the fact Ham and William never really fitted inside the stylish expensive restaurant of Karen's choosing. The fact they were both now on their own added to the mystique of the moment. In typical blokes-on-a-mission fashion, Ham and William carried on chatting and munching, oblivious to the other guests using them as a gossiping focal point.

Upon leaving the restaurant, Karen decided she needed a pick-me-up, and had always fancied an apartment overlooking the Thames in London. That day was the day she decided to look. She had a friend who was an estate agent. She decided she would look and do some controlled dreaming. Karen had the funds available, and she was about to press the button on the sale of her sister's cottage. So why not look; it suited her mood.

It was time to let the past go, and her thoughts regarding relocating from the Kent village of Hawkswold were gathering momentum within her private mindset. Was the London apartment dream a real option? The difficulty was she preferred the country setting, but the idyllic countryside now reminded her of her sister far too much, and a dramatic change was in order. Karen had to make a difficult decision.

With the key in her hand from the estate agent, she took the lift to the eighth floor within the swanky apartment block on the riverbank.

Upon leaving the lift, she opened the door to the apartment her friend had recommended to her overlooking the Thames. She stayed for a while inside, looking in drawers in the kitchen, trying to size up the rooms imagining her pictures on the bare walls. Whilst the apartment was very stylish, it felt somehow clinical and not as appealing in the flesh as the glossy brochure portrayed. The view however was stunning, that was where the money went. Very interesting, with something always happening outside the large panelled window with the familiar London backdrop framing the scene.

An ideal room for an exhibitionist, she playfully thought. Memorable, however quite a bit different to what she had been used to, perhaps that was the point! Karen was not yet doing cartwheels. She would need more time and perhaps another visit to really get an appetite for it.

# 24

Karen's thoughts regarding her future bounced around her head as she returned back to her faithful doorstep at ten in the evening. She opened the front door, thinking it was great to be back home and relished the feeling we all get when we return home from a visit away, delighting in the accustomed warmth, familiarity and security.

As Karen entered her front doorway her positive bounce took a major dive as she saw a blue piece of paper face down on her carpet. It was the same sort of paper she had seen with threatening notes before from her assumed perpetrator, Collard.

The note read: *It is time to hand over my money. C.*

A cold feeling filled Karen's entire body, she began to shake and where once she may have allowed tears to flow, this time she felt deep-rooted anger. She would not allow emotional anxiety to get the better of her. Her thoughts once again began to race: Was this note real? Was it an old note she had just discovered, moved from under her seating by the draft from the front door when it closed? Was Collard still alive? Was it Collard who wrote the note? Questions, questions, questions.

Typical, she thought, she never saw this coming. She could really use Ham or William right now for support, even just to bounce thoughts off them. Could she confront the horror on her own, if this note was fresh and authentic?

Pulling herself together, she walked through to her kitchen. It was time to put the kettle on, have a coffee and do some lateral thinking. Perhaps cracking open a good quality bottle of white wine would have been more appropriate, however coffee would have to do.

Karen flicked the switch to turn on her kitchen light, and it flashed, the bulb blew immediately, plunging her back into darkness. Karen remained stationary and took a deep breath. Stop being silly, she reminded herself as she felt increased tension. It is just a light bulb that has blown. It is strange how when you are alone in your house innocent noises take on a new theme, and darkness enhances trepidation, allowing your conscience to be over creative. Karen's pounding heartbeat took on a vibrant tempo as all her senses went into overdrive.

She walked over to her middle drawer, in her poorly lit darkened kitchen, and rummaged around for a fresh light bulb – she knew she had a few spare. Whilst doing so, she felt a presence behind her and the very slight sensation of the floor move under another person's weight. Was this a reality check or her emotions playing games again? Her natural assumption was her mind tricks were spooking her, which is easily experienced when you are home alone as isolation adds weight to any minor drama.

Karen went to turn to see who was behind her, but she felt the air move fiercely and a sudden thump to the back of her head, similar one could imagine to being hit by a baseball bat shrouded in soft velvet. Someone wanted her hurt, not necessarily killed. She felt the air around her head swish past with violence, the heat of a sudden impact was evident, acute pain and a wave of concussion were all sensations vying for attention as she dropped like a stone to the floor in a random heap. Her vital systems seemingly shutting down one by one, and her firm grip on her perceptions waning.

Memory, recognition, and a grasp of reality all fought for

her full awareness. Karen's senses were muddled and pain was a very real sensation, masking other things she should have been thinking about, such as self-defence or more importantly long-term self-preservation.

The voice of the man in the room was not immediately recognisable. He sounded like a middle aged man, perhaps forty years old. He was English, perhaps local. Who? Who was calling? Who was speaking?

Timeframes were difficult to manage, Karen's head ached and her vision was spinning. She was in darkness sitting upright in a chair with her muddled hair flopping over the front of her face. She felt physically sick and wanted to vomit. Her hands had been tied tightly to the chair arms, and ankles restrained to the bottom legs of her chair.

Karen was running through a mental checklist in her mind, having regained consciousness. She ran checks on the movements of all her toes, fingers arms and legs to see if anything was broken. All appeared present and working, albeit bound and aching with a passion. Her right ankle hurt, probably from careless carriage into another room.

Karen rapidly tried to get her thoughts together and everything back in order. Her senses were regaining their sharpness. She then tasted her own blood from a cheek wound and her abrasive swollen tongue filled her mouth. She needed water, she was parched. She could only assume her injuries in her mouth were caused when she fell over as she was unable to break the fall. Her head really hurt, and was throbbing, she needed to feel it and inspect it for her own peace of mind and assess the potential for damage. That luxury was not afforded to her. She was bound too tight for any movement to be feasible.

*What the hell is going on? what the hell is happening?* Karen kept thinking to herself. *This must be a nightmare, this cannot be happening. It is not real.*

In silence, and in darkness, she forced herself, in excruciating pain, to fall asleep. Her sleep was short-lived. Whilst it enabled her a brief term of escapism, her nightmare demons stirred her mind into thinking several men were standing around her, pushing her, cajoling and prodding her. Intimidation and emotional sacrifice were the order of the day. Punishment, upon endless abuse and excruciating pain, rocked Karen's world to its unstable creaking foundation.

An unfamiliar voice woke her and got her full attention. She groaned in disapproval, her head spinning. She was understandably livid, however in alien territory, she was cautious and wanted to be restrained in response. She failed miserably.

"Where am I?" Karen screamed. Her thoughts were contaminated, roaming under the influence of some drug-induced confusion.

"You are in my home. You are in a bad way, aren't you?" responded the captor in a calm voice, underlying his position, a position of rude control.

Karen felt the arm of the chair and it felt too solid to break. With dim lighting, she could make out a large open-plan kitchen to the far side. She was currently placed in the living room area of the adjacent room. She tried to absorb the lie of the land, so if an opportunity arose to get away from this mad man, she had half a chance to escape, even in darkness.

"The arrangement was simple, Karen. You chose to mess me around. Now you pay, now it is time for me to mess you around," the captor said, sounding increasingly pissed off, which was gratifying, as it mirrored Karen's outlook completely.

The mystery man then ran his hands down Karen's face, down over her covered breasts and then in an act of utter disgust, proceeded to run his hand slowly and purposefully up the inside of Karen's skirt, chasing her thigh. Karen tried in anger to push herself away, forcing her legs closed and the chair backwards, but the beast kept pushing his luck and thrust his hand ever further higher inside her upper thigh above her stocking tops. Stopping short of further shocking behaviour and torture, he removed his hand as swiftly as he had placed it within her intimate area.

Was this a forerunner of more mistreatment to come? The captor stood up and laughed and walked away, enjoying the spectacle and the dominant sensation of control he exercised.

Karen, fighting back her tears, asked, "What do you want? You're an animal. Why have you chosen me?"

"What do I want? I want ten thousand pounds, at least I did. I am not sure I want the money now. You had your chance!"

Karen confused, scared, and increasingly baffled by the unprovoked attack, enquired again, "What are you going on about? Ten thousand pounds. I do not understand you."

The abductor, becoming increasingly unpredictable and sounding more alarmist by the second, turned and held Karen's arms forcefully, digging in his fingernails into her forearms, almost drawing blood, standing in front of her head on, maximising the intimidation.

"You agreed to pay me ten thousand pounds if I hurt your lover, Michael, in the village. The job would be a better one if I killed him. That was your prescription for a better life and I took you up on your offer. Do not deny that instruction now, I am no idiot."

Incarcerated in panic with a maniac in her face, Karen thought very quickly regarding what she could say to try and turn events around. She flicked her head in distress, trying to move some of her troubled hair away from her eye line, to improve her impaired vision.

Karen rolled the dice, upping the tempo. "Treat me like an idiot. I do not remember the conversation we had, I must have had too much to drink. Tell me what I asked you to do!" shouted Karen, pushing her distress threshold ever higher, striving to get a reaction.

Looking straight at Karen, invading her personal space, pushing his nose up against hers, the both of them locked in eye contact. "You told me Michael went back on his word to leave his wife for you. He simply could not do it. Your response was hurt him, really harm him, kill him, for all you care."

The hostage taker went on to explain he had left things for three to four weeks, unsure whether to take the bait and action the crime. Following a blinding evening, courtesy of some cheap, poor-quality cocaine which had fallen into his possession, he had had the courage and the motivation to act out Karen's wish.

That evening, he had snatched the keys to the cottage from his mother, who was the housekeeper for the Stansfeld's at the time, crept inside the cottage, which was in darkness, and set about using his gun to full effect.

"Wow, what a buzz that was," he mused. "I am going to be famous! Michael was screwing his wife on the bed, and I carefully walked into their bedroom and watched them. He was on his back looking at her, she was on top facing the wall, looking away from me. They had no idea I was present. It was amazing, quite funny really. I intentionally let them enjoy themselves. It was the ultimate-pleasure-with-impending-pain scenario. I waited for one of them to turn to see me holding the gun towards them. It seemed like ages. I was running the escape route over and over again in my head. Ready to run at any moment. Heartbeat pounding, light headed, the coke was still pumping my brain, egging me on. It was a truly fantastic merging of emotions and I was the one in control. I loved it."

The killer went on to describe the moment he fired the first shot, hitting Michael's wife Helen in error. His aim was that of Michael, but he missed. He had no intention of killing Michael's wife, it just happened that way. There was the muffled shot followed by the thud of her body slipping off the bed and hitting the polished wooden floor. It was a close-range shot of course, and a single round took her out easily.

"After the fateful first bullet hit its target, I panicked, and fired more rounds until my handgun was fully discharged, and both bodies lay motionless riddled with holes. I wanted to stay and just look at them, look at what I had done, look at what I had achieved. I stayed with them for several minutes, just looking. However, the clock was ticking and I knew I had to go and make good my escape."

Karen was weeping and shaking uncontrollably. What she had just heard was an appalling first account of her sister's murder which was upsetting beyond belief. This was a nightmare, veiled within a nightmare and it was not getting better anytime soon. If ever you could find yourself in spiral descent into freefall chaos and concern, this was it. The ride of your life nobody ever wanted.

Karen bit her lip, held herself together and said with staggered emotion, "You have done what you have done, and now you need to be paid for it."

Her sentiment licked her imagination, and flourished her thoughts into bold action.

A softly spoken, tearful, compassionate Karen requested, "Untie me. I cannot pay you if you do not untie me."

The torturer and killer, a young man, unfamiliar to Karen, wielded a knife at her, making feint moves trying to spice up the relationship between them still further.

Karen was looking at vermin, and she was not about to let this rat slip away if she could help it. The knife held by her attacker pierced the holding tape, releasing her restrained legs and arms from her chair. For the moment, the knife had done its job and she was free. She rubbed her hands over her arms and legs, she tasted freedom once more as she fully removed the cut tape and was able to stand proud from her prison seat.

"I need to get my handbag and I will write you a cheque," signposted Karen, keen not to make any violent moves which could provoke further annoyance from an already unstable host.

"I want cash. Whoever heard of a killer, a hitman getting paid for a job by cheque?"

Karen, slightly disorientated and getting more frustrated

by the minute, replied sternly, "I do not carry ten grand in cash around with me, you fool. If you want cash, I will get it for you tomorrow. If anyone asks where you got the cheque from, just say you did some landscape gardening for me. The cheque will not bounce. If it did, I know you would be back. Neither of us want that, do we?"

After a slight pause and a licking of his lips, the hired killer responded. "A cheque is fine. Just give me a cheque, I will accept it." *Bitch!*

"Whose name do you want on it?" Karen enquired.

Slightly bemused, the reply came, "My name of course, Christopher Brown."

Karen, standing at the other side of the room, reached over to her handbag, rooting deep inside for her chequebook. Without hesitation she pulled out her gun, pointed it immediately at Christopher, paused, savoured the moment, enjoyed the fleeting alarm and frightened disbelief which filled his face. She knew she had to act quickly – there was only one opportunity to get this job done. Karen then pulled the trigger, three times, and watched Christopher slump to the floor. Bang, Bang, Bang, it was over.

She dropped her gun on the floor, turned and walked out the room clutching her handbag. As she made good her escape, she never turned her back once or regretted her actions one little bit.

Relief and pleasure in equal harmony, this was closure for Karen, real closure. She was on top of her game and in control of her life. She needed to look at her head, she had an unsavoury bump on it and her neck was killing her.

As she left the house, she turned right and ran down the country road. As soon as she was outside, she knew her location, she was on the outskirts of another local village, approximately a mile and a half from her house. She tried to run as fast as she could, breaking her heel, discarding her shoes, running barefoot for most of her journey home.

All sorts of thoughts filled her mind as she made her way

228

home. She vaguely remembered the attack in her kitchen, the bulb blowing out, being dragged through her house, amazingly having the presence of mind whilst suffering excruciating pain to grab her handbag as she knew she had a one of William's guns in it. She remembered being bundled into the back of a car, feeling drowsy and in pain, thinking she was about to be murdered and she was suffering, clinging on to her last moments alive.

What had she been drugged with? She must have been drugged with something. Her uncomfortable whirlwind experience played over again and again.

She then thought about her attacker, a proper gorilla type aged about forty. He had a shaved head and an imposingly large frame. He was impulsive, rude, and an arrogant meathead.

Karen ended up walking back to her house. Her feet were killing her, she had a headache and her arms and legs still felt pain from where they had been taped up tightly. At least she was free, she could taste the fresh night air and she was alive.

Karen was so exhausted when she got home, she never bothered going upstairs to bed. She just crashed for the night on her sofa. Was she safe? She hoped so. Would she suffer another encounter? She was totally exhausted, both physically and mentally. She hoped her ordeal was over. She needed some sleep.

Karen awoke the next morning, head in hands, trying to be strong, however despair and confusion were now ruling her head.

She had been a bloody idiot, she thought. She had shot a man, in a rage of distressed anguish, dropped the gun next to the body, with her own fingerprints on it, and left the scene at speed. How could she have been so bloody stupid? The thought kept rolling in her mind. Why didn't she keep hold of the gun? Why did she leave the weapon behind, the one item which could link her to the scene of the crime and the act of murder?

Yes, she was under pressure of a hostage situation, with a maniac bully who was capable of exacting all manner of nasty disciplines on her. With hindsight and a clear head, one can make these observations with stark clarity and think retrospectively how easy it would have been to have avoided making a simple error.

Karen reasoned, when you are in the heat of the moment, distressed, under the influence of something distasteful, shaking, terrified and staring down the barrel of potentially your last minutes on earth alive, it is just possible we do not all act as collectedly or as precisely as we would like.

Karen was frustrated with herself, and remained a little scared with life and fearful of what she could encounter around the next corner. She was trying to act tough, however when you are at the sharp end of an acute situation, with unsavoury obstacles being thrown at you, one after the other, robust decisions need to be made and sometimes you make the wrong call for the right reasons.

Karen started questioning herself: why had she fired the gun? In the great scheme of things, people do not go around killing each other, just because they fall out of have a row. Disagreements are disagreements after all. That said, Karen thought, if a man bundles you into a car, and tapes your hands and feet to a chair, drugs you, teases you, provokes anger from you and threatens sexual intimidation and violence, perhaps a bullet is the answer, or if not the answer, it is a very close second. Karen knew she had to stand by her actions and live with all the twisted consequences.

Before she had the opportunity to tie herself up in more knots of guilt, regret and extolling the virtues of self-defence for the armed bystander, a knock at the door broke her concentration. She re-focussed her attention on the unravelling drama within her life and answered the beckoning caller.

William was standing at her front door. "Hello, Karen," said William enthusiastically as Karen opened her door. "I thought I would take you out for the day."

A face full of tears, exposed bruises, a makeup malfunction, and dragged through-a-hedge-backwards hairstyle told William all he needed to know. Karen had suffered one hell of a night and she was in no mood for a day out.

Karen lunged at William, put her arms around him hugging him to death. Tears flowed.

Karen remained silent, battered and withdrawn. Not so much looking for self-inflicted sympathy, genuinely she felt she had reached her limit of life.

"Karen what has happened to you?" asked a concerned William as he entered her house, her unexpected grip loosening and she walked with William into her lounge.

Karen pressed hard against William again. She not only needed the comfort and the support, she needed to feel the warmth from someone she could trust. Karen felt as if she was dipping her foot into the deep end at the swimming pool as a child and she was rapidly falling out of her depth. Her rational thinking and level-headed responses were fading.

Karen was overjoyed to feel William's warm embrace again after a traumatic night, and in a moment of weakness, Karen's lips met William's and they kissed passionately. Karen thought, *I have never kissed an accountant before. He actually tastes nice!*

Whilst the embrace continued, Karen stated, "I think it is time to call the police. My life is too complicated right now. I cannot cope with this anymore. I have killed another man. When does this all stop?"

Raw emotion and sexual tingles die quickly when the lady you are with makes a statement like that. Karen went on to explain the previous evening's events: the kidnapping, torture and uncertainty she had felt. Attacked by an imposing careless oath who had claimed to have killed Michael and Helen. The injection of fear into Karen's life was not welcome, stark realisation followed that playing detective had risks, and Karen now craved to have her old life back. Boring her old world may well have been, but her quality of life had now suffered with too many numerous threats, close calls, and near-death experiences, all factors which outweighed what she had expected to gain from asking a few questions and allowing her family to rest in peace.

William responded with heightened concern. Informing the police of any involvement with a murder was a recipe for disaster, even if mitigating self-defence was a remote angle on a claim. Far-reaching consequences for both William and Ham would be problematic for all of them at best, leading to a jail sentence at worst, potentially leading to retaliation from the effected villainess wider community. This was a complication with a twist, exposing William to hard-edged reality he did not have on that morning's agenda and he could well do without. Police involvement was not an option, William had to act and act fast.

It was clear from what Karen had told William that morning that the house which harboured the body of the deceased and the crime scene appeared unoccupied.

William reasoned with Karen that any man who picked on women, such as Collard or this latest maniac she had got involved with, deserved the worst. Whilst you might not have acted totally legally, you might just have to park your history and as hard as it may sound, just get on with your life. Attackers and intimidators might well deserve the death sentence. Karen, however, did not.

William had a long-standing basic rule, never return to the scene of a crime, this discipline was critical he believed for his long-term survival and continued freedom. That morning, however, he decided he would break this rule and go to the scene of Karen's recent torment and recover her firearm. Naturally, he would try his damnedest to avoid capture and had no intention of disturbing any evidence at the scene or adding his own unique material to the mix.

It was important for him to recover the gun. Whilst it was unlikely any clues would link back to him, Karen had almost certainly left trace forensic evidence which could incriminate her, once the police got their claws into the formal investigative proceedings. William did not want her exposed to difficult questioning which could implicate him and make Karen feel all the worse for what was likely to be certain linked exposure for Ham and William.

With heightened tension, Karen drove William back to the house which was the scene of her hostage and torture episode. The house was situated on the crest of a hill, and was the first property you came to when entering the next village in the urban chain south from Hawkswold.

William got Karen to park the car in a wooded off-road area just down from the target house. Karen would then remain at the wheel, ready for a swift getaway should things turn ugly. As Karen pulled into the agreed parking area, edging the car backwards taking care to be as discreetly parked as possible, all signs were good. The area was quiet and there were no obvious signs of activity at the venue.

William put on his regulation hitman leather black gloves, got out the car, and headed across the road, planning to walk around the back of the house and into the rear kitchen entrance. The grounds and house were silent. William entered the kitchen and paused. Leaking body fluids from Karen's latest victim filled a stench in the air which was guaranteed to churn your stomach and leave you gasping for fresh gulps of air.

William was playing things over in his mind, his focus to recover the gun Karen had fired and his random eyeball scanning of the area quickly allowed him to hone in on the weapon. Before he could reach the gun, he was careful not to slip on any spilt fluids. The dead guy was a mess. William allowed his mind to wonder about Karen's predicament and was baffled by the attention she had got from this guy and the demand for money with menaces.

It made a lot of sense for Collard to be calling the shots, and for him to be ring fenced, adding gravity to the assumption he was the guilty culprit.

Why was this new victim lying before William? Who was he connected with? Why would he be demanding money from Karen? Where did he fit into the proceedings, was he one of Collard's men? Surely not! It all made very little sense and William was starting to ask himself, was Karen being as transparent with her facts as she could have been. Was she holding something back, intentionally or otherwise?

William was starting to think Karen could evolve into a liability and he would have to talk to Ham. Karen was certainly exposed to serious fear and she was stressed out, understandably. The loose ends which were now being exposed were likely to be their downfall if things were not shored up soon.

Crouching down in the kitchen, William reached under a small bench seat, and recovered the gun which Karen had discarded from under a small bench seat by the breakfast table.

Upon elevating himself upwards to stand upright again, he felt the barrel of another gun unexpectedly being forced into the left side of his neck and the voice of the man holding the gun stating calmly and matter of factly, "Drop the gun, face the wall, and do not try anything silly. I will use this thing if I need to."

William was annoyed that he had put himself into a position of vulnerability, and reluctantly did what the gunman asked. Dropping the gun to his feet, he looked out from the corner of his eye to see where the gun had fallen and checked what position it was now in, just in case he got an opportunity to grab it again soon.

"Why did you kill him?" the gunman asked, prodding the barrel of his gun evermore uncomfortably with increased force into William's neck.

"I never killed him. If you checked the dead body you idiot, you would see the man was killed hours ago, he is stone cold, stiff and still weeping!" William responded in an irritated, abrupt tone.

"If you did not kill him, what are you doing here?"

"I am a friendly neighbour, that is all. Let me leave. You do not need my dead body on the floor complicating your life," proposed an increasingly aggravated William.

The gunman kept the relentless pressure onto William's neck, seemingly not allowing to give up his latest catch.

With welcome timing, Karen appeared in the kitchen doorframe, holding another of Williams guns she had found in his glovebox. She pointed it with reassuring stable precision at the gunman who had his focus and his handgun barrel squeezed into William's neck.

"Drop it," came Karen's sharp instruction.

Karen remained silent and still, targeting her gun with desperate purpose. This was a challenging negotiating ploy by Karen. In the movies Karen had seen, the villain was supposed to cave in, drop the gun and surrender to whoever was pointing the gun from behind and giving out the orders.

Reality was somewhat different. Firstly, Karen did not want to increase her victim body count by killing anyone else. To kill two people within a fortnight was bad enough as it was, taking the tally to three was hardly desirable. Her conscience could hardly take any more and had experienced a rough ride already. Her emotional strings had after all been pulled to the brink of snapping from her previous outings wielding a gun. Secondly, by design or indeed by accident, the gunman was firmly wedged up against William and made it very difficult for any bullet to be dedicated to him as an isolated target.

William was sure to be inflicted with some sort of fallout should bullets start flying, and Karen did not need reminding that if she thought things were bad now, they would almost certainly be worse if her tally of dead bodies was taken that morning from two to four. Given her current run of luck and her questionable shooting accuracy, it was a very real possibility. If Karen found herself counted within the ever-increasing body count, then her outlook would change markedly to a less damaging, spiritual level. She would never moan about gloomy wet Monday mornings, holed tights or burnt toast ever again.

The gunman, willing to test Karen's commitment to firing her weapon, responded with purpose. "No, you drop yours or your friend gets it," forcing William's head to one side in a retaliatory act of defiance and reasserting his passion to inflict pain on William at all costs, even risking the instant death penalty himself.

*Shit*, Karen thought. *What do I do now?* She was comfortable handling a gun, however she was less comfortable when involved with others who were with her doing the same. She immediately made the assumption that the other people in the room could probably handle a gun better than she could. If the gunman was not willing to take direction, this situation was sure to spiral into another sphere of chaos anytime soon.

Karen, perplexed and unsure what to do, racked her brain for inspiration. *Think girl, think*, she thought.

William, concerned that Karen had gone momentarily quiet, decided to offer her some disciplined guidance, shouting, "Shoot the bastard, Karen, do not worry about me." William got another barrel-shaped dig in the neck and a knee wedged up his arse cheeks from his captor for that remark.

Karen instructed the gunman to drop his gun one more time and move away from William. She reminded him she had a loaded gun and was well prepared and capable of using it.

Her target gunman then made a suggestion in his thuggish gravelly voice, "Let us put both our weapons down together, and be adults about this. If we do that we can both walk away. Is that fair?"

A flicker of humanity raised its head within the gunman's soul. Perhaps he could be rational and compassionate after all with his fellow gun-wielding fraternity. Was his suggestion sincere?

William was having none of it, and was not prepared to trust the guy, shouting at Karen, "Do not do it, Karen! It's a trap."

In an attempt to underline his good intentions, the gunman moved away slightly from William, and began making a slow-motion action, indicating he was placing his gun on a bench seat near to where he was standing, outstretching his arm fully.

William did not like this development, and was prepared for the gunman to put one gun down and take another one out concealed about his person. William was sharp eyed and scanned his part of the room for anything he could grab as a weapon, anticipating an opportunity might arise soon for him to strike out and gain control. William's concern was that Karen may not have read the play correctly, and might attempt a pot shot at the gunman after feinting conceit. If William rushed the gunman, then he could put himself into the line of fire, should Karen panic and fire the gun, the subsequent mess and tangle of who shot who? And why? Could develop into genuinely confusing bloodstained bun fight.

Karen did not know what to do for the best. She quietly moved away from the doorframe and positioned herself behind the kitchen breakfast bar facing her threat head on. She felt comfort using the dining area as a short-term barrier, cautiously mirroring the actions of the gunman by attempting to disarm herself. Acting in blind faith, she began to place her gun down on the breakfast bar she was now behind, being careful to ensure the barrel was still pointing in the direction of her and William's adversary.

Karen with right arm outstretched, sensed her trigger finger was numb and was not sure how much pressure she had weighted on the trigger as she lowered the gun down to the table top. As the gun was about to leave Karen's hand, the slight impact of the gun hitting the table was sufficient to tension the trigger to accept the bite to fire.

The distinctive handgun crack filled the kitchen as the bullet left Karen's gun, simultaneously forcing the gunman and William to flop to the ground in unison. Both seemingly taking the force of the bullet and receiving Karen's unintentional immediate punishment.

Karen froze, disbelieving what her senses were telling her. Were the gunman and William now dead? Silence was now her enemy. Karen desperately wanted to know, was William still alive? Was he seriously hurt? Double jeopardy ensued; she knew she had to proceed with extreme caution.

Both men's bodies remained motionless, their clothes not revealing any bloodstained evidence of contact with her bullet. Their awkward position on the floor gave no clues to Karen as to who had been hit or the severity of the wounds received. Karen noted the weapon the gunman had been holding was not visible. Where was it? The continued silence and lack of stirring movement did little to reassure Karen the gunman was dead.

Karen began to shake, fear taking hold as she walked from around the breakfast bar, feeling exposed without the flimsy barrier to protect her. With her gun now firmly back in her hand, she was ready to dish out bespoke retribution should the gunman try something.

As she got closer to both men lying next to one another, William's foot moved and caught her attention. In the blink of an eye, the gunman moved with urgency, turning to face Karen, raising his gun in despair. William was too fast. Catching everything seemingly in slow motion, he fired twice squeezing the last two bullets from his gun, destroying the gunman's grip on his firearm and rendering his final opportunity useless as his life-force was terminated.

A groan and a moan from the gunman were his final audible signals, as he died the death of an undesirable thug.

Karen, who had dropped to the floor during the final bullet exchange, got up quickly to make sure William was unhurt. She rushed over to see him and threw her arms around him in delight, thankful he was alive and seemingly unharmed. The mutual meeting of the lips between them was a typical enthusiastic greeting of a couple who were great friends, who had been through a lot together and had just experienced a thoroughly challenging, personal ordeal, and more importantly had survived it. Karen held her head back from William, and looked knowingly into his glorious eyes. She liked the tasty sensation of his lips and the feel of his arms around her. Karen again closed in on William. This time they kissed with a real urge of passion, which aroused her senses and his grip tickled her attention.

After a brief stolen moment together, William pushed Karen away without explanation. Karen, sensing rejection, dropped her eye contact from William in immense disappointment.

"Do you not find me attractive?" enquired Karen with genuine concern at being pushed aside.

William's unhappy face already held the answer, "No, you stupid woman, I have got cramp in my leg and I need to stand up. Give me some room, will you."

William dropped Karen's first-fired gun in one jacket pocket, and the recently used gun in his other side pocket. He then stood up, walking over to both deceased bodies and proceeded to rifle both dead men's clothing.

Karen enquired, "What are you doing, William? What you looking for."

William made Karen aware he was looking for any clues, or identity indicators such as driving licences or similar.

Professional villains never carried any form of identity. If these guys were professional henchmen, they would be hard to trace. Both men were clean; by luck or by judgement, they were not giving their identities away easily.

William reminded Karen that it was never in a killer's interest to take anything of value from a corpse's body. You never want to have something on your person which can connect you to the dead party.

Karen replied, "You really are a slippery one, aren't you."

William looked at Karen with purpose. "I am careful,

Karen. That is all. There is method in application, pulling a gun on someone is a serious business, with stubborn consequences to match. I shoot to kill, not to maim and ask questions later. If your target does not fall with the first shot, they have an opportunity to take you down with their first firing. You rarely get an opportunity for a second round, I always make the first one count."

William, having finished his impromptu corpse frisking, straightened his back, stood up, and took the lead to exit the house, grabbing Karen's hand in the process as they speedily ran round the back of the property, across the single-track road back to William's car.

As William fired up his still warm Maserati, Karen looked at William and barked at him, shedding a tear, reaching out to restore in situ a few of his hairs which had stepped out of line. "For one moment in there I thought you were dead. I thought I had lost you, you crazy fool!"

William explained that by some act of blind judgement, he'd fallen to the floor at precisely the moment Karen's gun fired. William's intention was to fall and grab the gun Karen used to kill her hostage taker earlier. His act of surprise was masked and undermined by Karen's feat of firing, inspiring pure shock. Her actions surprised everyone. Touché.

William responded, "If you had not banged your gun on the table when you did, you might have fired it by mistake later and killed me!"

Karen responded, searching for William's softer side. "Do you like women who surprise you?"

William answered, teasingly, "I do not mind women who provide surprises. You, however, are bloody dangerous!"

Karen enjoyed the final word, spurting velvet-tipped tones as carefully as her eye contact would allow. Flirtatiously, she rested her right hand on William's inside leg. "I might be dangerous with a gun, however I am even deadlier in the bedroom."

Looking over from the driver's seat William's playful reply came, "It is back to your place then, Karen!"

William selected first gear and screeched down the road with amusing urgency. Destination Karen's house, tyre squeal and a crackling exhaust note doing their best to wake the sleepy early morning woodland inhabitants. William, that morning, was definitely on a mission.

# 25

William turned into Karen's drive to reveal Ham polishing his recently acquired classic sports car. Whilst William may have had other priorities on his hit list, this was an ideal opportunity for the three of them to get together and discuss the morning's successes, near misses and challenges. Once again, Ham had bypassed most of that morning's action.

Once back inside her home, Karen provided ample fresh coffee and sat in the company of her two men. Whilst general chit-chat filled the room, she remained quiet with an excitedly fidgety facial expression that was poised to reveal some answers.

Karen announced to her assembled crew that it was time she provided some background clarification to her sister's death. She went on to highlight the fact that, whilst the official line was that the Stansfelds' family housekeeper, Mrs Brown, had found both bodies of Karen's sister Helen, and her husband Michael early in the morning as she started her housekeeper duties, what Karen had not revealed before was that she had found the bodies at a little past one in the morning, some six hours before the housekeeper started her work.

Karen, upon stumbling into the murder scene, disturbed nothing, it was clear both Helen and Michael were dead when she arrived, and both of the victims were beyond help. She was distraught with her sinister discovery which was totally unexpected, her world caved in and rational thoughts, for the moment, evaporated within the confusion of the moment.

With retrospect, the advisable action to have taken would have been to have contacted the police to raise the alarm immediately. Karen however chose not to – what could the police do? She naively thought letting her annoyance and hurt get the better of her.

Karen chose to leave the scene. She went to her home, in tears, wrapped in pain, and chose to rock herself to sleep. That was how Karen dealt with her grief initially. Grieving is a very hard emotion to deal with, especially when confronted with a murder scene, witnessed in all its jarring, untidy anger.

"I hope you understand my behaviour," came a stark comment from Karen, spoken with regretful admittance.

William and Ham remained silent, slightly mystified by Karen's confession, which aside from a lack of contacting the police in a timely manner, seemed like no disclosure at all – they did not get it!

Karen qualified her actions by alerting Ham and William that her mind was a mess, and her soul had been strangled with pain. At about eight o'clock in the morning, the police had knocked on Karen's door, accompanied with Mrs Brown the housekeeper, and they relayed to her the terrible news that Helen and Michael had been murdered. We looked very similar you see, especially without our makeup.

Ham and William's twitching went up a gear. William requested clarification. "What do you mean you looked similar?

A tear gently rolled down her face, the anguish of it all reaching a climax for her. "Don't you see? Michael was not in bed with his wife the night he got murdered. He was in bed with his wife's sister, my sister, Karen!"

Ham immediately stood up and went to Helen and cuddled her, wiping away her tears, in a gesture of support.

Ham was very apologetic. "I am so sorry, I never realised. You know, I thought something was different about you, however I just put that down to your grieving."

Ham explained to William that Karen and Helen, the sisters, were aged two years apart, Helen was thirty-nine, Karen was thirty-seven. They both had similar build, similar hair, they shared the same lovely dark brown eyes. However, Karen was slightly more extrovert and wore a little more makeup and, being critical, had larger curls in her hair.

Helen explained she never planned to deceive anyone and it was never her intention to pass herself off as her dead sister Karen, it just happened that way.

When Helen had left the murder scene, she walked directly to Karen's house at the other side of the village. Once inside, she found herself in Karen's bedroom, and started applying her sister's foundation, eye-liner and trademark red lipstick. Helen, as a rule, never wore a great deal of makeup – it was not her style. However, fighting with her emotions, she decided to put on some of Karen's makeup, to see if it transformed her. Did it make her more attractive? Helen conceded it did make a difference. It brought her closer to her sister.

After all, why would her husband find her sister more appealing if they were similar? It must have been the makeup!

The knock at the door, after Helen had applied her sister's makeup, sealed Helen's fate.

Helen explained her housekeeper wrongly introduced her as Karen to the police when they'd arrived to inform her of her sister's death. With hindsight, perhaps she should have corrected them there and then. She never did and it just snowballed from there on. Next she was being interviewed with the police and meeting friends and family, and of course it became harder for her to correct everybody and make them aware who she really was.

Nobody seemed to have guessed Michael would be having an

affair and so it made perfect sense for Michael to be sleeping with his wife.

William asked, "Helen, I do not understand why you never phoned the police after discovering the bodies, you had nothing to hide. Phoning the police would be the most natural thing to do, surely?"

Helen paused, collecting her thoughts before stating, "I was furious, more so with my sister Karen than my husband. How could they do such a thing? I lost control briefly and had a crazy couple of hours. We all deal with death differently. Sometimes the whole episode just grabs you, distorts you. That is what happened to me."

William thought about the whole circumstances very carefully and never took any story he heard at face value. Was it possible Helen had discovered her husband was having an affair, and plotted to kill them both in the act? Was Helen capable of committing the murder? She had proved she was lethal with a gun. William kept prodding his thoughts, his mind was buzzing.

Helen knew William would be thinking the worst – he was very clever and thought-provoking kind of guy. However, his face said it all.

In addressing both men, Helen tried to justify her actions. "I never suspected my husband was having an affair, there were no clues at all. That is why I never called the police; it was the exposure to extreme shock that got to me. I was upset of course, but when I found my husband's dead body with another woman, I was bloody angry. The bastard, I wanted him to be alive so I could kill him. Do you understand that?"

Helen kept her composure and was genuinely relieved to be telling someone the truth. She continued. "Then moments later, I discovered the dead woman he was with was my sister. My loving sister, the thoughtless bitch. Can you imagine what that does to you? Betrayal does not cut any deeper or sting you any greater than this. Your husband cheats on you, your sister cheats on you, and then they both get taken away from you. I defy you not to go crazy for two hours if your loved ones or close family imposed this scenario on you."

William and Ham took a consolatory view regarding Helen's actions and remained silent, nodding quietly in agreement. William tried to change his facial expression, so his thoughts were not so transparent. Ham naturally looked sympathetic to all natural disasters, so continued looking on wearing his traditional face of comfort, agreeable support and global acceptance.

Helen went on to explain she was torn, wrecked and hit for six with what she had been confronted with that night. It was late, she was tired, and she did not need this drama to deal with. She wanted to get away, curl up and forget it. It was her way of dealing with a very personal, high-profile tragedy.

Helen reflected on her view regarding her love for her husband and her sister. "It is so frustrating when you cannot shout at them, you cannot quarrel with them, you cannot reason with them, because they are no more, they have left you. I keep asking, Why? Why was he unfaithful to me? Why did she sleep with him? How long had it been going on? Who murdered them? Why would someone want to kill them? The whole thing was a bloody mess."

A pot of drama with no answers. Helen was a proud lady, she felt humiliated her husband had cheated on her, and as a result of the murder, her private life would instantly be thrust into the public arena. The thought of all the curtain twitching, finger pointing, and gossip mongering churned her stomach. Her distress could lead to acute depression if she allowed her misery to spiral.

It was also clear in Helen's mind that if the police knew she was the dutiful wife who had been on the murder scene first and chose not to report it, there would have been a lot more questions than answers coming from the constabulary. Helen was trapped and had little option than to go with the flow – she chose to continue under the masquerade of her sister Karen's identity. For a short period it seemed like the right thing to do, and nobody without exception, challenged her status as her sister Karen. Why would they?

The subterfuge of her status provided a useful buffer against the rest of the world, at least it seemed that way for the short term.

Ham enquired, "Helen, why were you not at home on the night of the murder?"

Helen mused to herself, then replied, "Karen had asked me to visit mutual friends who were based a two-hour drive away to provide administration support for their small business. Their company was doing well, and the paperwork was getting beyond them. I was happy to help. For once in my life, I made the right choice and spent an evening away from home."

Helen pondered. "What a devious ploy to get me out the way for the evening, so Karen could entertain my beloved husband Michael. This request backfired in spectacular fashion when the gun for hire arrived, with his scatter gun, destroying his targets' lives."

Ham asked, "So who organised the hitman?"

Helen replied sharply, "It was Karen. She inadvertently arranged her own firing squad, bringing her personal invitation to her untimely funeral."

William interjected, "That does not make any sense. Why would she want to harm herself?"

Helen went on to explain that Karen's intention and her instruction to her chosen gunslinger, was to shake up Michael, not to kill him. She wanted him rattled, that was all. Reading between the lines, Helen could only surmise Karen had asked Michael to leave Helen for her. Michael probably made a few false promises to Karen and may have threatened to break their relationship off. Karen would not have liked that, she enjoyed getting from life what she wanted, rather than what she deserved. She enjoyed chasing rich pickings and if something belonged to someone else and she wanted it, she would try every trick in the book to take the advantage.

Helen continued enlightening Ham and William with her thoughts. It was Karen who had got ideas above her station, and decided to call on the services of a local lad who was one step removed from being the village idiot. He knew about guns; in the past he had killed a few wild rabbits. Helen had heard rumblings that Karen had enjoyed the odd covert night out with him. He could have been her bit of rough for all they knew, they never discussed it!

It was sensible to assume the lad she had employed to frighten Michael was probably given a remit to scare him whilst he was out walking or outside somewhere, it was unlikely he would have been given the full story as to why he was to be targeted. Clearly her chosen hitman thought better of her instruction and advice given and decided to attack Michael whilst in the confines of his own bedroom.

In the attacker's eyes, by killing or heavily wounding Michael, he was doing Karen a big favour. By killing or hurting what he thought was Michael's wife, in bed with him, was an additional bonus, sure to impress Karen, which he secretly hoped would bring him tasty treats later.

If only he knew!